CASSY PLAYS

Her Cards!

M R Westover

CASSY PLAYS HER CARDS!

© 2023, M R Westover.

Print ISBN: 979-8-35092-048-2
eBook ISBN: 979-8-35092-049-9

Contents

Prologue

THE BEGINNING OF THE END

August – The Day before the Party

"Should I, or shouldn't I?" Cassy has been arguing with herself since the moment she got up. Finally, with her fists balled up and waving in the air, she shouts, "YES! I must give it to him today—before the party and when no one else is around."

She quickly showers and ponders a moment before putting on her black leggings, a gray y-strapped tank, and her black nylon jacket. Should anyone question why she is there, she could say she had been running and got carried away and just stopped for a drink of water.

Opening the thin, black, linen-like box, she takes a moment to admire the inscription on the letter opener she is giving to Ron. Surely, he will understand the significance and appreciate the sentiment engraved on it. She stuffs the memento into her inside jacket pocket, laces up her running shoes, and races out the front door. The route is so familiar to her that she makes great time and plans on catching him before he goes to make rounds at the hospital. With all the party preparations for later and things to attend to, hopefully everyone will be out except Ron. Winnie is probably at her regular stylist appointment, and the boys—well, Phipps loves to go to the gym, and Trey is always looking for a tennis game at the club or playing his guitar at the Daily Grind. The house should be empty, except for Ron.

The house sparkles in the morning sunshine as it always does—stately, well-manicured, and inviting. Having been Phipps and Trey's nanny for so long, Cassy knows the four-car garage has a small side door to the east that is hardly ever used; she prays it isn't locked. The knob turns easily, and she slides in, setting her sights on the back stairs.

Most likely, Ron is in his office. She scurries up the polished mahogany steps while checking to see if anyone else is at home. The house appears abandoned, although there is ample evidence of pre-party preparations: white linen-covered round tables and modern Chippendale chairs, each set off with an angular-tied purple or blue sash, grace the great room. The alcove shows promise of music from a grand piano and multiple stands awaiting sheet music, and the bar appears, at a quick glance, to be stocked with choice liquors. Only the best for the party!

Pulling the personalized silver-plated letter opener from her jacket, she turns into the office, hoping to see Ron. No one is there. She makes a quick decision to lay the open box right in the center of the leather blotter. Admiring the look of the knife-like opener, she is sure he will grasp the meaning of the engraving, "TIME VIII."

Pausing, she remembers the first time Ron had touched her. He had come home late from a party at the club, and she was there, as usual, serving as a nanny for the boys. She even remembers wearing cut-off jean shorts and her yellow halter top that accented her pert breasts and her tanned, bare midriff. She sees herself dozing on the white leather loveseat in the family room. As always, he had offered to drive her home. However, the look in his steel-blue eyes was the only thing that registered.

She closes her eyes to savor the feeling of his tanned, muscular arm as it brushed against her chest that first night. He had been reaching to pick up her rainbow woven beach bag and straw hat and carry them to the silver Maserati. By then, Cassy had tired of fumbling high school boys and was longing to experience a "real man." And, oh, what a man Ron had turned out to be!

Forcing herself back to the present, Cassy fears she has stayed too long. She turns to escape before anyone sees her.

With her head slightly down, she zips her jacket and runs smack into Ron. "Oh, Sass," he says with a devilish grin on his face, inviting her into his embrace. She has rehearsed and rehearsed what to say to him, but being caught like this throws her off. She splays her hands on Ron's chest and gives him a slight but determined push.

"No more, no more," she chokes out as she shakes her head, and a tear slides down her cheek. "Eight years is enough! We had our time, and I do love you, but it's my time now. I want to build a family with someone who is mine!"

She sidesteps Ron, but he grabs her arm. "Sass, you can't mean this!"

"I do mean it, Deuce," she stammers and races to the front stairs. Tears are now streaming down her face, and she has a death hold on the banister as she scurries down the beautiful, curved staircase. She's always admired it with its decorative iron scroll spindles and white newel posts, but today nothing captures her attention except retreat! She doesn't see the town barista walking through the front door, carrying a large box with everything he needs to set up the coffee bar for the party. Renaldo recognizes Cassy immediately. Just as he starts to call out her name, Cassy reaches the bottom step, turns, and disappears toward the back exit.

Stunned, it takes a moment for Ron to run after Cassy. He first checks out the windows on the balcony overlooking the kidney-shaped pool and the manicured English garden, both already decorated with tea lights. Not seeing anyone, he pivots and peers over the front railing.

Busy with coffee preparations, Renaldo senses someone watching him, so he looks up and sees Ron on the balcony above the living room. Their eyes meet—Ron's penetrating and obviously perturbed, and Renaldo's questioning. Without a word, Ron is the first to break the connection, stomping back toward his office.

Shaking his head, Renaldo wonders, "What is going on?" He was sure Cassy was crying.

Chapter 1

MAN OF THE YEAR

The Day of the Party

G aiety and laughter spill from every open window as Renaldo makes his way across the lush green lawn to the party for "Man of the Year," Dr. Ronald Edwin Phillips II. As he passes by the window, he catches a glimpse of the honoree on the balcony, almost in the same spot Dr. Phillips had been standing yesterday morning. Not stopping to ring the bell, Renaldo steps inside and is not surprised to see everyone who is anyone already there. His entrance is unnoticed, and he immediately goes to check on the status of his coffee bar.

Ron, with his usual arrogance, is surveying the crowd and muttering to himself, "I deserve this. After all, besides being the town's preeminent OB-GYN, I have served as Meadowbrook School Board President for the last seven years; I'm a past president of Rotary. I spearheaded the fundraising for the Children's Hospital Neonatal Unit that opened last year, and I always sponsor and support school events. Yes, I deserve this!"

The only thing that surpasses Doc Ron's cockiness is his handsomeness. Almost every woman in the room secretly drools in admiration as they picture his taut, tempting body under that deep charcoal bespoke suit that he'd gotten hand tailored in New York on a secret trip with Cassy, his Sass. He also wears the cobalt blue tie Cassy had chosen for him on that escape. It matches his piercing cobalt blue eyes. Tonight, he sports a purple rose in his lapel, Cassy's favorite flower. He wants her to know that he still desires her and isn't willing to let her go so easily.

Peering over the banister, Ron recognizes his wife's bridge club as well as her tennis partners. Hell, he had "bedded" most of them at least once since he and Winnie had moved to Meadowbrook more than twenty years ago. His golf and tennis buddies are all mingling around the pool and nearby buffet, nursing their favorite drinks. Most of their wives, modeling the latest fashions and facelifts, have at one time or another availed themselves of his "late-night appointments." Thank God they are discrete. This is still a small town. As his eyes move from one beauty to another and as he visualizes the variety of ways they have shown their appreciation, he feels his testosterone level begin to rise. He smiles like a Cheshire cat and congratulates himself on his sexual prowess.

His friends call him Doc Ron. Winnie, his wife of more than 20 years, calls him Ron, and Cassy calls Ronald Edwin Philipps II her Deuce. Everyone else calls him Doctor Phillips. His right hand is wrapped around a crystal glass, but it isn't filled with champagne. Tonight he is drinking expensive scotch—18-year-old Glenlivet. Ron is tall, tan, and muscular. His dark hair sports silver at the temples; his square face is patrician; and outwardly, he exhibits an easy "bedside" demeanor that belies the turmoil he is experiencing since seeing Cassy yesterday. Where is she? He searches the room until he spots her. She is stunning, framed by the last of the sunlight pouring through the floor-to-ceiling windows overlooking the pool at the back of the great room. He silently vows, "I will not give you up, Sass!"

Winnie's eyes are drawn to their guests. First are Tom and Joey, Ron, and her dear friends since medical school, who always seem to be in a world of their own. Their heads are tilted close, their eyes are focused only on each other, and their body language says, "You are my Happily Ever After; I love you." Winnie wonders if she and Ron ever had that cherished connection, or was it more lust? She further contemplates, "Did he just need a trophy wife, and was I settling for status and money?" She turns to further scan the gathering, and over by the fireplace, she spots her second son, Phipps, and his girlfriend, Claire. Winnie stares for a moment, and while she's observing them, a thought stabs her. Those two look at each other just like Tom and Joey do. "They can't, not yet; they are too young. They have college and his athletic career to embrace," she whispers defiantly to no one. The stained-glass double doors open, and she returns her attention to welcoming newcomers to the party but silently vows to further examine Phipps and Claire's relationship.

At five feet ten, Winnie, with midnight black hair pulled into a perfect chignon accenting her beautiful long neck, a size four figure, violet eyes, and full curved lashes, still turns heads. Tonight, her Vera Wang custom cocktail dress is black with shiny black ribbon trim. Around her slim neck are two strands of perfectly matched black pearls. On her left wrist is a black pearl and diamond bracelet that accentuates her 7-carat emerald-cut diamond ring Ron had given her on their 20th anniversary, and on her right hand is an oversized luminous black pearl ring surrounded by diamonds.

Winnie, always the perfect hostess, mingles among their guests while keeping an eye on the front entrance so she can greet latecomers. She catches a glimpse of Axel, her masseur, entering the kitchen from the back entrance with additional hors d'oeuvres. She thinks to herself, "He must be helping the caterers tonight. I would have thought we had him on our guest list."

She appraises the elegant party setting that overlooks the pool area. It's perfect, just the way a person of her stature should entertain. There is the tinkling of tall champagne flutes offered by the white-jacketed servers. The dazzling chandeliers cast small rainbows in the amber-colored flutes and put a subtle glow on the beautiful cocktail dresses and smart suits of their guests.

A thirty-foot professionally prepared sign hangs from the balcony declaring, CONGRATULATIONS, MAN OF THE YEAR! DR. RONALD EDWIN PHILLIPS, II. Large, fresh flower arrangements of white peonies, blue tulips, and purple roses grace every table, cover the mantle, and line the banister—manly but elegant touches of color. Specialty hors d'oeuvres tempt guests into savoring tiny bites of unique combinations: spicy shrimp with candied pineapple, beef tenderloin with balsamic dressing on crisp bread, vegetable tarts, and bacon-wrapped scallops.

The Phillipses' Steinway grand piano that sits in the front window alcove has been joined by a four-piece instrumental group. Their instructions were to play the latest hits by artists like Michael Bublé, Harry Connick, Jr., Celine Dion, and Adele. The enjoyable music lends a festive, happy vibe to the party, and the Persian rugs mute the sounds of people mingling.

Son #1, Trey, can't keep from tapping his foot to most of the songs. Finally, one of his friends grabs Trey's guitar from its stand over by the piano and brings it to him. "You play at the Daily Grind; how 'bout you play one for your dad's special day?" Trey starts to shake his head, but a chant rises: "Trey, Trey, Trey!" The other musicians wave him over. Trey looks up to his dad, salutes and launches into a sterling rendition of "Hotel California" by the Eagles. It's a song he knows his dad has always liked.

Like everyone else, Winnie's eyes eventually land on Cassy, Meadowbrook's anointed princess, escorted by Phipps's Coach Brock Taylor. Cassy's flowing, light blond, wavy curls are held back at her right temple with a pearl-encrusted hair comb. Winnie must give the former nanny credit for dressing for the occasion. She stands out in her robin's-egg blue cocktail dress, matching slingbacks with silver five-inch stiletto heels. The dress flatters her small waist and then flares into a short, satiny skirt, accentuating her long, toned legs and slim ankles. The off-the-shoulder Bardot neckline of the dress showcases an emerald-shaped diamond pendant that was an unexpected and much-loved gift from her favorite boys, Trey and Phipps. The diamond studs Ron bought for her when they were in New York sparkle and complement the pendant. Winnie can see the admiring glances of many of the men in the room, including her Ron.

The soft muting of the guests and their movement toward the table where the award is prominently displayed indicate the party is poised for its intended purpose: honoring the Man of the Year. The mayor's booming voice and the clinking of champagne flutes call the assembled guests to attention. Mayor AG Williams is personable, attractive, and charming. Everyone knows he works hard at his primary occupation as a realtor to showcase their community. In fact, he had overwhelmingly won the last several elections to be their mayor. However, AG certainly is not self-centered, having been the caretaker for his wife, who succumbed to cancer two years ago. He had met Winnie during their freshman year at college. They had dated until Ron came into her life.

On occasions like this, AG is at his best. He quickly quiets the crowd with his smile and calls Dr. Phillips to stand beside him. Holding a small microphone, he goes right to the heart of the award, congratulating the doctor for being selected as Man of the Year. He then enumerates the many accomplishments of Dr. Ronald Edward Phillips II, ranging from committee chairmanships, volunteer leadership in organizations like the Lions and Rotary, substantial donations for community projects, and most recently, serving as School Board President. Anyone who wanted to take the measure of the man could have just turned to view the shelves on each side of the fireplace, which held a myriad of past awards. AG presents to him the beautiful glass obelisk with a solid black base of marble. It has a very life-like etching of Dr. Phillips's face, and his full name, Dr. Ronald Edwin Phillips, II, is cut just below the declaration, Meadowbrook Man of the Year.

Members of the press, of course, click away with their flash cameras to capture the moment the award passes into the doctor's hands. Doc Ron picks up the microphone, clears his throat, and, in a very strong and authoritative voice, begins to thank people. Covering his bases, he first looks adoringly at his wife and two sons, saying, "Without you three, this would not be possible." He goes on to thank the "little people," of course. "A special thank YOU," he emphasizes, "to those of you who carry on the real day-to-day work that sustains Meadowbrook and particularly our exemplary school and health systems." As he mentions the schools, he turns his beaming smile to School Superintendent Monica Woodland, and he doesn't leave out AG, praising his tenure and work as their chosen mayor. He also offers his thanks to his office staff and, of course, his long-time friend and colleague, Dr. Tom Redford, and his wife, Joey. Holding the obelisk above his head, Ron demonstrates his skill in evoking emotion. "This one belongs on my desk upstairs, so I can see it every day!" With a final thank you, he gazes directly at Cassy, adjusting his tie to say the secret "I love you," and she quickly dips her head and lowers her eyes, knowing that she cannot respond anymore with her own telltale wink. Doc Ron turns and begins the short walk to the landing. He is stopped numerous times with handshakes, brushed kisses from the females, and embraces from those who have known him forever.

At the top of the stairs, he turns right and steps into his office. He feels a presence but dismisses it because there are so many people in the house. He proceeds to his desk, a massive, polished walnut masterpiece. It would easily rival the one in the Oval Office at the White House. When he had finished his residency and opened his current practice, he had splurged on this symbol of success. The desktop sports a large leather blotter with onyx side pieces, a matching leather pencil holder, and a stapler. Beside his Howard Miller chiming clock lies his favorite Montblanc pen.

This desk doesn't see much work activity, but Ron's office is his sanctuary. His favorite books fill the built-in bookcases behind his desk and are framed by large green plants that give the room a feeling of freshness. As he eases into the executive black leather chair, he places the award to the right of the clock, in case some of the partygoers come up to see if he had been serious about where he was putting it. He still feels a bit uneasy, but the rich green walls, ornate crown molding, and Hemingway leather chairs in front of him lull him into a moment of reflection. What a week it had been! Too many issues, and now he had to figure out how to deal with them. In the next moment, he remembers the letter opener gift from Cassy. He leans back and pulls out the desk drawer; the box lies empty. In the next instant, he registers a sharp pain in his back, convulses and involuntarily slumps over the desk.

One of the periphery guests, a former worker from the bank who usually waited on Dr. Phillips, spontaneously decides she will go upstairs. She's been dying to see the rest of the house because of its grand furnishings and designer look. She can snoop without anyone protesting because her ready excuse can be to get a closer look at the obelisk and congratulate the award winner. As she tops the stairs, instead of turning to the right, where it appears the office would be, she eases left and goes into a beautifully appointed bedroom. A four-poster bed claims the center of the room, with a white linen-like canopy embossed with gold threads. The two nightstands are also antique white with gold trim and hold tall, fringed lamps. Billowing like a cloud, the coverlet is silky and completes the gold-trimmed theme. Betty can't help but wonder if this is their (Winnifred and Dr. Phillips's) bedroom, or does Winnifred keep one of her own? Before Betty can leave, she hears rapid footsteps outside the door she had partially closed to conceal her whereabouts. Carefully peeking out, she doesn't see anyone but decides she should at least try to locate the office and be able to say she personally talked to the award winner.

Moving down the west wing of the house, she is surprised she doesn't encounter any other well-wishers. She spots the corner of the large bookshelves visible from the office's open door, so she steps forward and hurries into the room. Her practiced congratulatory speech dies on her lips as her unbelieving eyes take in the scene. Folded over the desk lies Doctor Phillips with what looks like a large knife protruding from his back. Blood is trickling down his side, pooling on the chair. Opening her mouth, she tries to scream, but only guttural sounds emerge.

Spinning like a top out of control, Betty forces her legs to move and finally utters a convulsive scream, "He's been stabbed! Dr. Phillips has been stabbed! Somebody, help!" She careens down the wide, curved staircase and falls into the guests gathered below. Someone lifts her under the arms as she gasps, "Dr. Phillips ... office ... stabbed!" His best friend, Dr. Tom Redford, takes the stairs in great leaps and rushes to verify Betty's declaration. He comes around the corner of the office yelling, "Call an ambulance and the police RIGHT NOW!"

The downstairs gathering has taken on the look of a frozen tableau. No one moves, no one talks; all that can be heard are gasps and muted inquiries, "What did she say? What's happened?"

Chapter 1

TRAUMA AND TRANSPORT

Night of the Party (*continued*)

The emergency unit—both the ambulance and the fire truck from Meadowbrook Rescue 456—arrives within minutes of the 911 call. Cars are parked everywhere, making it almost impossible to maneuver their vehicles to the front steps. It is just as difficult for the emergency team to make their way through the crowd of guests huddled in small groups, all wondering, except for one guest, who could have done this.

The two EMTs, dressed in their blue uniforms, scurry up the stairs toward Dr. Tom Redford, who is frantically motioning them to hurry. They carry a gurney and their medical bags. The firefighters remain on the first floor until the EMTs can give them further direction. Crowd control is their goal at this moment.

As the EMTs enter the room, they register Dr. Phillips slumped over his desk with a knife-like object protruding from his back. They swing into their emergency medical routine, one checking on his temperature and blood pressure, the other monitoring Ron's carotid pulse and his respiration rate, and then, carefully turning the victim's head, flashing a light into his pupils to check for dilation. The vital signs establish Dr. Phillips is alive, but barely. They both examine the wound, finding that the blood has pooled. They know better than to remove the weapon; they must immediately transport him to the hospital.

The taller EMT steps out onto the balcony and motions the two firefighters to the second floor. Jennie, the smaller of the two, runs up the steps first. Art, her partner, is on her heels. Both know time is of the essence. Tom stands back in shock. His best friend is alive, but would he die? His last words with Ron earlier this afternoon had not been good. Tom hadn't meant all he had shouted at him, but he regretted none of what he had said. Someone had to make Ron see he was losing a lot—he was losing his family if he didn't make some changes, and who knows what else—and he needed to make those changes fast. Now Tom worried that he and Ron's family—and all of Meadowbrook—would be losing him.

With hesitation but total control, the four-member medical team lifts Dr. Phillips and places him face down on the gurney, carefully turning his face to the right. With firm grasps on the stretcher, they move Dr. Phillips down the stairs, where they snap open the gurney's wheels.

One by one, the guests stop whispering and break open a path as the medical team guides the gurney toward the ambulance. Doc opens his eyes for one instance and sees Cassy with tears streaming down her face. He remembers the first time he had kissed her and how passionate she was and how his passion matched hers. Unlike the kisses of his previous affairs, this one was awash with unfulfilled desire and longing for more. The drug in the drip the EMTs had initiated took over, and Ron closed his eyes, wishing Cassy would be there when he awoke.

Tom and his wife, Joey, hustle the distressed Winnie into Joey's Volvo SUV as the medical team rolls the gurney into the waiting ambulance. The boys rush to Trey's Mustang. The multi-colored lights on the ambulance begin to flash, and the sirens scream as they speed to Meadowbrook Hospital, a place so familiar to both Tom and Ron. This time, however, the roles are reversed; they were now the receivers, not the givers, of the medical attention.

Ronald Edwin Phillips II lies in a bed in the emergency room at Meadowbrook Regional Hospital, surrounded by a cacophony of the doctors' demands, nurses' responses to those orders, and the onslaught of testing and life-support apparatuses. Medical staff in white coats rush in and out, hovering over Doc's arms, his head, and his back. He has lost a lot of blood and looks like a drained milk glass—pasty white and completely inanimate. His primary doctor, whom Ron would have recognized if he were conscious, is trying his best to determine exactly what has put Ron in a comatose state. The knife, carefully pulled from his back, turned out to be a letter opener with Time VIII engraved on it. Thank God both his heart and lungs had been missed and no major arteries were involved. It could have been a traumatic injury. So what has put Ron in a non-responsive

MR WESTOVER

state? It is a puzzle that will take days to unravel, assuming Ron awakens and is able to help them.

Trey and Phipps had raced into the hospital ahead of their mother and their godparents, Tom and Joey. Hurling themselves at the nurses' station, they demand in unison to know where their father is. A very calm, no-nonsense nurse informs both boys, "The patient is being treated by the medical team. You certainly are welcome to wait in the sitting area right next to this room." The boys start arguing with the nurse, but Tom, rushing through the emergency room door, intervenes with authority and escorts them to the waiting area. The now-empathetic nurse shares with Joey that she will check on Ron's status regularly and give them updates.

Phipps never could just sit. He starts pacing back and forth for what seems like hours but is only minutes, and at the same time the boys turn to each other and appeal to Tom, "Who could have done this?"

Before Tom can even reply, Dr. Jensen enters the waiting area. He detects anger and fright in the boys' body language. There are others congregated; the doctor recognizes many of them, but he immediately goes toward his colleague, Tom. Joey brings Winnie and the boys into the huddle. Dr. Jensen shares, "Winnie, the weapon has successfully been removed, and Ron is stable but still unconscious." He goes on to say, "We will be reviewing a multitude of tests before we know how to proceed." He encourages the immediate family to go back to see Ron for a few minutes but reminds them Ron is unable to respond at this time. "Please, take my advice; go home and get some rest, as this could be a long haul. We will call you with any updates or changes."

17

As Dr. Jensen leaves the waiting room, he recounts that Winnie was as stunning as ever, even under these conditions. He had noticed her talking with AG, who appeared to be reassuring Winnie that all would be fine. Dr. Jensen hopes the tears Winnie has been silently patting away are sincere. He has known the couple long enough to entertain a thought, wondering if she is crying out of love, duty, or fear for her future standing should Ron die.

AG, having seen Winnie safely in Tom and Joey's care, decides he should really get back to the party to share what he knows and determine if he can be of help. As he pulls up, he sees many guests have left, but there is still a large number of cars in the lane and driveway. The police vehicles' lights continue to flash, and it looks like some of the officers are trying to clear the house entrance so they can string yellow crime tape. They have already placed it across the stairs leading to the doctor's office, the pivotal point of the crime scene. As AG approaches, the officers wave him through. Being the mayor does have some perks.

Stepping into the house, AG observes total chaos. The caterers and servers are trying to clean and pack up; the band is attempting to put away their instruments; the barista is tearing down the coffee bar; someone is gathering the flowers and putting them on a single table; and individual groups are still bantering about what just happened.

AG spies Detective Michael Finley at the top of the stairs visiting with several officers and two additional men, who he presumes are plain-clothes detectives. He's gesturing like he is giving them orders. They are shaking their heads and pointing to various places in the house. Seeing AG, Mike motions for him to join him as the others scurry out to their assigned tasks.

"Hi, Mayor," greets Mike. "Is this a mess or what?"

"I just left the hospital, and Doc Ron is alive, just unresponsive right now. I came back to see if there was anything I could do here to help you."

"That's great, AG. I need to get to the hospital, too. Is there a possibility you could capture these last remaining guests' attention and get them to go home? I want the forensics team in here shortly. I also need to talk to the party planner, so we have a current list of the guests."

"I can do that," offers AG. He steps to the top stair and lets out a piercing whistle. Everyone comes to an immediate halt and stares up at their mayor. "I know we are all stunned and wanting answers. I can tell you Doctor Phillips is alive, has undergone surgery and multiple tests, and is still not talking or awake, but his physician, Dr. Jensen—lots of you know him—is very optimistic after securing a read on Doc's vital signs.

"You can really simplify next steps if you can please get out of their way and let the caterers, servers, and clean-up crew complete their work. This home is now a crime scene, and the detectives and law enforcement want to bring in the CSI professionals to collect evidence and begin the task of finding out who did this. I will come and escort you out a few at a time. Thank you so much for your cooperation. Be careful and drive home safely."

AG stays until everyone is gone except the Phillipses' house-keeper, Maya. He cautions her to not "cleanup" or move additional items until it is cleared with Detective Finley. Maya is trembling, and AG pulls her into a comforting hug. "Don't worry," he whispers.

"Doc is strong, and his own doctor is very highly thought of. He'll get the best of care."

"I know, I know," she sniffles, "but the boys and Miss Winnie will be lost without him. Should I go home, too," asks Maya, "or stay and protect the house? The family will probably stay with Dr. Phillips at the hospital or go to Dr. Tom's. I'm not sure what to do."

"You go home, Maya. You've had a terrible shock, too. I will speak to Detective Finley. I'm sure he'll station officers here until they feel they have covered every inch of it."

Maya dabs at her eyes and profusely thanks AG. As she walks away, she reflects on what a nice man he has always been to her and Miss Winnie.

Back in the hospital, Ron's eyes won't open, but he hears fuzzy, quiet conversations going on around him. He cannot move but senses he is in a hospital and people are attending to him. He tries to remember what has happened but cannot recall anything. After a few minutes, he drifts into a quiet, calming place with nothing but darkness.

As Tom and Joey whisk Winnie out of the waiting area, Tom reminds Trey and Phipps, "Meet us back at our house as soon as you can. We have lots to discuss. Joey and I want you two and your mom to stay the night with us."

Trey drops Phipps at his pickup, which is now parked in front of Claire's house. Phipps tosses small pebbles at the second-floor window of Claire's bedroom. She recognizes the familiar tattoo, and within seconds of seeing him on the lawn, she races downstairs, knowing that he needs her right now as much as she needs him.

Seeing the dim lights at the Daily Grind, Trey stops at the coffeehouse to talk with Ren. It is about 3:00 A.M. when both Trey and Phipps show up at Tom and Joey's, exhausted but ready to support their mom in meeting the unknown, appreciating the mainstays in their lives: Tom and Joey, Claire, and Ren.

The next morning, when Tom goes to the hospital, the first thing he does is check on Ron. He finds it ironic that his best friend is lying in the hospital he and Tom had specifically chosen for their careers. More than twenty years ago, both Tom and Ron, new physicians, understood their university steered graduating doctors to choose the metro, with large hospitals and ample clientele available to fill their private practices. However, Ron and Tom knew immediately upon touring Meadowbrook that it was the perfect size for them and their future. There had never been any question they would seek positions in the same hospital; why break up a forged brotherhood? After all, they were in different medical specialties—Ron's in OB-GYN and Tom's in internal medicine. Meadowbrook Hospital was thrilled to get two highly acclaimed graduates to add to their roster. Both wives had also fallen in love with the town, and Winnie especially liked that it had its own country club. Joey was more interested in the schools and the community's emphasis on the arts.

Tom wonders, "What has become of the perfect life we began more than twenty years ago?"

Chapter 3

CASSY AND RON – THEIR BEGINNING

Late That Same Evening

Cassy left the celebration for the Man of the Year as quickly as she could. "What have I done?" she screams as she slips into her used Audi sedan. She heads for the hospital, leaving Brock on his own, driving as fast as she can, wondering all the time if Ron is alive in intensive care or dead in the morgue. She cannot think about his not surviving; she knows she would be guilt-ridden, especially after their encounter yesterday.

Still in her party clothes, she enters the hospital by a separate door her mom, Megan, the head night nurse, always uses. Cassy goes in search of Ron, showing a confidence she really doesn't feel. She finally locates him; he is in an ICU room, and she knows better than to go into that area; it is for hospital personnel and immediate family only. No one is in the room with Ron. As her heart pounds, Cassy steps in. Ron appears to be asleep. She grabs his hand, holding it to her cheek. "Did you just give my hand a squeeze? Maybe it was an involuntary jerk because I moved your hand."

She knows she shouldn't stay much longer as her mind skips back to their very first personal encounter. The one where she was finally more than the boys' nanny. It would promise eight years of clandestine meetings and deep desire by both.

Cassy's mind plays like a technicolor motion picture as she stares at Ron, remembering everything that was said and done that night eight years earlier.

I was descending the wide, curving staircase while marveling, as I always did, at the plush, formal living room with its snow-white matching sofas. I knew I would be most comfortable in the cozy great room with its leather chairs and white love seats, so I set out in that direction. Yawning, I curled up on one of the loveseats. I was wearing my usual summertime attire of short jean shorts with pockets longer than the shorts themselves and a tied-behind-the-neck halter top in my favorite color of lemon yellow. It accented my bronzed figure and hugged my just-developing curves. I had been there only minutes, it seemed, when I felt someone take hold of my shoulder and, with a gentle shake, whispered, "It's time to run you home, Cassy."

I knew that voice, although it was slightly slurred that night. It took me a few moments to reconstruct that I was still at the Phillipses' home, where I nannied Trey and Phipps. I adored those boys and hadn't really admitted it to myself yet that I harbored a huge crush on their dad.

Cassy's squeeze of his hand registers with Ron. Highly impacted by the drugs dripping through the IV, he still remembers the first time he and Cassy connected. His out-of-body review of the night causes him to twitch as he remembers . . .

I moved back to give Cassy space to grab her flip-flops and prepare to leave. I was a little rattled by the thoughts that were surging through me when I first looked down at Cassy on the love seat. It took all my willpower not to reach over and untie that beckoning halter top, which would unleash her perky breasts. I tried to tamp down my thoughts by searching for my keys and asking the typical parent questions: "How were the boys tonight? What did you do?"

"Oh, we played tag football in the pool and then played video games for a while," she had responded. "We kicked butt on the XBox with Madden's NFL 12. Then we watched that crazy movie, Weekend at Bernie's, for the hundredth time. Oh, and Trey serenaded us with his new songs, Blake Sheldon's 'Honey Bee' and Eli Young Band's 'My Old Man's Son.' He is getting pretty darn good."

Cassy's own reminiscing continued.

I couldn't help but remember all the times Doc Ron, my Deuce, had stood on the balcony watching the boys and me playing water volleyball, tag football, or Marco Polo. The kidney-shaped pool with a diving board in the deep end easily accommodated the boys and all their friends. Doc, like always, had his favorite drink, Glenlivet, in his crystal whiskey glass—neat, no ice. He'd twirled the scotch around and around in the glass, accompanied by a serious look on his face, then took a generous sip. I had seen him in that stance so many times, and not just above the pool. In fact, I had often brought him that same drink when he requested it. The boys always begged him to join them in the pool, but he would wave and step back toward his office. I cherished the picture I held of the boys' father as a man who was strong, accomplished, and admired by everyone in the community . . . and coveted by me, I finally admitted to myself.

"I didn't mean to startle you a moment ago," Doc uttered. "I know it's late, and you probably have big plans at the lake tomorrow with your boyfriend."

"No problem," I replied as I turned to smile at him. I remember thinking I felt his hand brush against my breast, and then I decided that it was just my wishful thinking.

"Oh, uh, September's extra warm days just add to the fun," I stammered. "I have plenty of time for hangin' out with my friends at the beach. The sun feels so good, and my favorite is dancing at night around the fire pit. We blast our favorite tunes on the boombox: Black Eyed Peas, Katy Perry, and Usher. Speaking of night, did you and Winnie have a good time at the party?"

"Oh, Winnie is fine—just a few too many white diamond martinis," Ron shared. "Let's jump in the Maserati, and I'll take you home."

Ron recalls his silver convertible, his pride and joy.

It said to everyone in the community that I had arrived and was a virile man who savored life. I have to admit, it brought out the carnal feelings I am forced to control in my everyday work world, especially that first night with Cassy.

Cassy continued tvo grasp Ron's warm hand as she relived their first night, filled with electricity that she could still feel.

It wasn't just the beautiful house, the boys, and Doc Ron himself that made me happy. I loved it when he took me home in the silver Maserati. Ron was always, well, almost always, a gentleman. He went directly to the passenger's side and opened the door for me. It was a tight space, and I had to swing my legs to settle in the bucket seat. I couldn't help but admire his physique.

"Tell me how school is going. I saw you on Friday night at the homecoming game. You were having a great time cheering on the team. Did you have fun at the dance?" And then with a little chuckle, he queried, "Was your date the perfect gentleman?"

Ron remembers quickly rounding the back of the car and slipping behind the wheel, expecting no response from Cassy.

My mind was on much more than her homecoming dance. She was a beauty—long blond hair, a gorgeous figure with just the right curves revealed—especially when I saw her in a bikini around our pool. I tried to rein in my thoughts. "After all, she is the boys' nanny, and I am old enough to be her father," I silently chastised myself.

Cassy turned toward me, and I sensed her delight and full-of-life exuberance as she threw up her arms and shared with enthusiasm, "It was a fantastic weekend! The dance, the game (we won), the parties, all the excitement. My friends and I had the best time."

When Cassy threw up her arms, her books fell to the floorboard. She bent over to retrieve them, but they kept sliding away. I slowed the car and reached over to help her. I couldn't help myself. My arm pressed against her breast. She tensed at first, but I was sure she was feeling the same thrilling tingle that I felt gliding through my body. I picked up the speed of the Maserati, neither of us saying a word—both lost in our own thoughts about that first touch.

I promised myself as we pulled up in front of her house that I would jump out of the car, gather up her books, and thank her again for staying with the boys. That was it; that is what I planned. Instead, without thinking, I leaned over and kissed her inviting lips. Complete silence followed, and then I heard myself apologizing, "Oh, Cassy, I'm so sorry. I should not have done that. Can you forgive me? I guess I had one drink too many."

I bowed my head, but out of the corner of my eye I saw Cassy move closer and reach over to lay her hand on my leg. She couldn't help but notice that my dick was hard and pressed tight against my zipper. She took her hand and gently turned my face toward her, initiating a kiss that was an unbelievable spark—a fire had ignited. "Definitely," I thought, "not the kiss of a typical teenager."

As she exited the car, Cassy pivoted to lean on the door and asserted, "I'll wave when I am safely in my room." She paused and looked directly into my eyes. She then added, "Our time will come!"

I was overwhelmed with emotions, pondering the phrase, "Our time will come." What exactly did she mean? Then I remembered she had said she would wave. I scanned the house window by window and stopped when I saw the soft glow of a light, and there she was. She waved. As I waved back, Cassy untied her halter top, gazing at me as she touched her breasts with her left hand and threw me a promising kiss with her right.

With my eyes glazed and my blood pressure raised, I whipped the Maserati into a wide U-turn and started toward home. It was impossible for me to concentrate; I knew I couldn't make it home with my cock in this condition. X-rated thoughts of Cassy raced through my *mind as I replayed her touch and kisses and the innuendos that came with "Our time will come." My erection begged relief as I imagined Cassy riding me.*

Cassy remembers the night eight years ago as if it had just happened.

I turned to learn my own form of release was coming up the stairs. The football quarterback, who was the homecoming king and my current boyfriend, gave a quick knock and entered my bedroom. He has been a steady at the house and the beach for months, so even at this late hour, he knew his way around. He was aware I had agreed to stay with the Phillipses' boys tonight, so he texted a moment ago to see if I was home. I greeted him in my gossamer white nightgown, which hugged my body and revealed my developing Marilyn Monroe curves. I was beckoning him with smoldering eyes that were persuasive, "I want you." He had seen that invitation often and realized his timing was perfect as we moved to the bed. As he lowered his muscular body onto mine, he felt my hands begin caressing every part of his body. "Man, Cassy, I have hit the jackpot tonight. You are hot, beautiful, and love to make me happy." He didn't realize I was picturing Deuce, not him, in our sensual connection.

Before Ron drifted off with the IV summoning a deep sleep, he felt Cassy's hand in his and remembered she wasn't his anymore, but with Luke Bryan's "Strip It Down" echoing in his head, he admitted that he still wanted her as much tonight as he had wanted her that first night.

As I neared home, guilt started to gnaw at me. As a prominent doctor, I had had my share of dalliances with the country club women,

*my golfing buddies' wives, and even the nurses at the clinic and hospi-
tal. None of those had ever stirred the desire I felt for Cassy.*

*Entering the house for the second time that night and going into
the master bedroom, I once again realized I was probably the reason
Winnie always drank too much. She was still beautiful in her own way.
Not now, of course, with her mouth hanging open and the smell of too
many martinis emanating from her lips. I really had worked hard to
give her everything she had missed as a child and all the things I knew
she desired to be accepted as a doctor's wife. Every day she was free
to play tennis at the club, lunch with other prominent wives, shop for
designer clothes, play bridge, or visit the spa. Often, she would meet
me for dinner, but our conversations had become sporadic and stilted;
I was constantly interrupted by what many called "my adoring fans."
We talked about the boys, Trey and Phipps. Winnie doted on those two
boys; she never failed to attend their activities—community theater,
guitar lessons, basketball, and tennis for Trey, and Phipps was every
father's dream—an all-around athlete in anything he tried, even as a
nine year old. Since I was often called away on emergencies, Winnie
kept me up to date on their activities. I had missed so much.*

Ron remembers shaking his head that night and asking himself, "What am I doing?"

Chapter 4

WHO COULDA' DONE IT?

The Day After

It is the day after the stabbing, and Detective Mike Finley stands in the never-ending hallway by Doctor Phillips's room. He notices an IV dripping into the doctor's arm and hears the varying sounds of machines checking vital signs. He is shocked that no family members are by Doc's bedside, only nurses filing in and out every few minutes. Finley makes a mental note to check the waiting room for the doc's family and friends.

Mike is certainly no stranger to hospital rooms and vigils over victims. He leaves for a few minutes to check with Ron's doctor. He knows better than to insert himself into a medical situation without the doctor's OK.

Finley remarks, "It looks like he is more than just sleeping, maybe even in a coma." Dr. Jensen just nods. "So how is he doing?" asks the detective.

"You know I cannot share that information with you because of HIPPA. I would love to tell you but cannot. You need to talk with Ron's wife."

Finley makes a mental note: must check with Winnie to learn the prognosis. This is now a waiting game.

Mike can just imagine what happened the minute the call came into the police station; the name of the victim would have certainly caused everyone to jump to attention. He had been contacted immediately because as senior detective in the Meadowbrook police department, every major case fell to him to solve. It hadn't always been that way; he started out like everyone as a rookie years ago and, over time, had moved up the ladder.

Mike Finley certainly matched the description of a seasoned detective, much like Columbo with his ill-fitting, well-worn brown suit, old-fashioned unpolished wingtips, and his ever-present London Fog khaki raincoat. He wore that coat whether it was the rainy season or not, and always with the belt hanging loose. In his mind, the coat helped when he was interviewing suspects. It lolled them into a casual rather than an official visit feeling and helped them open up.

What many people miss, however, is how sharp and observant Mike is in any situation, from a small petty crime to a complicated murder. Years of experience have honed his skills in detecting the slightest nuance in someone's tone or demeanor, and he has an eagle eye for details others overlook. His gravelly voice never gives anything away. It is steady as can be, even when he has gathered lots of information and is interviewing a likely suspect. Going from beat cop to lead detective during the span of his career means he knows everyone in Meadowbrook, and they know him.

Finley has never made a lot of money, but his kids are grown, and his wife has stood by him all these years. Money isn't his motive; his own code of integrity and upholding the law has carried him this far. His favorite activity now is volunteering at the high school for the forensics class and coaching those with an interest in going to the police academy.

Right now, he stands looking at the ever-present small notebook he has taken from his inside suit pocket. He has been to Doc Ron's house, but he will go back when the CSI team has completed their scrutiny of the crime scene. The officers at the site haven't given him much information other than a description of the chaos that had ensued when everyone realized what had happened. He is aware the weapon is a letter opener because he'd had a cursory view of it at the station, and he also noted it could easily have passed for a knife. What disturbs him now is the list of partygoers who attended the Man of the Year celebration. He'd gotten it from the party planner, who is still at the house trying to put everything back in order. What a list of suspects!

Mike isn't at all surprised that he and his wife hadn't been invited to the party. The list holds the names of the elite of Meadowbrook who frequent the country club, or the people close to the Phillipses and their boys. Right now, he is hoping this will remain an assault case or maybe an attempted murder, but not a homicide. Murder in Meadowbrook has been reserved for a different class of people, and in this circle, it would cause endless speculation and finger-pointing. It isn't going to be easy; these people all feel they are above such a thing and will resent being questioned. Of course, they will protest; while they want to help in any way they can, that doesn't mean Mike can pry into their personal lives, or so they think.

He looks up to see a couple of reporters from the *Meadowbrook Gazette* coming down the hall. Of course, they would show up. Earlier, they had been snapping pictures and phoning in copy during the Man of the Year festivities. Now they want a much more sensational, headline-producing story. Finely doesn't want to think it, but knowing the way the press is always searching for dirt, corruption, and intrigue, he is glad Ron can't be interviewed right now. The head nurse, Ava, is quick to shoo them away. "Have some decency," she snaps. "He's fighting for his life!" No one knows—not even Ron—the secret she has carried for so long.

Since Ron is in no condition to help him, Mike decides he should start with Ron's best friend, Tom, who had verified that Ron was alive when he ordered the call to 911. He is headed toward the nurse's station to find out where Tom's office is when he spots him talking to who he assumes is Tom's wife. They are engrossed in what appears to be a private conversation.

As Detective Mike draws near, Tom turns and sees that the man approaching has his badge in his hand. Mike expresses, "Dr. Redford, I'm wondering if I can speak to you about the incident with Doctor Phillips."

"Yes, of course, but I only have a few minutes; I am due for surgery. Oh, forgive me, this is my wife, Joey," Tom adds as he wraps an arm around her and draws her close. Mike observes that Tom's wife, Joey, is just as striking as Winnie, but in an innocent way. Her shoulder-length hair is the color of wheat kissed by the sun. High cheekbones and a ready smile certainly draw people to her, even Mike. She seems so much more down to earth than Winnie.

Joey extends her hand and comments, "No one can believe what happened. We really hope you can find out who did this. I was just leaving after Tom and I stopped by Ron's room to see if there was any change." She comments to Tom, "I'll see you at home, honey."

Detective Mike remarks, "Nice to meet you, Joey, even under these circumstances. Hopefully, I'll be able to talk with you later. I understand you both are quite close to the Phillipses."

"I'll help in any way I can," assures Joey as she turns toward the elevators.

Mike questions, "Is there anything you noticed, Dr. Redford, that could give me a lead on this? I understand you were the one who rushed to Dr. Phillips's side."

"I am. Like Joey," declares Tom, "I'll do anything to help you, Detective, but I was so busy getting the paramedics and firefighters orchestrated to rush Ron to the hospital that I didn't take note of the scene. If you have a card, I will give it careful thought and call you if I think of anything. I really do have to scrub for a surgery now." Just then an announcement could be heard over the speaker system: "Dr. Redford to OR 2, Dr. Redford to OR 2."

Mike waves Tom on and remarks, "We'll talk later," as Tom rushes down the hall.

Mike is ready to make a move toward the exit door when he finds himself surrounded by the newspaper reporters with at least seven or eight microphones in his face. The thought tickertapes through Mike's mind that he didn't even know Meadowbrook had that many news outlets.

"OK, OK," he spits. "I know you all have jobs to do, just like I do. But you also have to know it is too early to have any real information that you aren't already aware of." Everyone starts talking at once, and Mike tries to discern a question he can answer.

"Was the murder weapon really a knife?" one of them yells. "Where did it come from? Did it match any of those from the house?"

"Does Dr. Phillips know who stabbed him? Did he get a look at the perp or struggle with him?" asks another.

"Is his family aware of anyone who had a grudge against the doc?" asks a third reporter.

"Look," Mike joins in holding up his hand to quiet the group:

"A. First of all, there is no murder weapon, as Dr. Phillips is not dead.

B. We will, of course, fingerprint the stabbing weapon, hoping it gives us a lead, and at this point we do not know where it came from.

C. Dr. Phillips is in no condition at this point to be grilled about what took place. As soon as we are able, we will garner all we can from him. Plus, we don't know it was a HIM; it could have been a HER.

D. The family is in shock and coping as best they can. I will personally interview each one of them when I feel it is right. Now, please let me get on with my work."

Mike again heads for the exit, still surprised that there is no one in the waiting area.

Mike has investigated multiple stabbings over the years that had stemmed from a close-range betrayal. Could this be true of Tom and Ron? All the family members would also fit that category of close range. Winnifred and Ronald had been married for more than two decades; could there be a motive there since Ron is known for his many amorous conquests? And what about Trey and Phipps? Could they have a motive for stabbing their father? As Mike scans the guest list, his eyes land on Cassandra Carstens's name. He knows she had for many years nannied the boys. It wasn't that many years ago when she had been known as Sassy Cassy, but she had gone away to college and is now a respected teacher at Meadowbrook High. And what about the husbands of all his conquests—or even one of his conquests' jealousies?

The mantra running through Mike's mind is, "Who coulda' done it?"

Chapter 5

WINNIE, THROUGH THE YEARS

Later in the Week

Maya, the Phillipses' housekeeper, hands Winnie the ringing cell phone as she lounges by the pool and lunches on blue crab and shrimp cakes and a small wedge salad. "Good afternoon, Mrs. Phillips. This is Detective Finley. I need to schedule a time to interview you about the events surrounding your husband's attack." Winnie had known this was coming, and she has been dreading it.

"Surely, Detective. Do you want to stop by the house at about 4:00 P.M. today?"

After ending the call, Winnie takes a long drink from her stemmed wine glass filled with a favorite Chardonnay, leans back in her lounge chair and closes her violet eyes, shielded by her lush lashes. A wide-brimmed hat safely protects her porcelain skin. Her thoughts drift back to when she had first entered college at Northeast State University near Chicago. It had been a miracle she was even there. It marked the beginning of her real life—the one for which she had known she was entitled but was so afraid would never happen.

Shivering even in the warm sun, she pictures the small, cramped house she had grown up in as an only child. How could she have come from such a timorous but beautiful mother who never worked outside the home and a mailman father who spent his nights drinking beer and watching endless hours of sports? She squirms a little as she pictures the hell it had been going to school in hand-me-down clothes from the Salvation Army, wearing ugly scuffed shoes, and having very few friends. Actually, it was OK not having a lot of friends at the new upscale high school the town had built. It was asier to hide among the mass of students who never gave any thought to her. Her house had fallen just inside the school district's boundaries, which kept her from going to the "old" high school where all her elementary and junior high school classmates and friends attended. Nevertheless, she studied hard, excelled in art and its history, and had spent hours in museums and galleries, knowing she never had a chance for college, only work.

It was her great-aunt on her mother's side who had come to her rescue. Aunt Agnes had never married but had inherited money from her father. She had a position as a professor of history at a private university in New England until she retired. She had held Winnie's chin in her hand and expressed, "A pretty and smart girl like you needs a good education. You can't count on those looks forever, but you can establish a career, like I did." It was Aunt Agnes who had financed

Winnie's four years of college, including the sorority she had pledged. It had changed her life forever.

Sorority life had sculpted Winnie's social skills, and her part-time job at Neiman Marcus in downtown Chicago had steadily pushed her desire to dress in the latest fashions. With her art history major and multiple art classes, she respected how the play of colors could create beauty, how lines could showcase a collection, and how different fabrics created a mood. This had made her the perfect consultant to help wealthy clients with their designer clothing requests. She had vowed then that one day she would have designer everything; however, she really couldn't complain because her great aunt had been more than generous in funding her sorority wardrobe and her entire education.

Winnie took care to capitalize on her natural beauty by experimenting with make-up that enhanced her flawless ivory skin and only purchasing ensembles that flattered her model-like figure. She had adopted Joy by Jean Patou as her signature perfume. She used it sparingly because of the cost. George, her boyfriend, whom she called AG, told her every time he saw her that she was getting more and more beautiful. He was at State, too, but had never joined a fraternity. She remembered him always as adorable, comfortable, and devoted. He made her feel loved.

Having been with AG since coming to State, she seldom noticed the admiring, almost gaping, attention she received when she and AG were out on campus or on a date, usually at the college bar and grill. Then, like a tornado, everything changed during a sorority/fraternity mixer early in her sophomore year. Senior fraternity brothers from one of the more elite houses had decided to check out the new "stock" at her sorority. AG had been out for a guys' night at the fights, so she had decided she could turn the tables and scrutinize the "big boys." She had worn her hair down and casual. The ebony tresses fell in soft waves just past her shoulders. Her dress, a cranberry red sheath, hugged her body, hit her mid-calf, and had a deep but respectable V-shaped opening. She liked to wear the simple, small diamond studs and pendant that had been a gift from her grandmother for high school graduation. The silver chain was the perfect length to call attention to her cleavage and highlight her graceful, swan-like neck.

She had been standing at the punchbowl—spiked with vodka, she was certain—deciding if she really wanted something to drink when someone cupped her elbow and slowly turned her around.

It was Ronald Phillips II. Everyone knew him. He was a big man on campus, had any number of girlfriends, and was pre-med. Oh, how handsome!

"I don't believe we've formally met. I'm Ron Phillips and you are . . .?" There was a long pause as Winnie registered that he was actually addressing her. She had been immediately lost in those piercing, cobalt blue eyes and felt the masculinity oozing from his body; he was standing so close.

"I'm Winnifred," she stammered.

"Well, Winnifred, you and I have to get better acquainted. In fact, I think you will be my Winnie." He had led her over to a chair, and the rest, as they say, was history. She hadn't wanted to hurt AG; however, Ron had been persistent, bringing her flowers, gifts, begging her to go out with him. Her sorority sisters had been positively green with envy, but a few were even genuinely happy for her. By the end of Ron's senior year, he had made sure to put an engagement ring on Winnie's finger. He had been accepted to a small but prestigious medical school in Chicago, and he wanted to "lock down" this stunning woman.

Winnie was enthralled by Ron and was swept up in all the excitement and plans for their future. However, at times she was still drawn toward AG. For his part, AG had known immediately he was outclassed and vowed to remain Winnie's friend even though he longed for more. Whenever Winnie sought him out, even though she had scarred his heart, he gave her his listening ear and comforting advice. Only once had they stepped back in time and made love in college like they used to. Without words, both understood it was their final goodbye to a physical relationship.

Ron and Winnie had married the summer after his second year of medical school. It could have been a double wedding with their friends, Tom and Joey; the couples spent all their free time together, or what little they could carve out. They had stood up for each other, Tom and Ron as best men and Winnie and Joey as maids of honor. Of course, the actual weddings had been as different as the two brides— Winnie with her demand for elegance and Joey wanting a more meaningful experience.

Winnie's great-aunt had stepped in once again. She was elated to plan, execute, and, to Winnie's relief, pay for a glamorous event that befitted her great-niece, who was marrying a doctor to be. Ron had charmed Aunt Agnes just as he did most women. He never failed to kiss her hand, thank her for having such a fantastic great-niece, and tell her how much she meant to the both of them. He knew his charm would pay dividends later.

The venue was the beautiful non-denominational church on the university grounds. It had soaring wooden flying buttresses, red tufted pews, a gold-enhanced lectern, and gold sacrament vessels. The stained-glass windows rivaled even the most impressive ones found in a European cathedral. All the gifts of a very generous alumna.

Winnie chose black, ivory, and gold as her colors, with just subtle explosions of red. The flowers seemed so simple, but the ivory tulips placed on an ornate, wrought iron holder at each pew bent forward like they were bowing to the couple as they walked down the aisle. Adorning the front of the church were huge ivory baskets overflowing with red tulips and tied with gold lamé bows. The same gold lamé fabric served as Winnie's runner down the aisle. With the candles glowing at dusk as the wedding took place, the church seemed to vibrate with a love-filled expectation.

The groom was already so handsome that "he hurt," but in a black tux with an ivory silk tie, he stole everyone's admiration. However, when Winnie entered the church, there was an audible gasp. To say she was angelic and radiant would have been a misnomer, as she floated down the aisle on her great-aunt's arm. Her mother and father had been killed in a tragic accident earlier that year. There were three perfect red roses in a crystal vase on the piano to pay homage to her parents and to her grandfather, George, who had always protected her heart. As she passed Ron's mother and father sitting in the front pew, she gave them a heartfelt nod.

The dress? All the women waited to check out the dress. Winnie certainly didn't disappoint them. She wore a trumpet/mermaid scoop neck gown with a full-length veil. It was the same ivory color as Ron's tie, and when Winne passed her guests, they were treated to a flawless lace back with covered buttons reaching to the hem of the gown. Her hair was loosely pulled into a swirl of curls, and her ears held pearl drops hanging from diamond studs. The effect was breathtaking; however, right now she was staring at Ron. She really wanted to marry this man and build a life with him.

The reception at a local country club was a blur—cake cutting, photographs, dancing, going from table to table to greet guests—but thank goodness it came to an end. Ron and Winnie could now look forward to flying away to a private villa in St. Lucia. This had been a gift from his parents, and he couldn't thank them enough.

Joey and Tom were cut from a different cloth. They were already deeply in love, and each knew they had found the right person for the rest of their lives. The wedding would just be a validation of their commitment to their relationship. Tom, as a gifted doctor to be, and Joey, as an accomplished musician, were one in thoughts, aspirations, and kindness.

Joey's mother had come to help her plan their simple but very meaningful wedding. They had decided on the park in the center of their university town. It was English in style, with different hedges and rows, each rimmed with a watercolor painting of wildflowers. There was a small but ornate gazebo right in the center and plenty of room to set up white folding chairs on the lush lawn.

Joey had a hard time picking colors for her wedding; wildflowers made her happy and came in every color. She and her mother finally decided, with Tom's help, that the gazebo would be decorated with yellow and blue ribbon-tied wildflower bouquets. The yellow and blue would represent the sun and the sky. Tom and Joey had always found their peace and happiness in the outdoors—walking, talking, and holding hands.

Tom, as handsome as Ron but always carrying it in a more subtle way, had decided to wear a pewter gray tailored suit with a yellow boutonnière. He didn't care what he wore as long as he got to marry Joey. They were so happy; it could only get better. Tom's mom and dad had always supported him in anything he pursued, and they constantly let him know they were proud of him. They would be front and center at the wedding, and what was really great is they loved Joey, and the two families got along so well. It was a blessing for Tom and Joey's new beginning.

Joey had selected an understated but striking gown. It had a white lace bodice with a boat neckline and a tulle skirt—not too full, just enough to say "beautiful and feminine." She carried yellow roses surrounded by wildflowers. Her dad was in a slate gray suit, and the two of them exuded happiness as they came forward to meet Tom. He had tears in his eyes as he lifted Joey's veil; his Joey was even more stunning than she had ever been.

Ron and Winnie, their dear friends, had opted for the traditional wedding vows. However, Tom and Joey felt more invested sharing their own written vows. He pledged to cherish her all of her life, and she pledged to love him all of his. There were certainly tears in everyone's eyes by the time Tom and Joey finished their full vows. The words and sentiments were so touching and sincere—those who were happy in their relationship were renewed, and those who weren't wondered why they didn't have that sacred connection.

It was a gorgeous day; the sun had truly shined on them. Tom and Joey's reception was held in a huge white tent featuring a dance floor, a live band, and a buffet line catered by their favorite Italian restaurant. Their friends and families gathered around tables dressed in sparkling white tablecloths. Beautiful clear vases filled with greenery and wildflowers lent a festive aire to the event. Tom and Joey personally served their guests the bride's strawberry creme wedding cake and the groom's double chocolate cake with ganache icing.

The dancing and celebrating ended late that night as the guests formed a double line saluting Tom and Joey as they headed to their decorated car. The next morning, the newlyweds were going to an uncle's cabin in the Colorado Rocky Mountains. They had been there once before when they were first dating. It was the perfect place for a honeymoon, with lots of privacy, a pristine lake to canoe on, and myriad wildlife to study. The wedding and the honeymoon promised Happily Ever After for Tom and Joey.

Settling into Married Life

Winnie, now married, had continued to take classes at State and still enjoyed her work at Neiman-Marcus. Plus, that job gave her some of her own money, and she didn't want to lose the opportunity to observe how entitled women spoke and behaved. Joey had also kept busy giving music lessons and composing songs on her own. She looked forward to teaching at a school and inviting students to love music.

Time had flown by during their husbands' residencies. The couples had been inseparable. The Redfords didn't care about recognition as a future doctor and his wife; the Phillipses craved recognition, so the foursome didn't have to compete with each other. Tom and Joey introduced Ron and Winnie to the simple things. Neither couple had lots of expendable money, so entertainment had to be on the "cheap side." They went fishing; Winnie hated it. They went to the medical campus concerts, which were free, and they all enjoyed the local bands. Joey took them to museums, especially in Chicago. Ron was always looking around to see who was there, always looking for possible connections. Tom enjoyed picnics by the river and a lazy afternoon watching the clouds roll by. Winnie would take Joey shopping at upscale stores, but she never bought anything; she just liked to look around.

During this time, Winnie had given birth to Son #1, Ronald Edwin Phillips III, or Trey for short.

Unable, at this time, to conceive their own child, Aunt Joey and Uncle Tom were the natural godparents and adored Trey. Winnie had comforted Joey through multiple fertility treatments. Both Tom and Ron had then accepted appointments to Meadowbrook Hospital—Ron as an OB-GYN and Tom in internal medicine.

Ever since then, Ron had been taking advantage of women at the hospital, the country club, tennis courts, and community committees and events. Winnie didn't need to hear the constant whispers to know her husband was a philanderer. Oh, but they had had some good years, and she loved being a doctor's wife with all the perks.

She stops reminiscing for a moment and looks at her surroundings. This house and its grounds have been a wonderful home for someone with her background. She remembers how gratifying it had been to help design it. By then money had not been an obstacle, and Ron only wanted to keep her happy. Besides, she knew it stroked his ego to have the most prestigious house in Meadowbrook.

The two-storied house honors its Georgian heritage, finished with a red brick exterior and white shutters to frame the mutton-barred windows. The entrance is an impressive half-moon portico supported by four white columns. Large hundred-year-old oak trees provide a green canopy, and the manicured bushes make the front walk a focal point for the arched doors. The requisite magnolia tree stands just to the right of the front entrance, and ample dormers with large custom windows announce the second floor. The entrance itself is a masterpiece of white oak with a half-round glass inlay with matching inset side lights. Claiming an imposing position on the highest hill, the forty-acre estate is a refuge for the family and definitely a showpiece, as the owners had intended. From their vantage point, the family can look out at the shimmering lights of Meadowbrook, reflecting on the winding river. Guests are greeted at the circular drive, and many of the parties are hosted around the massive swimming pool, imposing pool house, and expansive flower gardens.

Yes, the house, country club, cars, jewels, and status were what she had so longed for way back at the beginning, and she and Ron were voracious where sex was concerned. Winnie thought, "*Were* is the key word." They practically devoured each other every time they made love, which was anytime and anywhere they had a chance. But over the years that had certainly changed, and her heart had started yearning again for an attentive, passionate lover. Ron hadn't filled that place for several years. Instead, Winnie focused her time and energy on raising her boys, her true source of joy.

Breaking her private reminiscing, Winnie notices the sun is much further down in the sky, and she needs to get ready to face the detective. She will ask him to respect her sons' trauma at seeing their father so viciously attacked. Winnie believes only she knows they have life issues of their own.

She, too, must guard herself, but it doesn't keep her from wanting to blurt out, "That bastard, he deserves this!"

Chapter 6

AG – THE FAITHFUL LOVER
. . . AND?

Early September

AG was checking on the price of a real estate property on the MLS (Multiple Listing Service) when he reminded himself he probably better get his story straight. He knew sooner or later Detective Mike would get to him. AG had come to Meadowbrook right after college intending to work in the bank, but people and real estate were the perfect connections for him.

AG had a manly face, with gentle dark slate gray eyes, a friendly smile, and silver hair. He usually wore a simple dark blue sports jacket with a baby blue chambray shirt open at the collar. He exuded the air of a man who was secure in himself and who also loved to put others at ease. His kids thought he was the world's best dad. If you couldn't find AG at the real estate office or City Hall, you could just drive out to Meadowbrook's public golf course. He was addicted to the game, and his buddies were quick to include him in a foursome. One of AG's thrills had been teaching his son golf and seeing him excel at the game.

He and his wife, Audrey, had had two children, whom they both adored. His daughter, Janet, was at Stanford majoring in English literature, with the goal of becoming a book editor or even writing her own novel. His son, Drew, had a golf scholarship to Penn State, majoring in "who knows what—it changes every semester." It had been so hard on all of them when Audrey, three years ago, had been diagnosed with aggressive metastatic breast cancer. She fought hard through chemo treatments and radiation. She even agreed to experimental trials with new medication, but the odds were against her, and she died far too soon.

Everyone in Meadowbrook knew AG and encouraged him to fill the void of losing his wife by running for mayor. He had already established a solid reputation for being honest and trustworthy with his real estate dealings, so it seemed a natural step. He hadn't even had to campaign because everyone else backed off, and he was elected in a landslide. Not wanting to interfere with or cast a shadow over his duties as mayor, AG had continued to work with a well-established local realty firm. He had no desire to run his own company with all that paperwork and headaches with closings. AG was satisfied with the split the firm offered on proceeds from a sale.

If he were honest, he would say his hardest times were when he had to interact with Winnie and Doc Ron. Like recently when he had to represent Meadowbrook in congratulating Ron as Man of the Year. He could tell all those people a few unsavory aspects of Ron's character, but he knew most of them would not believe it, or maybe they would but not say anything.

AG had been Ron and Winnie's agent about twenty years ago when they bought the 40 acres for a new home they planned to build near Meadowbrook's city limits. Now with the city's growth, the Phillipses were a few miles from the town center. Of course, AG loved the big commission that sale had produced, but whenever he was around Winnie, his mind and body would go back to the time they had been together in college. Such sweet and gentle lovemaking they had shared.

"Winnie, let's skip classes this afternoon and head to the city— just you and me and all the art galleries you want to see," I shared on the phone.

"Done deal," she had agreed without hesitation. "How did you know I don't have to work tonight, and the Museum of Contemporary Art would be the perfect start to the weekend. I cannot wait. Pick me up at 12:30 in front of the library?"

And a perfect afternoon and evening it had been, especially the time alone when we got back to my off-campus apartment. My two roommates had left for the weekend. The night was ours—Winnie's and mine—starting and ending with lovemaking that was tender and sweet—the kind I would remember forever because it was just that—tender and sweet—and her first time. I knew I needed to be patient and reassuring; her head was pushing back, but her eyes and heart were saying yes.

She melted into my arms; her hair smelled of wild pears and cucumbers. Our kisses began with teasing each other's lips, but those soon deepened with our tongues exploring each other, battling for dominance.

I pressed my arousal against her as I nuzzled her neck with what I hoped were intoxicating kisses. "AG, I want more tonight," she whispered as she began to unbutton my shirt. "I want to feel you inside of me. I want you to make love to me." As she raised her arms, I pulled off her tank top and unclasped her pink lace bra. Then I hurriedly dropped my khakis and boxer briefs to the floor. She slid off her shorts and her matching lace panties. Her naked body invited butterfly kisses on her nipples, heightening her need—and mine. My desire for her was all-consuming, my erection as hard as steel. I needed to consume her as much as she wanted me. My fingers entered her wet folds and caressed her clit until she came on my fingers. I enjoyed her O, I think, even more than she did—seeing her body arch and her head roll back, her loss of control, her need satisfied at least for the moment.

With my cock sheathed in a condom, I began to tease her sweet spot again—slow circles at first and pressure that caused her hips to gyrate and her lips to beg for more. I slowly entered her, pausing to give her time to adjust to my rock-hard cock. We soon found a rhythm that began with slow thrusts, becoming stronger and deeper with every plunge, taking us both over the edge at the same time.

Winnie spent the night; when she entered the kitchen where I was making coffee, she was wearing one of my old State T-shirts that hung almost to her knees, hiding her perfect body but revealing her tanned legs.

This was the woman I was going to love forever.

And then life happened. Ron entered the picture, and Winnie and AG's life together ended at college. Oh, there were still several rendezvous over the early years when they both lived in Meadowbrook—moments of making love, Winnie trying to deal with her husband's constant sexual entanglements, and AG struggling to provide for his family but feeling overwhelmed.

"I cannot take anymore," Winnie sobbed on the phone. *I could imagine the tears streaming down her cheeks and recognized her pent-up need for reassurance. "Ron seems to think a diamond bracelet, a pearl ring with matching earrings, and even a trip to Europe will erase all his affairs. The latest one has been tougher than usual. I know he has been spending late-night 'office hours' with the head nurse at the hospital while I am home chasing Trey, the most rambunctious two year old. Most adorable, too, I admit, but most trying at times,"* she added so as not to sound too pitiful.

"Let's meet in the city tomorrow," I offered on a whim. "Let's take a day like we used to do during what we thought were 'stressful days' of college life. We can do the hop-on hop-off for old times' sake, go see the updates on Wacker Drive, enjoy the architecture of the city, and even hit a few art galleries. The Museum of Contemporary Art is one of your favorites. You pick wherever. Let's go and just remember the good times while we make new memories."

"I shouldn't, but I will. I know Joey would love to have Trey all to herself for the day. I will meet you on the front steps of the Art Institute at ten. Cannot wait," she said, hardly believing what she had just offered.

And what a perfect day it was, AG remembers. To others, we looked like a couple in love—holding hands, laughing at each other's jokes, just enjoying being together. And we were, at least for that day that ended with a late lunch and an afternoon of making love.

We both walked away with intense fulfillment, revived spirits, and a secret that would be kept for years—one that we didn't even know at the time.

Rekindling those same feelings these last few months had been amazing—no longer sweet and gentle, but intense and so satisfying. Both Winnie and AG knew they had to be careful, but it was just so hard to be around each other in public and not long for those stolen moments.

AG didn't take his appearance too seriously; however, the years had been kind to him. Many of his constituents, especially the lonely widows, gathered around him whenever he was out and about. He couldn't even guess how many invitations to coffee or dinner he had turned down, and he was always answering the door to find someone with a pie or cake saying, "I had just been baking and thought of you all alone." AG certainly wasn't lonely though; he was a member of Rotary, Knights of Columbus, and was constantly helping at Saint Augustin's Catholic Parish he and his family had always attended. If anything, he was having trouble squaring what he felt for a married woman, his Winnie, with the tenets of his religion.

Thinking back to the reason for this whole train of thought, AG felt he could certainly deal with the detective unless someone knew about Winnie and him. It would cause such a scandal and force them to make decisions that could change the lives of so many others. He would have to tread carefully to maintain his easygoing manner. He knew the detective to be a thorough and perceptive interrogator.

AG spent most of his day going from one listing or showing to another, and usually there was an official task of some type that required the mayor's attendance. He had lots of time to contemplate where things stood right now.

As he was rushing across town for the third time today, he heard himself say what he had so often thought through the years: "I always knew I would do anything for my Winnie."

Chapter 7

SON №1 - TREY, RONALD EDWARD PHILLIPS III

Still Early September

Mike Finley had handed over to one of the other detectives on the force the assignment to interview those on the guest list of the Man of the Year party, so he could concentrate on the family and closest friends. Also, a male police officer had been assigned to guard Dr. Phillips's room for protection purposes, and Mike could gather from him information on who was coming and going. Mike reminded himself how much these cases were like a puzzle: you had to select the interviewee, gather what each knew,

CASSY PLAYS HER CARDS!

pick up on the nuances they wouldn't say outright, and then put together a solid picture that showed everyone's motive, the weapon (he had that), and the opportunity.

In Mike's first interview, Winnifred certainly had played coy about her boys, simply saying over and over they were good kids. "Why then the dramatic reference to them having their own life issues?" he wonders. He had called the Phillipses' house to find Trey, and the housekeeper had offered, "I think he is probably at the coffeehouse playing his guitar."

"Was the Daily Grind his employment or just enjoyment? Was he seeking a full-time job in the musical field? I guess if your parents want to support you, you can do what you want," thinks Mike.

Mike is looking at a picture of Trey that had been in the local paper touting his musical performances at The Daily Grind. Trey is quite a handsome young man. Obviously, good looks run in the family. He has golden bronze hair, cut short but flipped back at the top, light sage green eyes, chiseled jaws with a dimple in the center of his chin, and facial hair shaved in a trendy five o'clock shadow. He had been photographed in tailored pants and a preppy, light green linen shirt with the collar standing open, his guitar draped over his shoulder. "WOW! The girls must have fought over him in high school and college," mutters the detective aloud.

Through Trey's former teachers, Finley has discovered that Trey was a stellar student who excelled in drama and the visual arts—he probably got that from his mother. He had led a popular band in high school, *Trey's Huggers,* and they had even played area proms and local school dances. Mike knows Trey drives a midnight blue Mustang GT. It is parked in front of the Daily Grind, just as Maya, the housekeeper, had suggested.

As soon as Mike walks in, he sees Trey on a small but well-equipped square stage in the corner. The coffeehouse itself is uptown, with barrel-shaped leather chairs grouped facing a gas fireplace. Bistro tables and chairs are scattered throughout the shop, and the aroma of freshly ground coffee beckons customers to sit awhile and enjoy the music. Mike recognizes the barista from the coffee bar at the Man of the Year party and recalls that he has often accompanied Trey to the hospital to see Doc Ron.

"Wow, nice place," thinks Mike. "This guy must have money, or someone is backing him." Everything is new and trendy. He's heard about the Daily Grind, but his usual coffee is out of a "thousand-year-old pot" at the police station and has the consistency of tar. Looking up at the menu, he has no idea what to order: Cafe Latte, Cafe Mocha, Cafe Chai, Espresso, Cappuccino, Coffee Americano—maybe that is what they now call "regular" coffee. You can also get Italian Soda, Acai Antioxidant Smoothie or Caramel Apple Macchiato. "Isn't that a dessert of some kind?" he sighs, realizing he might be dating himself a bit.

Trey knows the detective is here to see him. The housekeeper had reported to Winnie, and Winnie had warned Trey. "Heed my advice, Trey," texted his mother. "Be calm, and remember you don't have to tell him everything. He's trying to find your dad's assailant."

His mother has always been his comfort and support. For years, she has carried a picture of him with golden curls and a cherub-like smile. When Trey was seven, his father had finally insisted his hair be cut so everyone would know he was a boy. Trey automatically heard music in his soul before he ever realized it was coming from a radio, TV, or musician. He gravitated toward the softer side of life, like reading and composing songs. His sport had become tennis.

It was so much more gentlemanly than the contact sports Phipps gravitated to. As he got older, his father had tried to sign him up for little league baseball and pee-wee football, but Trey never made it past the first few practices. He was too young then to sense how deep his dad's disappointment ran, but he would certainly know later. It's amazing that his relationship with his younger brother, Phipps, had never been affected. They were not only brothers but also best friends.

Trey reminds himself not to let on with the detective that he is gay. It had been so hard during those high school years, the reason he had immersed himself in his favorite sport, tennis—at least Dad approved of that. The country club always had willing opponents, and some of them even interested Trey, but he was far too afraid his father would be livid if he found out. Trey hadn't allowed any of his feelings to manifest themselves until he had gone to college, where he had discovered the love of his life. Only one other person besides his mother had known he was gay, and she wouldn't tell anyone. She had promised, and he trusted her. Before Trey left college, he had been so afraid of losing his partner and the relationship they had developed that the two of them had plotted until they came up with a reasonable plan to stay close to each other. Both wanted more openness about their relationship but knew it was best to prepare Trey's family first to accept it.

Trey had always hoped he could return to Meadowbrook after he graduated from college. He didn't have dreams of sports fame like his brother. All he really wanted to do was write and play music in his hometown. He had had several songs played on the local radio station, but none had really taken off. His favorite one was called "Different," a song about two true loves that find each other."

Coming back to the present, Trey announces to his audience he is taking a break, then looks over to Renaldo, who gives an affirmative shake of his head. Anyone seeing that would just assume Trey is verifying his break with his boss. He sets his Gibson guitar on its base next to the Fender amp, turns off the microphone, and walks over to shake Mike's hand.

"How can I help you? This whole thing with Dad has me rattled and really upset. Playing my guitar takes my mind off it. Can you tell me what you've found, or better yet, who did this?"

Mike proffers consoling words to Trey as he motions him to take a seat at one of the bistro tables. "No new information, but I'm finding out just how popular your dad is in this town—no wonder you are frustrated and demanding answers. Can you think of anyone who might have done this?"

Trey keeps it short. "No, he's always helping people around here. He has never been home much because of his medical practice; still, he has always given Phipps and me a good life." Before going any further, Renaldo walks over and puts his hand on Trey's shoulder.

"Can I get you two something on the house?"

"No, thanks," both Finley and Trey reply at once. Mike takes this opportunity to speak with the barista. "It's great of you to go with Trey to the hospital to check on Doc Ron."

Renaldo steals a look at Trey and then says with a South American accent and a confident demeanor, "I'm glad to do it. Doc Ron is one of my most steady customers. Unless he is out of town or called in on an emergency, he stops by before going to the hospital to get his usual, a cappuccino with an extra shot of espresso. And as for Trey here, he has been so good for business that I want to show my appreciation and concern for his father by being there for him, too."

Mike nods as the barista turns to go to the register. He notes as he watches him go that Renaldo's appearance is totally opposite of Trey's. Whereas Trey has blond features, the barista is dark. His hair is short, his eyes are deep, deep brown, and his musky skin is bronzed. He unquestionably fills out his work shirt that is emblazoned with the logo, Daily Grind, Best Grounds in Town! Every time Mike has seen Renaldo away from the shop, he has been wearing black cargo pants and a black skin-tight T-shirt. He sports the same 5 o'clock shadow as Trey, except he has a trimmed mustache. Mike can understand why the coffeehouse does such a good business, and it isn't just because of the music or the coffee. Renaldo has that can-talk-to-anyone style that men, women, even teens—especially girls—are drawn to. Mike turns back to Trey and delves, "So you never wanted to follow in your dad's footsteps and become a doctor? I know you had the top standing in your high school class, and your ACT scores obviously qualified you to move in that direction."

"Boy, you really do your homework, but why on me? Why aren't you out trying to find the person who did this to my dad? And just for your information, I never wanted to be a doctor. I love music and the arts." At that, Trey stands up. With a mildly disgusted look on his face, he offers, "I have two more sets. Gotta get back on stage." Mike also stands up and makes his way to the door as Trey begins to play Stapleton's rendition of the Beatles, "Don't Let Me Down." Finley is hoping he will have better luck getting information from Phipps.

Talking to the detective has brought up so many memories for Trey; as he plays, he lets loose the thoughts of his earliest inklings when he felt so different. He remembers how he gradually became aware of his sexual feelings for other boys and how excited he was when he was in the company of a boy he really liked. "I had no idea how to connect the dots, so I just went on with life," he mutters to himself.

He remembers entering middle school, where all his friends were panting after girls, talking about how stacked they were and designing ways to get noticed by them. "It didn't make sense to me. I liked talking with girls or being at social events, but I had no desire to 'date' one," he admits to no one. Thankfully, music saved him again. Being the guy leading a band gave him stature and a reason to be too busy to have a steady girl.

"Follow in my dad's footsteps?" He nearly skips a beat in the song he is playing, and a smirk plays on his lips. "That detective is so far off. I can't think of anything more disturbing than being an OB-GYN, always on call all hours of the day and being away from my family. Although the tangible rewards are plenty, and I have been the beneficiary of many of those, to me, the profession demands too much of a sacrifice. Me, an OB-GYN? Never!"

As Trey finishes the set, all he can think about is being in Ren's arms at their haven, their townhome. Ren had left earlier, knowing the shop was in the capable hands of his new manager. Both Trey and Ren had recognized the hunger for acceptance their new hire desired. He is just like them, trying to get his education and fighting to identify who he is and what he wants in life. He isn't as handsome as Trey or as masculine as Renaldo, but he loves the coffeehouse atmosphere and is so comfortable around Trey and Ren. And Renaldo knew from the start he would add a fun, lively vibe for the younger crowd who had discovered coffee.

As he packs up his guitar and music, Trey mutters to himself. "I didn't mean to do it, Dad. I just had no choice."

Chapter 8

SON №2 PHIPPS
... AND CLAIRE

September, and the Interviews Continue

Everyone he asks tells Detective Mike Finley if he is looking for Phipps, he should check first in Meadowbrook High's weight room. Phipps's given name is Thomas George Phillips, named for his dad's best friend, Tom, and for Winnie's grandfather, George— only two people knew differently.

Coaches and even the principal are quick to share with the detective that Phipps is looking at a Division I scholarship. Several football scouts have already been to watch him and assess his skills. Phipps is Meadowbrook's hometown jock, and they all turn out to see him play under the Friday night lights. He never disappoints them. Phipps has several pictures on the school's "Wall of Fame," even though he is just starting his senior year. As a multi-skilled athlete, he is all-state in football, basketball, and baseball and routinely plays scratch golf, which helped his high school team get to State last spring.

Mike remembers that his investigation of Phipps showed he is a good student, but nothing compared to his brother. His principal has described Phipps as hardworking, strong, good-looking, popular but quiet, and with a quick wit. He has dark brown hair with auburn overtones, and aquamarine eyes that mimic the blue of the Caribbean. He is everyone's friend—and a special one to Claire, the love of his life.

If you were to ask anyone in Meadowbrook, they would tell you Claire is a typical teenager. But there is nothing typical about her; she is simply dazzling. Her long raven hair is eye-catching no matter what style she wears. For school days, it is usually down past her shoulders in waves of curls; for cheerleading, it is in a high ponytail with a big bow sporting the school's colors; at the beach, Claire wears a tight French braid; and for formal school dances, it is styled in an upsweep with just enough loose tendrils to frame her infatuating face. Her eyes are turquoise, and her smile lights up any room she is in. To say she is popular is an understatement. And it isn't just her looks; students and adults alike see the special qualities she possesses inside and out.

Claire's list of extracurricular activities reads like a catalog. She is on a competitive dance team at the local dance studio, *Divas Dance*, often has a solo in the school's show choir called *Revolution*, can hold her own in any debate with her crisp dialogue and direct eye contact, and has a voice everyone tells her is good enough for Broadway or a recording career. On top of that, she is a stellar student who loves to learn and always gives help to others who are not as quick as she is to master skills. As a senior, she is exploring colleges, and with her credentials, the question is never which one will accept her; it is which one does she want. Her mentor and role model is Joey Redford. Joey always gives her extra time and support, pushing her just enough to enhance her musical, dance, and debate accomplishments.

Her mother, Ava, is the head nurse at Meadowbrook Hospital and has been putting away money for years for her only daughter's education. Claire is her true delight. She wants her daughter to have everything good in life. Claire has never known her father. The story told to her by her mother is that Claire was the result of an on-and-off relationship with a man who later turned out to be married. Ava tells everyone that the man for her is (and always has been) unavailable, but that doesn't stop her friends from trying to "fix her up." She herself is striking, with deep auburn hair, emerald eyes, and what many would call a voluptuous figure. Claire's mother also fills in at Dr. Ron Phillips's office when they are short on help or to cover vacations. Ava's priorities continue to be her daughter and advancing her own nursing career.

And, yes, the love of Claire's life is Phipps. Phipps has always displayed leadership skills. As a kid, he bossed Trey around and involved him in all kinds of shenanigans. After all, they had 40 acres to explore, a huge pool that provided a water playground and cooled them off on hot summer days, a game room to rival any arcade, several basketball hoops, a mowed football field, and every kind of sports ball. On top of that, their mother was always eager to chauffeur other kids to and fro, so the boys always had willing comrades. In fact, the Phillipses' home was *the* place to be. Trey loved his younger brother and appreciated his ready social skills. They were the scourge of Meadowbrook even in elementary, but nothing vicious—just fun-loving and mischievous. More than once, Winnie had had to go to the school to plead their case for leniency. Ron was always at his office or the hospital.

Both boys could have described in detail their childhood treehouse, which also served as a clubhouse for several years. Their dad had had it built for them in hopes it would corral some of their ramblings around the property. It was constructed of wood, 10 feet by 10 feet, with a railed balcony, two front and two side window cutouts, and one tall door. A fire escape slide had been added to the back; Winnie had insisted over the boys' objections. "Oh, Mom, we're not babies. We can escape if we need to." There were stairs leading up to the railing surrounding the balcony and ending by the half door. A bucket on a rope to haul up "essentials" and a tire swing had completed the exterior.

The boys had painted a primitive but effective sign: "Phillipses' Clubhouse, No Girls Allowed." That sign would get painted over several times, especially when the boys and their friends were in middle school and discovered girls. Inside the treehouse, there were crude but functional seats that Trey and Phipps had spent hours in the garage nailing together. They had conned their mother out of two navy blue serviceable quilts, a rickety side table from the basement storeroom, and an often-used set of walkie-talkies. She had insisted each boy have a heavy-duty, higher lumens battery-powered flashlight. Bulbs strung above the balcony also provided some light. Little by little, they had added unique finds to the walls, like driftwood from the river, an eagle feather, an old bicycle wheel, and metal images of their superheroes.

Many days were filled with make-believe as they became pirates sailing the ocean, castaways stranded on an island, or fighting off the "bad guys" with every type of Nerf gun that was stored in their toybox arsenal. For food, they raided the kitchen or ordered a pizza. Rain seldom derailed their plans for a day in the clubhouse. If the tree house could have talked, it would have been able to share the secret joys, challenges, and future hopes of a generation.

There was only one living thing that got a free ride up to their retreat—that was their beloved yellow Labrador, Champ. His outgoing, trusting, intelligent, and high-energy temperament had been perfect for the boys. One of their fondest memories was the Christmas they had pulled the red ribbon from a "barking box" and out bounded the cutest puppy. He had immediately licked their faces and jumped on each of the boys, wrestling them to the ground. From then on, he went everywhere they went. Champ had grown as they grew. He was happiest romping through the fields, chasing them on their bikes, or hanging his head out one of the windows of the clubhouse.

With all his talents, Phipps could be a snob or a bully, but instead he treats everyone fairly and genuinely acknowledges them. By high school, he is a shoo-in to be the captain of every team he is on, one because of his prowess at the sport, two because of his leadership, and three because he makes everyone, even the bench warmers, feel important. The coaches value his leadership and truly want him to succeed. His triumphs always manage to inspire his teammates to give their best.

In his freshman year, Phipps had created a tsunami in the student body, especially among the girls. Usually, the senior boys ruled the dating scene, and the rest of the boys had to settle. Not Phipps. In no time, the boys liked him, and the girls loved him. Those first few months, he had his choice of dates for all the parties and dances, even homecoming. He was so wrapped up in the whole experience that he hardly had time to breathe. Then, as the semester changed and he went for the first time to his required speech class, he found himself sitting next to Claire Davis. He had heard her name many times, usually associated with the dance team or music classes, but he had never really talked to her. As he slid into the desk beside her, she smiled at him and offered, "Hello, I am Claire Davis, and I believe you are—what's that everyone calls you—Phipps? Nice to meet you."

Phipps, even though he felt a little tongue-tied, pulled out a sincere "Hi." He was staring and couldn't stop. She was a vision; her long, dark black hair was pulled back, revealing her luminous eyes. He searched for a color—turquoise, like the stone. And that smile— he loved that smile. He was captivated, and he didn't know what to do with it. He was the one usually leaving a girl with a stunned look.

After class, he raced to catch up and asked what her next class was. Claire slowed and turned to speak to him. "I have dance class now. I don't imagine you will be in that one," she calmly remarked, giving a slight, not mean, but confident chuckle.

"So right," he stammered. "I'm off to football practice. Great being in class with you," tripping backwards but wanting another look at his future.

"Me, too. See you around," Claire smiled and moved toward the gym.

"How lame," he thought. "I could have come up with something better than that!'

Over the next month or so, Phipps made it a point to "bump into" Claire, and it wasn't long before they were comparing notes on everything going on in high school. Claire was so easy to be with; she knew and was known and liked by everyone, just like Phipps. They were never not a couple after that first year. By the start of their junior year in high school, they are "the couple"—he, the spectacular jock and she, the beautiful cheerleader. One can just imagine the envy with which other students speculate about the couple and their relationship.

Phipps and Claire are incredibly close. They understand each other and often share the burden of carrying high expectations from everyone around them. Many compare the couple to Phipps's godparents, Tom and Joey Redford. Phipps, like Tom, is a romantic who makes Claire feel extra special with his compliments and encouragement. Oh, Claire is no pushover, not at all, but she has a unique bond with Phipps, much like Joey has with Tom. Her mother seems to like Phipps, but she is always cautioning Claire, "Remember, you are on the verge of grasping an exciting, beautiful life, so don't get too serious. Especially leave room to learn what type of person you might eventually want to spend your life with." Ava admits to herself, "I knew someday I would have to tell her—this relationship cannot go any further."

Of course, the mother of a high school girl would say that, but Claire never pushes back with what she already knows: "I've found him."

Detective Finley checks the weight room where everyone had said Phipps would be, but finally finds him next door in the gym. He is wearing tight Roberto Cavalli jeans that hug his butt and sports a hoodie sweatshirt emblazoned with the school mascot. His tennis shoes are very expensive Nike Lebron Elites. Mike stands at the edge of the gym floor until Phipps notices him. Cradling the basketball he has been shooting, Phipps approaches the detective.

"You're mighty accurate with that ball," Mike starts the conversation.

True to his quiet reputation, Phipps replies, "I try. I imagine you're here to talk about my dad."

"Yes, for sure. Can you give me any insight into who might have wanted to hurt or attempt to kill him?"

"Not at all; my dad has so many friends in Meadowbrook. I just can't imagine anyone wanting to hurt him," he answers. In his mind he wonders, "Unless it is the husband of one of his conquests—and that might be one of hundreds, if the rumors are true."

"There is a pretty girl who accompanies you to the hospital to see your dad. I assume she's your girlfriend."

Phipps takes a few seconds before answering as he envisions Claire. He always thinks of her as his All-American Girl—with classic good looks, brains to match, and certainly an athlete being a cheerleader, drill team member, and accomplished dancer. And he loves her kissable lips. Then remembering where he is, Phipps replies with an edge, "That's Claire, my girlfriend. We are starting our third year together. She likes my folks, and they like her. There's no way she's involved in his stabbing."

"Oh, I don't mean to imply that she is," Mike quickly affirms, "but it is my responsibility as a detective to check on everyone I can to find your dad's assailant."

"My dad has been to every one of my games. We talk about sports constantly. I just can't imagine playing with the same passion I have now without him there. He must pull through." Mike offers that he has been to the hospital and talked with Dr. Jensen, who really believes he'll be OK.

"He just looks so helpless lying there. My father has always been a whirlwind: community activities, delivering babies, and shepherding the school district. He's taught me everything I know about leadership, and I can't stand to see him sidelined."

"What do you think could have been a possible motive for someone to want to harm him?"

Phipps isn't naive; he knows his dad probably "catted around some," but there had never been any solid proof, and he clings to the hope that his father and mother are happy together. "I truly don't know; he isn't in a dangerous profession, and it is his nature to be generous. I think that is why everyone is so shocked.

"Are you done with me, by the way? I gotta go see Cassy—Ms. Carstens. She was our—Trey's and mine—nanny for years and was always ready to play catch with me or tag football in the pool; now she tutors me in English. I have to keep my grades up to be sure I get scholarship offers."

"Well, I do have plans to talk with Ms. Carstens, but not right now. I'll walk out with you." Detective Mike is parked right beside Phipps. He admires Phipps's coal-black Dodge Ram pickup with a double cab. "Pretty sharp ride!" Mike shouts as they both leave the school parking lot.

As Phipps is driving away, he says under his breath, "Dad, is there something I don't know?"

Detective Finley heads for the station and Phipps to the Daily Grind to meet Cassy—Ms. Carstens—for his tutoring lesson.

Mike stops a few blocks away and makes some comments in his small notebook:

- No leads coming from family members

- Family issues with Phipps and Trey, neither one has alluded to any

- Check with Dr. Jensen at the hospital about Ron's test results

- Keep investigating the former nanny

- Winnifred appears to be very helpful but is holding back and is super protective of her boys

- Interview Claire

- Interview AG

- Interview the barista and the masseur; there is just something about those two guys

Phipps pulls into the Daily Grind. As he enters, he sees Cassy on one of the barrel chairs. She seems oblivious to the ever-present stares she elicits by just being there. He knows she is gorgeous, and he has great respect for her because of the way she treated Trey and him as a nanny and has always held their confidences. Yes, she wears the label of "best loved" teacher at the high school and deserves the title.

"Hey, Ms. Carstens," he saunters up as both break into grins.

"Cut that out, Phipps! How come you're late?"

"Oh, that Detective Finley caught me at the school and was grilling me about Dad. I know he has a job to do, but I have enough on my mind with school, sports, Claire, and passing these classes."

"Relax, I'm here to help you. You are a very capable student when you put your mind to it, and I have lots of techniques to help you conquer English."

They comfortably work for about forty-five minutes, only interrupted by the greetings of those who come in for their coffee fix.

Cassy is gathering up her materials when Phipps queries, "Cassy, you were at the house a lot. Did you ever see Dad . . . mm— how do I put this—with other women?"

Cassy secretly gulps, and her stomach does a complete flip. "What do you mean, Phipps?"

"Well, I've heard rumors about my dad, but I never believed them. Women do love him, but I think he is devoted to our mom. Surely no one would have a reason to stab him, would they?"

"I really don't know, Phipps, but I do know besides all of us, I never saw anyone else at your home." She can hardly breathe and is congratulating herself for breaking it off with Ron. She couldn't stand the thought of hurting the boys or being less in their eyes.

Cassy, shaking her head, thinks, "Oh, how could I get in this deep? The ramifications may be too much to bear."

Chapter 9

REMEMBERING
EIGHT YEARS EARLIER

Early September

I t is late. Cassy has learned from her mom, Megan, who is Ron's night nurse, that he has been moved to a private room. He is still in critical but improving condition. Cassy just wants to be sure he is getting better. She doesn't want him to die. She wants him to live, to have a good life, just no longer with her. And yet the days of old flood her mind.

"Supervise them as they entertain themselves, make sure they get dinner, and let them have some time in the pool; after all, the dog days of summer are upon them," Winnie had instructed me as she was getting dressed. Trey and Phipps, now 13 and 10, were growing older, and so was I. In fact, I was headed into my senior year at Meadowbrook High. It held so much promise. I was class president, head cheerleader, and dance team choreographer with my mentor, Joey Redford—the only person I trusted with my secrets.

Those were amazing accomplishments because I had worked hard to achieve them. I was even more proud, however, that I had maintained a perfect GPA and could start narrowing my choices for college. In the back of my mind, surfacing with some regularity, was my deep desire to be voted Homecoming Queen. Anyway, the boys usually swung the vote for queen, and I was in tight with most of the important ones. I will get to work on that once we are back in school.

Doc and Winnie had gone to a party at the country club that night, as they so often did. I knew they would be late tonight, so I enjoyed my usual activities with the boys—tag football in the pool, a couple of their favorite video games—and then scooted them off to bed. I ended up in the great room, stretched out on my favorite loveseat.

As Cassy muttered aloud her recollections, she felt him squeeze her hand. His eyes fluttered below his closed lids. She wondered if Ron, her Deuce, was now remembering that special night eight years ago that had catapulted both their lives toward this upheaval. They had talked about it several times, and she had her own part of the story to dwell on, but she loved hearing Deuce tell it his way.

The festivities were interrupted for Winnie and me—at least for me—when I answered my pager to find I was needed at the hospital. A set of twins just couldn't wait. As the primary for the OB-GYN team, I handled the more demanding deliveries, and my associates covered the routine cases. I had been expecting this one, but over the years of my practice, I knew you could never predict the exact timing of babies' appearances. I looked around for Winnie, but she was off somewhere, and I couldn't wait to find her. "Anyway," I remember convincing myself, "she will be fine. She has her martinis and lots of company." This same thing had happened many times before. After all, she is a doctor's wife and certainly expects or tolerates these interruptions. I passed Tom at the bar. "Hey, the twins are arriving - have to go to the hospital. Will you and Joey take Winnie home if I don't get back in time?"

Two hours later, after a successful delivery of the six-pound boys, I entered the house, heading straight for the great room. There was Cassy. I stared at her perfect face, beautiful hair, and very desirable body. She stirred and extended her long legs, putting herself in a very inviting position. It was all I could do to hold myself back from smothering her with my own body. I fought to maintain control, adjusting my dick and reminding myself I was supposed to return to the party. Gently, I woke her and apologized. "Sorry to disturb you, Cassy, but I was called to the hospital for a special delivery. Twins. They're doing great! I am going upstairs to take a shower and then head back to the party. I didn't want you to wake up and hear someone in the house without knowing it is just me."

Cassy sat up, yawning, and stretched her arms over her head, revealing a toned stomach. "Thanks for letting me know," she called out, as I headed up the stairs with some very inappropriate thoughts and a twitch below my belt that was becoming a steel rod.

Cassy recalled how suddenly she became alert when Ron had come home unexpectedly and how quickly she put her plan into action.

I was very much awake. I had heard the garage door open and secretly had wished far more times than I could count that Doc was alone. I shook my head to clear my thoughts. HE WAS! With an alluring smile on my face, I headed for the master bedroom. I could still hear the water running in Doc's private bath and figured I would have time to put my long-held plan into action. I knew I wanted a man to initiate me into real sex, and not just any man. I wanted Doc Ron. Our time had come.

A moment later, he walked into the room with only a towel wrapped around his waist. It was obvious that the shower had not cooled his ardor; his towel revealing a strong protrusion. I wondered why he moved toward the door, but I heard the lock click, and he turned with a hungry look in his eyes.

I had pulled back the king-size pewter-colored sheets and comforter with Doc's initials in the right-hand corner. I had centered myself on the bed, wearing only a seductive smile, a sexy red push-up bra, and a red thong with a heart that invited exploration. Our eyes locked. I patted the sheets and then motioned Ron to join me, my entire body seducing his thoughts and his manhood.

I could even recall my exact words. "Our time has come. I want to feel like a woman—a real woman—who has pent-up desire for sex beyond quick thrusts and it's over. My body longs to be caressed, stroked, and made to tingle all over." I reached behind my back, unsnapping my bra, revealing my firm breasts, my nipples hardening. In a sultry voice, I said as his towel dropped to the floor, "Look at you - all man! Take me hard and fast." What flickered through my mind was how many times I had practiced that come-on.

I remember Ron running his hand through his wet hair and shaking his head. "I shouldn't do this. I shouldn't be taking advantage of you, Cassy," he muttered as if trying to convince himself. But we both knew this moment was inevitable.

His eyes were devouring me. Doc began to cover every inch of my body with kisses and nibbles, his tongue circling my nipples and then nipping and sucking each until they were granite hard. He returned to my lips, where our tongues tangled with crazy desire. He explored with his hands my entire body. He was voracious while I had my hands locked on his head, moving him from place to place on my body. I moaned with ecstasy and invited deeper exploration. I could barely hold back my desire for him to enter me. In a short moment of lucidity, I whispered to him, "My thong is edible—scotch, your favorite." Ron made a beeline with kisses from my breasts to my thong and quickly devoured what hindered him from reaching my mound.

"You are beyond every dream I imagined. Are you sure you want this, Cassy?" I tilted my head toward him, my sultry eyes conveying that I wanted him as I captured his mouth with a deep, sensual, long-lasting kiss.

I felt his fingers slip inside me as I arched my back. "More," I encouraged, while my hands held him tight against me. I felt his tongue flick as he sucked my clit at the same time his fingers inflamed me, resulting in a toe-curling scream, "Ron, I am coming!" He reached up to muffle my scream - a quick thought about the boys entered my mind. I could only say a quick prayer that they were deep in sleep.

Ron continued to explore my body, teasing my nipples with his teeth and my swollen bud with his fingers several times before he *entered me with his hardened cock sheathed in a condom that came from nowhere and began to establish a sensual rhythm. His panting and moaning heightened my yearning desire. "Don't stop! Don't stop!" At the same time, we crested, held still, and tumbled sideways on the bed.*

Ron felt a little awkward, I sensed, as he started to get dressed. He looked at me and grinned. "What do you plan to wear for panties now?"

"Oh, don't worry about me," I said in a teasing voice, looking over my shoulder as I walked past him toward the stairs. "You'll find out when you take me home later."

Ron felt himself drifting into his own memory. "God, that night had been unbelievable. Cassy had always been fun and funny."

The trip to the country club had been a blur; I replayed every image and sensuous thought, but as I pulled under the entry to the club, I knew I had to put on my just-been-at-work face. I could easily talk about the long but happy delivery of the twins to proud parents. At least I had hoped I could. As I entered the club, I saw Winnie dancing with the local realtor and mayor, AG. "She probably hasn't even noticed I was gone," I thought. Still, I knew I needed to be attentive to her. I went to the bar to get her a white diamond martini, made with Gray Goose, of course. Every bartender there knew Winnie's drink of choice. I crossed the room just as the dance ended.

"Hi, AG. How's business?" I asked as I handed Winnie her drink and a 7 & 7 for her dance partner.

"Good, very good, Ron. Thanks for loaning me your wife. Winnie, you are a great dancer," he added with smiling eyes.

"No, no, thank YOU for keeping her company. I just got back from the hospital." I took a sip of my scotch, noticing Winnie's eyes meeting AG's.

"Uh, Uh, how did everything go, Ron? Was it a safe delivery?" Winnie stammered.

"Yes, beautiful twins. Did you save this next dance for me?" As Adele's "Make You Feel My Love" played, I set our drinks on the table by AG and whisked Winnie onto the dance floor. Winnie waved to AG. I noticed he gave back to her a half wave. "Are his eyes revealing a desire for Winnie? The song playing could easily have been their song," I thought. "AG and Winnie had history, but would my hold on Winnie ever be broken?" I noticed Winnie hosted the same look.

After the dance, AG approached with Winnie's martini as I headed to the bar to get a new scotch for myself. My phone pinged, signaling an incoming text. I promptly viewed it, and a mischievous grin and a short chuckle made me shake my head. There on the screen were two beautiful breasts, with the note "Come play with us!" Instead of the bar, I headed to the men's room because I could feel the twitch below my belt becoming rock hard.

In the stall, I snapped a picture of my erection and sent it to her with my own note saying, "Your Deuce is wild and will be there soon!"

When it was safe to leave the men's room, I looked for Winnie. I spotted her among a group of her animated friends. Winnie appeared to be listening, but I believed she was lost in her own thoughts. Going over, I coached her, "Wow, Winnie, it's later than I thought. We best go." I took her elbow, leading her toward the door. As we passed a table, I grabbed her half-empty glass, setting it on the table where AG appeared to be sealing the deal for a new home for a local banker. I noticed Winnie looking longingly at AG as she mumbled in my ear something about staying later. As we exited, I motioned for the valet to bring around my car. When my red Ferrari arrived, I gently assisted my inebriated wife into the passenger's seat, slipping the valet a tip before I started for home. I knew I had to go to the hospital—and hopefully make one more stop.

"You always take care of me, don't you, Ron?" Winnie could barely form her words, but she was in one of her martini-induced talking moods. "You danced with me!. You do still love me. Tell me, Ron, tell me. I love . . . ." Her words trailed off as she surrendered to the effects of the last martini. Maybe it was good I didn't have to respond; Winnie was in a fog. I had seen her this way so many times, but especially tonight, her words and actions didn't reach me. Someone else was holding my mind—and body—captive.

Once home, I carried Winnie to her bed, placing her under the lacy coverlet. She was still wearing her Chanel cocktail dress. I did slip off her stilettos and placed her Louis Vuitton clutch on her nightstand. I then quickly checked on the boys. Trey was asleep with the video game begging for a response and Phipps with a football in one hand and a basketball in the other.

I sprinted down the stairs to wake Cassy. She looked so innocent in her tube top, but her hardened nipples said she was ready for me. I knelt beside her and slipped my hand under her short skirt. I aroused her—and myself.

"Are you ready?" I whispered.

"Always," she replied.

"No bra?"

"It's hidden in your underwear drawer," her eyes laughing and seducing me at the same time.

"M-m-m-m." *I fought for words and finally sighed. "Maybe we better get you home."*

It took us only a minute to get into my new Ferrari and pull away. Cassy quickly started caressing my groin. The results were instantaneously evident; she seductively lowered my zipper and took a firm hold of my erection. All I could do was moan with much anticipation, as I pulled the car to the side of the road.

And she pulled on my shaft. Her fingers and then her tongue massaged the pre-cum moisture. She kissed the underside of my erection before her lips surrounded my hardness, and she devoured as much of me that she could. The push and pull were rhythmic, causing my guttural sounds that encouraged her even more until my release was inevitable. She stayed with me, swallowing my cum. Her return to my lips allowed me to taste my own climax. "Oh, Sass, our time has come," I moaned as I zipped my pants and pulled the car back on the road.

Ron surrendered to a deeper sleep, with an erection evident under the hospital blanket.

Chapter 10

TOM AND JOEY REDFORD – A PERFECT COUPLE

Through the Years

Tom and Joey are *the* couple everyone envies, even in college and all through Tom's medical school years—he, the dashing future doctor, and she, the accomplished musician. Tom has what you would call rugged good looks. He likes to wear his dark chestnut hair so it just curls at his shirt collar; his eyes are Montana sky blue, rimmed with navy. His smile's deep dimples always capture women's attention, and he carefully maintains a classy five o'clock shadow. Joey, now his wife, still takes Tom's breath away each time he sees her. She has a striking face with perfect model-like features. Her high cheekbones and constant smile give her an air of caring and compassion. Wheat-colored hair cascades in natural waves below her shoulders, and her eyes are coffee brown with hints of copper. On their wedding day—and every day since—she had seen in Tom's eyes his "Forever Now" love for her.

Everyone in Meadowbrook knows that the Redfords and the Phillipses are the closest of friends as far back as college and even having been in each other's weddings. Tom now works alongside Ron, and they spend many an off hour playing golf or tennis. The two are fierce competitors, always having a little wager on the side, but it never taints their best friends' status. Winnie Phillips and Joey Redford have also formed a very close and steady friendship. They now bond over playing bridge and tennis at the country club, and both are devoted to Trey and Phipps.

The Redfords' house had been the perfect find for them. At first, they had planned to build like Ron and Winnie; however, on one of their many drives, out looking for land close to Meadowbrook, they took an interesting turn off the main road and came upon a beautiful Victorian-style house. It sat in a flower-filled valley, had several other structures, and stood at the end of a large tree-lined drive. It could have been a two-page picture spread in one of those glossy magazines that touted stunning places to live.

No one seemed to be around, so Tom and Joey stopped the car, ready to explore when a man carrying a for sale sign came around the right side of the porch.

"Hi, folks, can I help you?" After a closer look, he exclaimed, "Oh, you're Joey and Tom from State. I dated Winnie until she met Ron. It's great to see you."

Tom and Joey broke into smiles. Tom remarked, "We know you are the mayor, but we certainly had not realized that you deal in real estate. So is this for sale? Is it a private residence? Who lives here? It is so amazing. We're in the market and have been checking out small acreages close to Meadowbrook."

"Well, you came at just the right time. Mr. and Mrs. Sutton lived here for about 50 years before they passed away. They had the house built and took immaculate care of it during all that time. Now the heirs are wanting to sell. Here is my card. I'll be glad to show you around if you like." Joey grabbed Tom's arm, and they both started shaking their heads. "Yes! Yes, please."

AG began delivering a rambling, but impressive, description of the property. "The Sutton House sits on five acres here in the valley. As you can see, it is true Victorian architecture with the tower, turrets, and dormers. You've already had a good look at this wide wrap-around porch with the decorative railings and turned posts. Ornate trim work around the porch includes gingerbread cutouts and spindle work. Notice the pointed arches and windows, which include diamond-shaped panes, then the steep, front-facing gable roofs, decorative eaves, and wooden board-and-batten siding."

Tom and Joey were still oohing and aahing over the outside when AG simply motioned and invited, "Do you want to see the inside?"

In unison, the Redfords again begged, "Yes! Yes, please."

AG started his same impressive description. "This house is three stories because it has an attic. The overall plan is very intriguing, and some would say rambling, but there are lots of specialty nooks and built-ins. All the woodwork is original, double doors, ornate stairways, and detailed hand-carved trim. The second floor has four bedrooms and two baths.

"As you can see on the main floor, there are high ceilings and deep archways, and the sparkling chandeliers are included in the sale price. This is the formal dining room, with the kitchen just through that door. And I am certain you've noticed that most of the rooms have fireplaces—all functional. About ten years ago, they tucked this bathroom behind the library on the main floor. That library with floor-to-ceiling shelves has one of those sliding ladders, so you can get to the books on the top shelves. Finally, this would be your parlor, or what today we call the living room or great room. There is wainscoting on all the walls in here. This fireplace has a carved mantel and a Tiffany Victorian beveled fireplace screen."

After a quick look at the upstairs bedrooms and baths, Tom caught a glint in Joey's eyes that telegraphed, "I want this; it is our future."

Once outside, AG said as he postured toward the house, "That's it in a nutshell. Any questions?"

Tom naturally asked what the property was listed for, and Joey, thinking of a music studio, asked about the other buildings, one obviously a three-car garage. AG pointed to the other larger structure and noted that it was used by Mrs. Sutton as a craft and quilting area. The smallest structure was a potting shed.

Tom and Joey thanked AG. "We will be in touch."

AG, like a good salesman, responded, "Don't wait too long; I expect it to go fast."

Tom and Joey talked excitedly all the way back to Meadowbrook. He was so impressed with the location of the house in respect to the commute to downtown and the hospital, and she was already in her mind decorating the inside in what she loved, a more modern Victorian style. Tom mused, "That garage is perfect for our cars, and the house is so unique. I can just see us sitting on that porch whenever I get a few hours off—coffee or iced tea and you and me."

"You do realize that the kitchen needs updating, the walls need lighter, brighter colors, and please, please, can we paint it yellow with white trim?" she begged. "All those rooms upstairs, we can fill them with little ones."

It went on like this all the way back to their rental house, and the first thing they did was call AG to put in an offer. They looked at each other with joy in their eyes as Tom whispered, "This is destined to be our happily-ever-after home."

Tom's secret car getaway, his metallic gray Corvette ZR, was the first car parked in the Victorian garage. He could hop in it, go just outside the city, and push it to full throttle. He had never envisioned owning one until he finished medical school and had a lucrative position. Even then, he had held off for a few years in hopes they would have a family—this car was clearly impractical for children! With the radio cranked to full power, he would sing to the music—he loves opera. His favorite is *La Traviata* by Giuseppe Verdi. To him, the music is passionate and transports him to another time. It is the perfect release from the many stressors that he deals with in his practice. Joey is such a supportive wife. She knows he goes way too fast, way too far, and dreams out of character in that Corvette; however, her love for him recognizes the peace it gives him, and he always comes home with a huge smile on his face. She kisses his cheek and jokes, "Aha, I know where you've been and what you've been doing." He hugs her and goes to change from his scrubs.

Joey certainly doesn't have to work, but she continues using her degree in music by volunteering at the high school. She loves managing and coaching the Meadowbrook High School Show Choir, choreographing their dance moves with the help of her gifted student, Claire. Although she knows she isn't supposed to have favorites, she can't help herself. Claire, Phipps's girlfriend, is super talented and always looks to Joey for support and advice. Joey is everything Claire wants to be.

Joey also has a real flair for preparing students going into speech and debate competitions. Her sharp eye can catch them on the slightest slip that might cause them to lose points. She is very well read and can converse on multiple interesting, challenging or downright confusing topics. She makes sure their research is up-to-date, accurate, and drives home the side of the issue they had chosen or been assigned. Right now, they are preparing for state competition, and she believes they have a strong chance to win it all.

The students really like her. She is fun, outgoing, and knowledgeable. Joey has studied voice and can sing anything. She is happiest with a microphone in her hand and an audience to charm with her dancing and songs. The students often beg her to perform for them tunes like "Shake It Off" by Taylor Swift and Beyonce's "Single Ladies Put a Ring on It." Her enthusiastic choreography and perfect pitch always get the high schoolers pleading for more. They are without a doubt her fan club.

There is one big cloud that hangs over the Redford marriage. Both Tom and Joey have always desperately wanted to have children. With Tom's contacts in the medical field, they had tried every fertility treatment available, including drugs, which made Joey sick;

experimental surgeries—four of them with no definitive diagnosis; and artificial insemination. That last one had been hard on Tom's ego, but he knew it meant so much to Joey. But nothing has worked.

Joey feels like she has been in a long, dark tunnel of despair recently, and has finally sought the help of a psychiatrist. She has been perfect for Joey, with a soft, easy style that made Joey feel comfortable pouring out her fears and hurts. Joey has shared with her the moments when she breaks down in tears going to her OB-GYN. The number of happy, pregnant women makes her wonder all over again, "Why? Why? Why? Going to a baby shower," she chokes out, "is torture."

She can't even look at the doctor when she shares her most troubling and heartbreaking fear—that Tom might leave her for someone who could give him children. Slowly but surely, the psychiatrist helps Joey realize she is a wonderful human being on her own. She begins to understand that her worth is not determined by the child she might bear or being a mother to her own child. She possesses gifts that enhance all children and her students. The psychiatrist also assures her that she has interviewed Tom, who has joyously expounded on how much he loves his wife. They appear to have found their own person. That helps Joey validate her feeling that Tom is her rock, and she knows he has never made her feel this was her fault.

So far, nothing has worked, and they just continue to hope. They have discussed adoption many times; however, both want their own children. They have cherished being involved with Trey, Phipps, and now Claire and treat them like they are their own. Winnie, of course, knows the situation and loves having Tom and Joey act as the "second mom and dad that the boys love and turn to."

Joey immerses herself in her artistic endeavors. Tom has little time to fret over something he can't change and so devotes himself to his demanding job and to Joey, of course. Secretly, they both keep wishing that it would just happen. There were many times when Joey, always working to make their new home their own, would break down in tears of frustration, pleading into the air around her, "Will we ever have our own children?" She wants to pass on some of her and Tom's childhood treasures that are stored in her cedar chest. A woman dreams of handing her daughter her doll that laughs and walks, and Tom has saved all his big metal dump trucks so his son could build roads and houses in the sand.

Recently, Tom has been worried about Trey and Phipps. They are more comfortable confiding in him and Joey than their own parents, and usually their issues involve minor obstacles for them. This time, though, Tom is torn between the love he feels for the boys and the trust they have placed in him, his responsibility to their father and the changes this would force Ron to face.

Trey had to confess to someone that he is gay and has a partner he loves! Not a huge surprise to Tom and Joey. They had discussed this possibility several times and marveled that Ron could not— or maybe would not—pick up on all the signals. Tom isn't sure if Winnie knows what is going on, but she has that intuition mothers employ, so she most likely is tuning in. However, she has never mentioned anything to them.

Phipps and Claire are the perfect young couple. Neither of the Redfords had seen this kind of devotion in other kids—well, young adults—their age. Tom and Joey secretly share Winnie's concern that everything for the two kids is moving too fast and could derail their plans for their futures. Too many early relationships falter in college, and some never even make it to the university. That would be a travesty for Claire, with her singing talent, and for Phipps. They are afraid he would regret having settled if he never got to play college and maybe even pro sports.

Then there is Ron's philandering, although lately he seems a little less assertive. Tom has always worried about Ron's extracurricular activities, but he isn't one to pry into other people's private lives, even if they are super close. During medical school, Ron was a different person at a conference away from home. Conquests were his cocaine, and he freely partook. Because of it, they no longer go to the same conferences together. Whenever Tom can, he takes Joey, and they have fun exploring the cities: New York, San Francisco, New Orleans, and Palm Beach. In fact, often they go early and stay a few days after to maximize their getaway.

Tom and Joey really enjoy spending time together, and each year they book a week in the winter on a beautiful island. So far, they have been to Jamaica, Antigua, Barbados, and Maui, and they are really looking forward to being in Fiji this coming winter. If they are honest with themselves, they always secretly hope that the change of environment will help them conceive.

If Tom and Joey aren't working, vacationing, or conferencing, they take the opportunity to go to Joey's family farm. Tom thinks of Joey's parents as the "salt of the earth." Her father, Steve, is a modern-day farmer with computerized equipment and a home computer to calculate his expenses and yields. Tom and Steve ride often in one of the big tractors with air conditioning and talk about world affairs. Joey and May love catching up and experimenting with new recipes, including baking one of May's prize-winning pies.

One year they had gone with her parents to the State Fair. It was an all-day occasion. The fair covered four city blocks and drew thousands of people. Tom, being a city guy, was fascinated by any and everything fried on a stick. His favorite was the pork chop on the stick, and Joey loved the fried Snickers. Her parents opted for the funnel cakes.

Tom's folks are just as solid. They live in Peoria, where his father works in management in the large CAT company headquarters, and his mother is a school administrator. She has a wonderful knack with middle school students and always strives to help her teachers get them ready for high school and for life. Her memory chest at the bottom of the bed at home holds hundreds of thank-you cards from former students. Tom's dad, Parker, and his mom, Pam, are prominent in the Lutheran Church, deliver Meals on Wheels, and volunteer at the local nursing home. Since Tom is their only child, they have totally spoiled him, but he has turned out to be this wonderful human, and he found another wonderful human to love and marry. Tom and Joey know how lucky they are when it came to both sets of parents.

Tom and Joey are well respected in the Meadowbrook community. They are not the elite like Ron and Winnifred, but their inviting and genuine personalities draw people to them. Every year Joey heads the food drive at Thanksgiving and the Christmas tree decorating fundraiser for the hospital. Winnie volunteers to help Joey, but most of the time begs off with other commitments. However, both Ron and she like being front and center when the press comes to report on the fundraising success. You would think Joey would get tired of standing in Winnie's shadow, but she never does. She is a true friend.

For several months now, Tom has wrestled with a nagging feeling that a life-changing storm is brewing for Ron.

"Why can't I tamp down this troubling feeling? My sense of dread for Ron just keeps surfacing."

Chapter 11

CASSY BEING SASSY – LOOKING BACK AT COLLEGE IN CHICAGO

Seven Years Earlier

As Cassy was making her final decision about college, she knew she wanted to be in the Chicago area—close enough that she could return to Meadowbrook on a weekend and still enjoy her anonymity in the large city. When she voiced this to Deuce, he quickly proposed a simple solution.

"Let's get an apartment in one of those nice Chicago sub-urbs. Then we can be together without worrying about logistics or prying eyes. You can decorate it any way you like, and, of course, I'll cover the rent." Holding her hands, he begged, "Say yes, Sass, say yes." And Cassy did.

In July when Winnie and the boys took their annual European vacation, Ron and Cassy sneaked off to the city to find the perfect place. After looking at quite a few, they agreed on a small one-bedroom condo on the ground floor in an older neighborhood. It was on a tree-lined street, came with a small private patio and a pool, and had recently been updated to a more modern open floor plan. Besides, it offered parking, internet, hardwood floors, a gas fireplace, and a stacked washer/dryer. Furniture shopping was fun, and she didn't need much. Whenever they returned from one of their shopping forays, they would congratulate themselves on selecting a place that could provide plenty of privacy and could be accessed through the patio doors.

In August, just before her first course was set to begin, Cassy spent afternoons searching in the local stores to buy items that would bring color and comfort to the newly furnished rooms. The bedroom had a neutral color scheme of gray and tan. A super soft and luxurious white comforter, beige sheets with white edging, a sand-colored duvet, and charcoal gray pillows certainly made for an inviting focal point. On the nightstand, Cassy had placed a picture of her mom and several of Deuce.

For the great room, they had purchased a tufted cream-colored sofa with a matching chaise, a black floor lamp with a marble base, and a 60-inch lift-top desk for Cassy's studies. The sofa sported at least five pillows in variations of robin's-egg blue, Cassy's favorite color. A plush area rug with large diamond shapes matching the blues in the pillows completed the cozy setting. Four large seasonal prints of Chicago accented the eggshell white walls.

A multi-colored vase decorated the small kitchen island, and Cassy vowed to herself to keep it filled with fresh flowers. Two ladder-back swivel stools in black were pulled up to the island overhang. An espresso machine promised the best early morning aromas, and a blender promised perfect margaritas.

Having established the apartment to her liking, Cassy decided to prepare herself to start classes at Buxton College, a small private university that concentrated on bringing in students with strong promise but limited funds. Megan was happy for her daughter but felt uncomfortable with the whole college scene, so she let Cassy take control, as she had with so many parts of her life.

Arriving on campus, Cassy checks in with her advisor to verify her fall schedule, then proceeds to the bookstore to purchase textbooks and supplies. She likes the vibe of the nearby coffeehouse, Grounds for Celebration, as she sips on an iced coffee and watches fellow students arrive on campus. It is obvious that several of the guys check her out, and she checks them right back. Returning to her apartment, she decides to put on her bikini and catch some rays at the pool. She enjoys chatting with several of the other sun worshippers, who encourage her to join them later at the local pub, Happy Daze, featuring local craft beers. Cassy finds she loves staying on her own, exploring the city, taking in events, or holing up in her now inviting apartment to begin her studies—and entertaining Deuce when he is in town.

Before classes are scheduled to start for Cassy, Ron arrives in town for a five-day medical conference. He attends sessions during the day. Even taking time to swap war stories over a scotch with his colleagues, he still has plenty of time to slip over to "wrestle" with Cassy. He cannot believe how satisfied he is with her—so much so that he has lost interest in other conquests, and that wasn't his pattern in the past.

Knowing that they want time alone tonight, they pick up Chinese: moo goo gai pan for her and Mongolian beef for him. Over dinner, they feed each other with their chopsticks and exchange taunting sexual innuendos. They read their fortune cookies, adding "between the sheets" to add a little spice. Cassy's reads, "Nothing is impossible to a willing heart . . . between the sheets." Ron's message reads, "Life is short. Break all the rules . . . between the sheets." "Both hold promise for the night," he teases.

"I like when you bite what I'm offering," she quips as she extends her chopsticks.

"You are going to offer me much more than that," he counters. "I've got a long, beefy morsel for you!"

"Oh, I like soy sauce on my meat, and a little sweet and sour sauce would add some tang," she pushes back.

Cassy jumps up to dim the lights as Gabriel's "In Your Eyes" echoes from the Bose speakers. They are both anxious for the real dessert, and they are ready to enact the fortune cookies' promises "between the sheets."

Ron reflects on the lyrics, "I see the light and the heat in your eyes." He discloses, "I want to be *that* complete in your eyes, Cassy."

She rushes into Deuce's waiting arms, pulling them both to the plush carpet. They work together in an I-can't-wait pace; Ron hurriedly undresses Cassy, ogling her body as he unclasps her bra and shimmies her panties to her ankles. Her hard nipples and her citrus fragrance heighten his arousal. Cassy gazes into Deuce's cobalt blue eyes as she pulls his Polo shirt over his head. His khakis and black boxer briefs drop to the floor, revealing his erection with its tip moistened by his pre-cum.

Both their bodies start to shake as he licks her nipples and asserts his claim, whispering, "I want to show you how good it can be when we're not in a hurry. We have all night." Ron possesses her mouth and tongue, capturing every sound she can't hold back. "God, Cassy, you are beautiful—so beautiful. You drive me wild." He takes control, and she loves it. He isn't the only one going wild. Neither can hold back. After assuring her nipples are hard with desire, he kisses and nibbles a trail to her stomach and then to her nub, where he tickles and encircles it, causing her hips to rise to meet his mouth, grinding for fulfillment. His long fingers slip through her folds. "You are so wet for me, Sass."

Two of his fingers enter her channel, massaging her sweet spot. She groans and begs him, "Please, Deuce, please. I need to come."

With his cock covered, like a steel rod covered in a condom, he penetrates her and sets up a fierce rhythm that has both begging, "More, more, harder, harder, faster! Don't stop!"

Their bodies quake, but they are far from finished. She drapes her legs over his shoulders as he captures her love bud with his teeth and lips and begins a new, conquering rhythm. His eyes are amused, and he keeps saying with his smile, "I want to watch you come again. It's so fucking amazing." She obliges him, and her orgasm makes her scream his name with satisfaction.

Cassy returns the favor, sucking on his cum-smeared shaft. He shouts wild protests of pleasure. "You're killing me, Cassy!" She continues to tease and tantalize with her tongue, licking his erection and then taking his cock deep into her mouth with his tip gliding back and forth on the back of her throat. "Sass, you are definitely killing me!" Then he bursts into an over-the-edge climax. They are satiated and lie tightly spooned in the queen bed. Their hands never quit savoring the feel of rubbing up and down each other's sweat-sheened bodies until they are finally lost in sleep.

Light through the bedroom window awakens them Saturday morning, the last day of the conference—and a day he is skipping. It is exciting trying to decide how they will spend their time in the Windy City. They want to walk, talk, hold hands and act like they really belong to each other. Ron, of course, has been to Chicago many times more than she has, so he suggests they take the architectural tour. He uses his phone to book it for later that afternoon, and then they duck into a little cafe to have breakfast.

Back outside in the cool but pleasant air, he turns to her and questions, "You know about The Bean, don't you?"

She laughs, puts a coy smile on her face, and chuckles, "Your bean? Do you have one? If you do, I know I would have discovered it by now."

"NO, no, it's a landmark. Come run with me and I'll show you." She is amazed and thrilled by The Bean's shiny exterior and the people of every age walking around it, laughing, posturing at their distorted bodies in the reflection, and taking photos. A friendly tourist takes Cassy and Ron's picture with their arms wrapped around each other.

Ron hails a cab to take them to the check-in point for the afternoon boat tour down the Chicago River. Upon arrival, they wonder why there are so few people—just one other small group of three queued for the architectural excursion. They get their answer when a steady rain begins to fall. The crew motions both groups to come aboard and stand under the overhang of the bar. While their drinks are being prepared, the trio introduces themselves to Ron and Cassy, sharing that they are from New Zealand and in Chicago for a family reunion. Before Ron and Cassy can reciprocate, the young guide points to the clearing sky and notes, "Let's begin the tour."

It is evident the guide truly knows architecture as he shares the history of more than forty buildings on all three branches of the river. Just as interesting is his knowledge of the major events that shaped Chicago. Ron, Cassy, and the trio reward the guide's expertise with ample gratuities.

Next, Ron and Cassy land at a rooftop restaurant on the Navy Pier. They are ready for drinks and starters. He opts for a Cabin in the Woods, featuring one of his favorite Glenlivet Caribbean cask scotch with gingerbread syrup and Tiki bitters. Cassy, wanting to stretch and try something new, orders a Whiskey Tango Foxtrot—Jameson with mango, ginger, and lemon. Together, they munch on crab maki rolls with cucumber, crab sauce, and tobiko caviar. As Cassy finishes her fourth drink, her eyes telegraph a message to Ron: "Deuce, I need you NOW!" Receiving the invitation, Ron immediately pays the bill and calls an Uber. It arrives almost instantly and whisks them off to the condo. He fumbles with the key while Cassy hangs on him, kissing his face and nibbling his ears. They never make it inside.

Ron pushes her up against the wall in the covered entry. Cassy wraps her arms around his rock-hard shaft, riding it strategically up and down her swollen mound. Ron rips off her lace thong and rams his cock deep inside her. A pulsing rhythm results in low, growling moans as they climax.

Once inside the apartment, Cassy turns and smiles at Ron as she stumbles toward the bedroom, stripping off her clothes and dropping them on the floor one item at a time. It only takes a moment before she passes out on the bed.

Ron shakes his head. "Four is just one too many." He wonders, "Will Cassy even remember this in the morning?"

Realizing he must go home today, Ron had packed his suitcase last night as she slept. It is morning, and he heads to the shower. Cassy is still asleep or four sheets to the wind, and he debates if he should wake her now or just before he leaves. As the water cascades over his body, he hears the shower door open, and Cassy slips in with him, making slow massaging circles on his back.

"Oh, Sass, you have the power to drive me insane. I'd do anything to take another ride like our very first one, where you literally drove me wild, but I have to get home."

"Deuce, you drive me insane, too. I must have a shower, especially with you. It will quench my desire and squelch my hangover. Don't deny me," she pleads as she kneels and massages the pre-cum at the tip of his steel rod. Then she takes him into her mouth, sucking hard and fast.

She licks his entire length until he pulls her up and turns her toward the wet tiles, allowing his cock to ram into her from behind and then pulling it out slowly, over and over. Cassy yells, "Deuce,

I am coming. COMING!" Ron slams into her three more times, chasing her climax with his own.

They exit the shower, toweling each other as they share sensuous kisses. Knowing it will be several weeks until he can hold her again, Ron gives her a deep, not-to-be-forgotten kiss. Both dress quickly. They cling to each other as he moves toward the patio door; they continue kissing until the last gap in the glass slides between them.

By noon, Cassy is ready to get out and see what the world has to offer. She returns to the coffeehouse where she had seen so many other college students, especially good-looking, viral guys wearing shorts and skin-tight T-shirts revealing their six-pack abs. One of the guys, obviously an athlete, approaches, recognizing Cassy as the babe in the pink bikini at the pool yesterday. "Are you planning to be around the pool later this afternoon?" he asks.

"About 4:00," she answers with a wink as she struts to the exit, carrying her salted caramel latte and spinach salad.

Chapter 12

CASSY BEING SASSY – THE MILE-HIGH INVITATION

Three Years Earlier - Heading to Maui

"Hot damn! That would be one great fuck!" he admits as he sips his Coke. And she struts toward him. He takes a gulp of the soda this time, wishing it was a Crown neat, but when you have to fly, you have to fly—and not drink.

Cassy is thinking the same thing: "Hot damn! That would be one great fuck—and perfect for the Mile-High Club experience that I have always wanted to have. Do I risk it? Oh, yes—and definitely my way."

Jack Thatcher, a successful pilot with the airlines and even more successful with the ladies, sports a chiseled jawline, eyes the color of teakwood, dark hair with a hint of curls around his ears, broad shoulders, and washboard abs. Staring at him steals the air right out of Cassy's chest. She congratulates herself on selecting him as her Mile High champion.

"God, she is gorgeous, stunning in fact," he mutters to no one but himself. "Those long legs ending in nude stiletto heels and her chocolate leather pencil skirt that barely covers her ass are causing twitches below my belt." Looking down, he concedes, "I gotta get him under control or I will be heading to the pilots' lounge to take things into my own hands. That long flaxen hair curls in submission on top of her blue-as-her-eyes sweater, revealing tits that are waiting for someone to tease them, suck them, and make her hot and wet. Someone like me."

Cassy strides over to the bar stool next to Jack at the Chicago O'Hare airport. She gazes purposefully at his visible bulge and immediately takes advantage of his smile that reveals deep dimples. Her nipples harden as she imagines his dick entering her on the plane.

"Hi," she begins, her sapphire blue eyes seductively saying much more than that. "My friend, Ali, told me you are *the* man to see when it comes to being initiated as a member of the Mile High Club."

She crosses her legs, causing her tight, short skirt to slip even higher on her thighs. At the same time, she places her hand on his thigh, knowing that the bulge is becoming even more evident, with his dick obviously wanting to stand at attention. As they gaze intently into each other's eyes, she leans forward and whispers in his ear as her lips tease his ear lobe, "I am enroute to Hawaii via Los Angeles and am wondering about the rules of admission to *the* club—the Mile High Club."

"God, my wish just came true," he thinks to himself. "Ah, well, I am *the* man for *the* club," he emphasizes. "Now just how would I benefit?"

"The best damn fuck you've ever had," she chortles as she watches his bulge escalate.

"2:06 in the front lavatory. Don't be late. And no panties!" he returns with a coaxing smirk.

"No problem, and I am always commando unless I am wearing edibles." And she disappears into the crowd of travelers, with Luke Bryan's "I Don't Want This Night to End" playing in the bar.

"Two o'clock—and in six minutes I am going to be joining a very exclusive club, 35,000 feet above Las Vegas. Hot damn, kudos to me for finding this one!" Cassy snickers to herself.

At exactly 2:06, she enters the lavatory and lays her eyes on the biggest erection she has ever encountered—the thickest and longest. Cassy lifts her eyes to Jack's sultry gaze. "Shall we get started? Initiation for membership in the Mile High is about to begin," he asserts.

He slides his hands up her hips, moving her skirt to reveal the prize of the encounter. His hands don't stop as they explore her breasts, hidden by her sky-blue cashmere sweater. He pinches each nipple, already hardening, as he places a sensual kiss on Cassy's inviting lips.

Cassy meets his gaze as she licks his precum, encases his cock with a Magnum XL condom, and then mounts his erection, unquestionably at full attention now. His hands go back to her hips, lifting and lowering them as she rides him, alternating slowly at first and then faster, and then back to slowly, tightening her pussy with the upstroke. Every thrust takes him closer to ejaculation; he sees in her eyes that she is near her own orgasm as his fingers circle her clit, teasing and massaging.

The steward hands Cassy an envelope as he makes his last check before landing. Cassy's nipples harden again as she reads Jack's note. "You were right—best damn fuck ever! Congratulations! You are undeniably a member of the Mile High now. A drink and dinner—at 8:00 P.M. in the bar of the Four Seasons? And wear the edibles."

As the passengers deplane, Cassy meets the eyes of the know-all steward and her conquest, Jack Thatcher. His eyes undress her as she sashays her swaying ass off the plane.

Cassy wears her edibles and a red shoulder-baring dress that minimally covers her ass but frames her curves and accents her breasts.

She eyes Jack sitting at the bar, nursing a Crown. With a heated gaze, he is enjoying her stroll toward him. Her five-inch gold-strappy stilettos accentuate her long legs and slim ankles. He is envisioning her beneath him, wanting him. He knows he wants her.

Jack slides off the stool, sauntering toward her and placing his arms around her waist, directing her to the dance floor. Cassy never loses a step as they dance to Michael Bublé's "Feeling Good." Their flirtatious smiles invite a night of fun—a long night of fun. The mood becomes more serious when Jack encircles her waist and pulls her close as they dance to Stapleton's "Tennessee Whiskey," their chests meeting and his tempting eyes devouring her body and promising a night she won't forget—even better than the Mile-High encounter—without any restrictions on their heated connections.

Cassy whispers in his ear, "I love it when a man places his hand on my ass like this when we are dancing. It tells the world, 'Back off. She's mine tonight.'"

Jack adds, "And I like it when your nipples are hard as granite against my chest. It tells me you are ready for *my* aching cock. He pulls her body even closer to him; she feels his bulging package intensify her own need. Their desires are rising, and they both feel a demand to exit the dance floor. They find solitude at the bar, where they both inhale a shot of Jack Daniel's Single Barrel before heading to the elevators, where Jack slips his hand across her bare shoulder and beneath the silky fabric, teasing her nipples even harder as he kisses and nibbles her slim neck.

Once in his room, as Marvin Gaye's "Let's Get It On" plays in the background and her taunting eyes connecting with his, she slips off her dress, standing only in her panties—her edibles, now wet. Jack pulls her onto the bed, kissing her deep, his tongue chasing hers as he then continues to encircle her nipples, taking her to distraction with wanting him and what he has to offer.

He continues his exploration of her body, distributing kisses down her belly until he spreads her thighs, devouring the edibles and giving her a teasing smirk. "Jack Daniels, even here?" He begins tantalizing her clit with his tongue, kissing, sucking, and taking her to an orgasm with his mouth that has her screaming, "More, more, don't stop!" And he doesn't. He does the same with his fingers, finding sweet spots she doesn't even know she has.

Jack slips the condom on his pulsing cock and enters her slowly at first, but as both their needs heighten, he lifts her legs to his shoulders and pushes deeper, harder, and faster. And just like on the plane, they both explode at the same time. All they can manage is to lie there, exhausted but wanting even more.

Jack knows he must get to the airport soon, so a shower seems like a great "last resort," where he soaps her breasts, kisses her creamy skin, cradles her ass, and caresses her clit with his skillful fingers until he pushes her against the tiled shower and enters her one more time. That feeling is right there again—mind-numbing ecstasy as they reach a crescendo together, continuing to moan each other's names.

Cassy notices that Jack is still hard. As he reaches for a towel, she tosses it outside the shower and kneels in front of him, stroking his shaft. She moistens his entire dick with his own pre-cum and then licks her fingers as their eyes meet. He groans and fists her hair, pulling her swollen lips toward his erection. She swallows as much of his dick as she can and then begins to suck—hard and fast, then slow, and then fast again. "God, Cassy, you are blowing my mind. I can't believe I'm ready. Oh, oh, I'm yours again. NOW!" She swallows his ejaculation and then rises to kiss him. He tastes himself on her lips. "God, that was unbelievable!"

"That wasn't God, Jack. That was all Cassy." Jack chuckles and then rushes to dress and pack his flight bag, knowing he is running late for the airport shuttle.

"Best damn fuck!" She smiles as she reads the note he left on the bedside table.

"Text me your return date. I'll meet you anywhere, anytime, even high in the sky. BDF."

Chapter 13

CASSY BEING SASSY IN MAUI

**Three Years Earlier
and after the Night with BDF**

"You've got to be kidding me! Damn, that is one perfect body!" yells one of the beach volleyball players, as another adds, "Is she for real?" Numbers #3 and #4 just stand with open mouths, and #5 falls dazed as the volleyball knocks him on his ass. Each in the female gallery just stops and gazes at the sun-kissed mermaid in her neon red thong bikini. They look fixedly at the jocks and then eye each other. "Oh, now what—or whom—do we have to deal with?"

Cassy doesn't even hear the bantering—or eye the desirous looks—as she strolls along the beach, her earbuds blaring Alicia Keys's "Girl on Fire."

Yes, Cassy Carstens is the fire, and her admirers are the moths.

It is like that every day. Cassy is the goddess who comes from the sea. Her blue eyes are the color of the ocean. Her golden blond locks reflect the sun's brilliance, and her eye-catching tropical bikinis perfectly accentuate her amazing body: skin bronzed by the sun, breasts that are pushed into an inviting cleavage, a thong that reveals her rounded, firm buttocks, and long legs begging to be opened and wrapped around the waist of her next conquest.

As she walks the beach, Cassy thinks about this special trip. Maui is the ideal vacation spot for her and Deuce—perfect white beaches, the warm penetrating sun on their tanned bodies, the fragrances of plumeria, pink cottage roses, and yellow hibiscus. Cassy spends her mornings lying in the sun, deepening her sun-bronzed curves, kayaking, and taking surfing lessons. She isn't a good surfer, but she loves the pounding of the waves on her body—and the adoring looks of the bona fide surfers.

Doc Ron has his medical conference every morning at a nearby hotel, but the afternoons and sunsets are all theirs. Winnie and the boys are on their annual three-week European trip, so these ten days are filled with Cassy and her Deuce's Hawaiian explorations.

One fun-filled day began with watching the surfers, both board and wind, at Ho'okipa Beach. Cassy concentrates on today's sky filled with the best kite surfers showing off their skills with rainbows of colorful kites. However, Deuce's eyes concentrate on his Sass, in her lime green one-piece that is sculpted to a "Y" shape for maximum tanning. It barely covers the parts of her body that he most covets, but he certainly doesn't want all these male surfers lusting after her. His bulge becomes evident to Cassy. She gives him a quick wink, scooting to a large rock, where she strikes a devastatingly inviting pose that promises more later.

Eventually, Deuce coaxes Cassy back to the car with a promise of a trip to Paia. Initially, in the late 1800s, it flourished as a bustling sugar cane operation, but as the plantation's days ebbed into the latter part of the 1900s, so did the town. Today, however, it is the hippest and hippiest community on the island. He can picture his Cassy strutting the streets with a hibiscus flower resting on her ear and a sheer cover-up playing between her legs as she walks.

Even though it is late in the morning, breakfast is on their minds, especially after Deuce tells Cassy about Charley's French toast, made with thick-cut Hawaiian sweet bread tossed in cinnamon and vanilla. Ron knows he is ready for the plate-size macadamia nut pancakes with coconut syrup.

When they pull up to Charley's Restaurant and Saloon, Cassy turns to Deuce with a questioning look that says, "This is special?" However, when she walks in the entrance, she falls in love with all the Willie Nelson memorabilia, including a large replica of Trigger, Willie's guitar, and the mural featuring famous people who have personally experienced Charley's—people like Yogi Berra, Joe Torre, Oprah, Michelle Obama, and more. After breakfast, Deuce buys Cassy a T-shirt featuring Willie Nelson performing at Charley's. It's one of her favorite keepsakes from Paia. They promise the waitress that they will be back for happy hour and hope to see Willie or his sons performing live music.

Deuce and Cassy spend the afternoon wandering in and out of the shops of Paia. They aren't looking for anything special, but the silversmith stores carry unique pieces with touches of Hawaii. They linger over a stunning sterling silver hinged cuff bracelet with blue topaz in Oceania and a set of sterling earrings with freshwater pearls in Sophia Grace Paia.

They stop for a quick drink at the Aumakua Cava Bar; Cassy's drinking a Kava Paloma, and Deuce's having a Zombie. Turning on the bar stool toward Deuce, Cassy remarks, "I would like to check out Pakaloha Bikinis. It's just down the street."

"Cassy, I love that idea," he replies as he hands her his black credit card. "I'll stay here and finish my Zombie and then meet you at Charley's in about 45 minutes." She jumps up, kisses him on the cheek, and scoots out the door. He waits a few minutes to be sure she is out of sight before he goes back to both jewelry stores and purchases the bracelet with stones matching Cassy's sapphire eyes and the pearl earrings she had kept holding up, turning this way and that with challenging eyes that said, "Look at me!" Oh, he was looking all right. How could anything as simple as watching her choose earrings lend him speechless with a rising excitement in his groin?

Walking toward Charley's, Ron is so proud of himself; he can't wait to surprise her. "She is going to love these," he thinks. "She gets beautiful reminders of our time on the island, and I get memories of her sexy, oh so sexy, body—as if I need a reminder. She is all I ever think of anymore." For a fleeting moment, he tries to visualize their future—no, no, he likes this arrangement.

Cassy enters Charley's and sees Deuce at a table near the stage. He stands to greet her with an I-missed-you kiss and guides her to the other chair at the table. "You've got to be hungry; it's been forever since breakfast. I'm enjoying a local beer; what would you like?"

"I'll have the same. I can't believe I'm famished. Let's eat now, OK?"

"They have a great menu; I've been checking it out." Ron goes on to share his choice. "I'm gonna order the bourbon barbeque ribs. It has Charley's own special sauce. You know I'll love the corn and the mashed potatoes and gravy. Can't get enough of that comfort food—Hawaiian style."

Cassy lingers on the menu, trying to make the perfect decision. She finally decides, "Deuce, it's buttermilk fried chicken for me. I cannot wait to try that applewood-smoked bacon doughnut with jalapeno-maple glaze that comes with it. Only in Paia."

Lukas Nelson and his band, Promise of the Real, are the perfect treat on which to end the night. He sings several of his dad's songs, two of which caused Ron to pause and think about his relationship with his Cassy—his Sassy Cassy: "Always on My Mind" and "All the Girls I Loved Before." Cassy loves Lukas's own songs, especially "Set Me Down on a Cloud" and "Can You Hear Me Love You." She, too, ponders her relationship with Ron, her Deuce—or is he?

When Cassy wakes up the next morning, lying by Deuce, she has to recalibrate where she is and what she is doing here. The days have become magical, and she knows they have several more ahead of them. He starts to stir, and she greets him with a kiss. "What, oh what, have you got planned for us today? I'm not sure you'll be able to top yesterday."

"Oh, you have no idea how creative and spontaneous I can be," Ron jokes.

"Oh, yes, I do. I love it when you build me up to one of those crashing orgasms."

"Not now—up and at it. We have things to do and places to go. Wear that heart-stopping, sun-bright string bikini you got yesterday, a cover-up, a hat to ward off the sun, and flip-flops. Oh, on second thought, throw in a pair of shorts and that new T-shirt we got yesterday. Can you guess where we're going?"

"No, no, I want to be surprised! It makes me feel so alive. Just make sure to leave time to give me one of your tantalizing fucks." She flips her hand at him as she saunters across the room. "I get the bathroom first."

He starts to chase after her, and now she is giggling. He almost grabs her, but she sidesteps him and shuts the door. In his mind, he muses, "How did I get so lucky? Cassy is without a doubt *my* Sassy!"

As they leave the hotel and drive to Lahania, Cassy is pumping Deuce for clues, but he offers just one hint: "We're going to catch the ferry to the island of Lana'i, the Pineapple Island."

As soon as they exit the ferry at Manele Harbor, Ron leads her to a jet-black Jeep Wrangler with the doors and top off. It's loaded with a picnic basket of fruit, cheese, fresh-baked bread, and several bottles of wine. Snorkel gear for two pokes out of a canvas bag sitting behind their seats.

"Your carriage, my queen," as he bows and helps her into the passenger side.

They are like two kids speeding around the bends and topping hills until Ron turns the Jeep down a dirt road, which leads to the stunningly beautiful Hulopoe Bay. They walk along the beach in the pearl-white sand with the crystal blue water lapping at their feet until they spot a secluded cove. They while away the morning swimming, snorkeling, and partaking in mind-blowing sex.

In the seclusion of the small cove, Deuce is lying naked on his back on the sun-warmed sand. He leans up on his elbows to watch Cassy frolicking in the warm ocean waters. He sees a mermaid—his mermaid—whose long golden curls cover her breasts, breasts he longs to kiss and tease. Sensing his thoughts and feeling her own mounting desire, she lifts her knees high and hurriedly splashes through the waves toward him. Her nipples peak in her wet bikini, water cascades down her flawless legs, and she captures Deuce's eyes with her I-want- you-too playful look. She can't help but bend down, scoop up a handful of water and toss it right at him. He jumps up, grabs a towel to wipe his eyes, and marvels as she slowly sashays toward him.

Standing right in front of him, Cassy slowly unties her bikini top, and in a seductive voice, she taunts, "I'm ready. Are you?" She already knows he is, his bare erection standing at full attention. She kneels beside him, massages the pre-cum, revealing his readiness, and then devours his lubricated cock, its tip pelting against the back of her throat with every suck she initiates. Deuce groans and nearly loses his balance as his body begins to pulse in rhythm with Cassy's delightful assault. He reaches down and pulls aside her thong so he can caress her clit and feel the silky moisture saturating her mound.

"Sassy, ride me, ride me now! I'm so ready to fuck you!" Deuce pleads.

She is enjoying the pleasure he is providing with his fingers and doesn't want it to stop, but she admits to herself that greater things will be "coming" if she is willing to wait while he slides on a condom. Cassy pushes him down and quickly straddles him, allowing him to guide his shaft to her eager opening. She envelopes his entire member and then begins the same cadence she had used with her mouth to get this rise. Deuce's hips jut up to meet her plunge, feeling the tension she creates when she pulls away. Cassy loves being in control of Deuce and his climax. She varies the speed of her thrusts. "Sass, you are the sexiest, most desirable woman in the world. Faster! Harder!" he groans as their hips grind together. And she does just that—faster and harder—until he yells, "Cassy, I'm gonna come!" She clamps down and milks his essence until he crashes. He pulls her into his arms, offering a sensuous kiss on her lips, and then nibbles the sensitive skin of her earlobe. "Let's play in the ocean, and then it's your turn, Sass."

"I can't wait, Deuce. I need you now! I want you to take me from behind—hard and deep, just like I did you, and I mean NOW!"

She quickly dismounts, releasing herself from his still-hard cock, and rolls over, leaning on her elbows and elevating her ass high in the air. Deuce stimulates her need as he caresses her clit. He finger-fucks her as he strokes his cock with his other hand. Cassy begins panting and gasps, "Deuce, I said hard and deep—give it to me! I'm ready, so ready!" He takes his cue from her and plunges deep into her channel. She meets each of his thrusts with her passionate push back and feels his balls slapping against her thighs. Her body begins to tremble, and her moans become screams. Her entire body shutters as she gives one last loud scream of triumph. Unable to hold back, Deuce gives his final push and falls over in a daze. As they slowly come down off their highs, they hold each other's gaze and let the waves lap over their entangled bodies.

Awakening from a brief siesta wrapped in each other's arms, Deuce looks at his watch. Jumping up, he grabs at her arm and begins gently pulling her up. "Come on, Cassy, wake up. I have another surprise for you and another reservation."

"I am not sure I can leave here; this has been perfect," Cassy protests with a sleepy yawn. She jumps up. "Ah, but you know how I love surprises. Let's go!"

Reaching the Wrangler, Ron pulls out two wrapped jewelry boxes with white ribbons. When Cassy opens the first, she lets out a gasp and starts crying as she sees the coveted bracelet. "Oh, Deuce, it's so gorgeous," she exclaims as he leans over to slip it on her wrist.

"You're not done," he says with a knowing grin.

From the second box, she pulls out the earrings and starts to once again tear up. "You are too generous. These are so perfect—just like you," she laughs and throws her arms around his neck, pulling him toward her to settle a sensuous kiss of thanks on his lips.

"Here in Hawaii, you are my ravishing mermaid, and it thrills me to see you adorned in island style."

"Now we have to get back to Lahaina in order to get to the other side of the island."

When Ron walks up to a doors-off helicopter, Cassy nearly faints. This time, she squeals with anticipation. Their pilot, standing close to the helicopter, postures to them and asks, "Are you ready for your once-in-a-lifetime experience? You'll feel the island breezes and see the towering waterfalls with their sparkling rainbows. You won't believe the homes of the rich and famous and the lush, unspoiled valleys and thick rainforests. Grab your camera or phone because you'll want to take plenty of pictures."

After the copter ride that fulfilled all the pilot had promised, Ron and Cassy exit the helicopter clinging to each other. They drive to Lahania where they have pupus, ahi poke and avocado stack and macadamia nut crusted calamari at Kimo's as they enjoy the ambience of a golden sunset. With their pupus, they sip on Kimo's Kucumber Koctails and finish off with coffee laced with Bailey's and Hula Pie.

Today is their last day, and then it is back to Chicago, where she will begin her final year at college. Cassy stands in front of their striped cabana, distant from the others on the beach. She twirls around as she unclasps her floral beach skirt, matching the thong bikini she got in Paia. Ron isn't here yet, so she uses the passing minutes to apply suntan oil as she listens to Hunter Hays's "I Want Crazy." She is massaging the oil onto her thighs, finding herself throbbing for his touch when her Deuce enters the cabana. "Oh, Sass, allow me," he vows with promises of satisfied lust.

And let him she does. He anoints her breasts with the Hawaiian tropical oil. Her nipples pebble and peak as hard as marble as he slowly teases each with first his fingertips and then with his soft, fish-like nibbles. She moans, raising her hips toward his obvious package, begging for more. His fingers continue the stimulation as he strokes her inner thighs. Deuce spreads her legs, sidelining the fabric as his fingers enter her. He loves her body when it arches, and she begs for more. "Sass, *look* at me. I want to savor these moments as you clutch and writhe with desire. I covet *seeing* you come on my fingers and my mouth."

Their eyes meet as her hips begin undulating in tempo with his fingers. She winks at him and chides, "You can go faster than that, Deuce!" as she clutches his head and lifts her breasts to his eye level.

"Hungry, are you, Sass?" Ron asks as she pulsates higher, faster, and harder than he has seen her do in a long time. He quakes with pleasure as he moves his mouth to her clit, circling it first with his tongue, then nibbling and sucking until she is close to another big O. "God, you are insatiable, and I love seeing you need me, want me. Come against my mouth, Sass. Fuck, Cassy, you are my sex goddess. I love you like this."

Deuce's own cock is pulsating and demanding. "I need to be in you, feel you, take you, own your beautiful sex!" He slips inside her, at first slowly and methodically but then faster and harder as she tightens with each stroke. "Look at me, Sass. I have to see your face and eyes. I'm not just with any woman. I'm with *the* woman every man dreams of." A moment later, together, they explode and then collapse.

Winging their way back to state side, Cassy replays the week and realizes her favorite was the privately chartered sunset cruise, where the crew made themselves scarce in a separate part of the Windjammer, and she and her Deuce were free to satisfy their lust with the accompanying sound of lapping waves and the brilliant colors catching the sails.

"Damn good — or was it?" she thought as Whitney Houston's "How Will I Know?" echoed in her head.

Chapter 14

BROCK - AN UNEXPECTED WRINKLE

B rock Taylor had come a long way professionally from his college days. He had great memories of playing for the University of Oregon as a linebacker but knew he would never make it in the pros. He had a killer body, having worked his way through school in construction, but compared to the "tanks" who were selected to be linebackers for the pro teams, he knew he didn't measure up. He had been smart in getting his degree, and coaching and refereeing lots of middle and high school games had strengthened his vita for teaching interviews.

Even though his life before playing for the Ducks had been spent mostly on the West Coast, he knew he would seek a position anywhere that would let him be a head football coach. Several midwestern openings had been given to him by his coach, his surrogate dad. He sent resumés to all of them; however, he leaned toward the one listed for Meadowbrook because it specifically advertised for a *leader* for their football team.

"It's a great place to start and build your résumé and coaching credentials," shared his mentor. "I went to school with a friend, Tom Redford, who ran around with another pre-med student. Tom never quit talking about Ron Phillips, who went back to Meadowbrook to open an OB-GYN practice and has a son who is a Division I prospect. Tom followed him there and made it sound like a paradise of opportunity." Brock didn't care about paradise; he just wanted to go somewhere he could build a football dynasty.

On the day of his Meadowbrook interview, he arrived early to check out the town and the high school facilities. He was willing to relocate, but it had to be for the right job. He found he was impressed by his surface review of the area. However, he would make his final judgment when—maybe *if* is the right word—they offered him the job. Brock was very sure of the strength of his credentials, and he knew how to interview, but you never knew what a district was really looking for.

He was greeted by the superintendent, Dr. Monica Woodland. His mind registered that she was quite good-looking, and she was very professional. She took time to explain the process: he would have three separate interviews, going before the school board, a teacher/administrator panel, and the coaching staff. "At the end of the day, I will go over the salary and benefits being offered and answer any questions you still have. Hopefully, we can make the final decision by the end of the week."

As all interviews tend to be, the day went by in a blur. When he took a moment to reflect, he knew he had nailed the school board's questions, wowed the other coaches with his recent expertise, and did OK on the certified staff questions. He had to admit his delivery in that focus group was distracted by one of the teachers. She was simply dazzling, and he had to keep reminding himself to listen.

Then, to his delight, he was told that Ms. Carstens would take him on a quick tour of Meadowbrook High and show him where he would be teaching and coaching if he were to be selected. The only thought Brock had was "Jackpot!"

"Please come this way," suggests Cassy as she led him down a long hallway. "I will take you to the health room. It's in the newer part of the building and has all the latest technology."

"Thank you," stammered Brock. He'd never had trouble talking before—why now? "What do you teach, and how long have you been here?"

"I came last year to teach English and coach cheerleaders but have lived in Meadowbrook all my life. I love it here," Cassy said with a wide grin.

"That's nice to know. Does the town support athletics?" Brock sputtered.

"Oh, please! They don't just support it; it's an integral part of the community, and a head coach must be able to handle lots of demanding parents." After showing him the classroom, Cassy remarked, "It's been great to meet you, Brock. I hope you'll consider us if you are offered the job. Bart, our current head coach, will be down in just a few minutes. He will give you a tour of all our athletic facilities. He is a super coach and an even greater guy. I know he wants a leader that will continue the athletic traditions and even take us higher. You'll like him; he's moving on to the college level and wants the best for the Cougars.

"Here he is now," gestured Cassy. "Bart, I would like you to meet Brock Taylor. He is our final interviewee for your position. She turned to Brock, "Good-bye, Mr. Taylor, and good luck."

"Thank you, Ms. Carstens. I hope our paths cross again, and, please, I would like it if you called me Brock." She blushed as she left the two.

"Welcome, Mr. Taylor, I'm happy to explain our program to you. As you can guess, I am quite proud of it. Follow me."

"Please call me Brock. I understand you are moving to a university."

"Yes, I am, and it's important to me to hand this team over to someone who can keep developing it. They have come such a long way, and I believe in the future with the right head coach we can be a strong contender in the league," boasted Bart. About an hour later, Brock was escorted by one of the football players back to the superintendent's office—none other than Phipps Phillips. Brock took the opportunity to pick this player's brain, knowing that he was the Division I candidate and captain of the team.

In the end, Brock really liked what he had seen and heard, so when the superintendent shared the salary and benefits of the position and asked him about his interest, he didn't hesitate. He liked everything and everyone, especially Ms. Carstens. "Yes, definitely." The next day he received a formal offer and said yes immediately. He couldn't wait to meet his team—and ask the beautiful blond English teacher to help him with the ins and outs at Meadowbrook High.

Coach, that's what everyone now calls Brock, is well on his way to his dream. He supervises the weight room, teaches health and PE, and has become well connected in the state through all the athletic conferences. He is learning to pull back with his confrontational and competitive personality, but he cannot suffer slackers. He keeps himself in great shape by swimming, lifting weights, and drilling with his football team.

Oh, Brock clearly makes a statement of masculinity, sitting on his prized Harley - the Road King, where he always draws a crowd when he stops in Brick Town. His chiseled face, incredibly dark chocolate eyes, and sandy blond hair draw attention to his tanned muscular body in a coach's standard uniform, PE shorts and T-shirts featuring the school's mascot. Every single female in his age group—not to mention the high school girls—find a reason to walk by. He really likes women and is unfailingly friendly. But since he had connected with Cassy at the new teachers' fall orientation, his dick twitches as he methodically schemes to win her over.

Brock lives in a two-level condo close to Meadowbrook High. His home is sparsely furnished, but the complex's pool has become a gathering place for his students and players. He has learned quite a bit about "Sassy Cassy," listening to the kids talk. Young people always assume that as an adult you aren't really tracking what they are saying. Brock is especially close to Phipps, Doc Ron's second son, because he is such a talented athlete, and Phipps is always telling stories about Cassy being his and Trey's nanny. Brock knows Cassy is well respected as a teacher at the high school, and her students really like her and her classes. She is always ready to tutor the kids when they need it, listen to them when their love life is challenged, and even talk with their parents when a little extra effort—a kick in the butt—is needed by her students.

He has initiated his plan to become the main man in Cassy's life by talking to her about classwork and asking for her help in reaching certain students. One student in particular garners both their attention. He is a gifted football player and a stellar student, but recently displayed a sour attitude that is beginning to affect those around him. He dates one of Cassy's cheerleaders, and she had come to Cassy several times, saying her boyfriend is changing so much she doesn't know if she can stay with him.

Cassy and Brock decide they both should approach the parents to see if there is a problem or anything new that they need to know. "We care very much about your son, and he certainly has a bright future in front of him. We truly do not mean to pry," Cassy offers.

"No, no," replies Brandon's father. "Please sit down." He went on to explain, "His younger brother has recently been diagnosed with MS, multiple sclerosis, and the whole family is trying to adjust to the prognosis. Brandon has expressed how guilty he feels that everything comes so easy for him. The WHY question is haunting him."

"How difficult this is for all of you." Cassy stands and puts her hand on his arm in a gesture of concern. "Tell us what we can do to help him and your family."

"We have set up counseling sessions for the whole family, and we are encouraging Brandon to share with his friends, his girlfriend, and school personnel. We are going to do everything we can to help his brother, but Brandon can't change things by being angry."

From that day forward, Cassy and Brock make Brandon a priority for their personal attention in helping him deal with this blow and still fulfill his potential. They show him how to share his hurt with his girlfriend and get permission from him to share with the rest of the faculty and the team. The situation and genuine concern bring Brock and Cassy closer together, and Brock forgets all about scheming to win Cassy. He is genuinely taken with her dedication, beauty, and personality.

Soon they are sharing lunch together, which leads to real dates, and now he knows he has a jewel—someone who mirrors his love of sex and can handle a professional as well as a somewhat "kinky" behind-the-scenes lifestyle. "Cassy smells good, too, like ginger and citrus flowers. And she can drink beer and play cards with me and my friends, then walk into parent-teacher conferences in a tailored suit looking fresh and intelligent." Brock has to admit that he has the same chameleon quality. The principal has come to rely on him, parents seek his advice, and he commands respect among his students. "And I smell good, too, like sandalwood and a hint of lemon peel," he jokes to himself.

One of his favorite pastimes with Cassy is their motorcycle rides out in the country, where they can rev up the Harley and let loose. Cassy clamps her arms around his 6-pack abs. Her beautiful breasts are almost bursting out of her tube top, and they are pressed against his sinewy back. Her tight buttocks point upward, and her ponytail whips in the wind as they speed down the highway until they find a secluded arbor that shelters them from discovery. Privacy is most important, as they both have reputations to protect. Cassy always brings them the local craft beer and munchies—tangy chicken wings, chips and salsa, salted nuts, chili cheese toast bites—because she knows their activities whet their physical and sexual appetites.

It's when they are free like this that both Cassy and Brock fall into a habit of teasing each other by acting out their fantasies. Hers is being the *femme fatale*, twirling her body to and fro, teasing him with a syrupy Southern belle voice, coming in close for a feather-light kiss and then squirming out of his arms as he grabs for her. Lying seductively on the flat grass, Brock leans back on one elbow, gives a slow whistle, and growls, "Come here, 'Miss,' I have something special for you."

Cassy slides down on her hands and knees and purrs, "First, show me what you got, 'Mister'!" Jumping up, Brock holds up his arms with their sculpted muscles; dropping his fisted hands, he hooks his thumbs into his Wrangler jeans' belt loops, and then swaggers toward her like a cowboy. At that point, they both break out laughing at their antics and catch each other in a torrid embrace. Kissing, fondling, and undressing lead them to a frenzied coupling and liquid-hot orgasms.

True love is budding. They lie on a flannel blanket, holding each other and talking about everyday happenings. They know so many of the same people, working in similar positions at the high school. They enjoy just being together at both school and town events and have reached the age where the future is calling their names—a home, a family, stability.

Brock eventually stands and offers Cassy his hand. "Hey, Baby," he smiles and then smirks at the same time as he presses her toward the closest tree, leans in, captures her lips, and tangles with her tongue.

As her body slams up against him, she hisses, "If I'm your baby, you are my king, so anoint me, take me. Make me your own!" His erection continues to engorge, and both begin panting in unison.

With the tree trunk as their support, they engage in fast and hard foreplay. Cassy grabs his ass, pulling him harder and harder against herself, and he is masterfully massaging her breasts in a circular motion. The tension continues to escalate as she unzips his jeans, and he pulls her shorts aside, entering her with a bellowing moan. She urges him on with her own moans and begging for more. They are matching each other thrust for thrust as they come to simultaneous climaxes.

Once again, they are still lying in each other's arms as the sun begins to set; neither wants to be the one to break the spell. It has been a perfect afternoon, and both are dreaming of the future as they head back to town and their responsibilities.

Brock already knows he is in love with Cassy. He has given her his all. She is there one hundred percent as well, at least most of the time; however, there are instances when she seems to pull away or go quiet. Often, it is when she comes back from out of town or they have to spend a longer stretch of time apart. He isn't naïve. He knows that as beautiful and sexy as she is, Cassy must have had plenty of men at her feet in high school and college, but is there someone still in her life that means more to her than he does? Pushing negative thoughts aside, he just keeps repeating to himself, "She is the one. She is mine!"

Cassy lays her head on Brock's back and hugs him even harder as the motorcycle flies along the dirt roads. Even in her happiness, she recognizes Brock presents a new complication in her life—one of two men claiming her as their own. One she could never fully have, and one who is showing her how good a *real* relationship can be.

Chapter 15

THE DAILY GRIND

15 Months before the Stabbing

Standing behind the espresso machine, mindlessly because he's done it so many times preparing an order, Renaldo gently shakes his head yes as he looks over the coffeehouse. The Daily Grind is so inviting, just how he had dreamed about it—the color palette is beiges and browns with little splashes of yellow for the summer iced-coffee crowd. The shop is easy to identify with the coffee cup sign swinging over the front door. Of course, there is a drive-up window on the south side, but most people come for the ambience. Other "quick-shack" coffee spots had sprung up as Meadowbrook grew, but you didn't just go to the Daily Grind for coffee. There are the homemade pastries and treats that Renaldo has contracted a local farmer's wife to supply. Her signature is the over-sized cinnamon rolls that ooze melt-in-your-mouth white icing. Kids love the cake pops and moms, claiming to watch their figures, go for the almond biscotti. The early morning runners and health fanatics stop daily for their power smoothies. Late afternoons are perfect for the middle and high schoolers to pop in for a mango blast or iced passion fruit smoothie along with their snickerdoodles, peanut butter cookies, chewy chocolate brownies, and cupcakes of every flavor.

The Daily Grind imports the most flavorful beans from Brazil: Santana, Santos, and Delta. Renaldo knows these growers and the quality of their products. However, when it comes to buying beans, anyone who tries to take advantage of him soon finds out he KNOWS the coffee industry! Stash Tea, a green tea from central Brazil, is his other favorite. The specialty plants had been imported from Japan and cultivated in the high plains of Brazil, providing a similar climate to those on the island. Renaldo never gets tired of the aromas that waft about the shop.

Sconces on the walls provide diffused illumination, with can lights hovering over each bistro table surrounded by soft leather barrel chairs. Decorative drop lights grace the coffee bar. Modern art covers the remaining walls. Renaldo is partial to Ceicily Brown, Gunther Fong, and Liu Lei and likes to support Sam Gillian, a black artist who is a pioneer in abstract art. His Blue and White prints are prominently featured and influence the dishes and cups, vases holding fresh flowers, and the area rugs. Renaldo has even devised a signature drink he calls the Daily Grind Blue Refresher...Beat the Heat!

After about one year in business, Renaldo knows he needs to add an outdoor patio to capitalize on traffic from the summer tourists. He decides on a large freestanding pergola that provides a semi-shaded seating area and allows for a breeze and protection from the harsh glare of the direct sun. The natural beauty and durability of the hard wood he selected has made it well worth the price. He has tasked Trey to select the right plants and outdoor furniture to complete the project. When completed, the two marvel at what they have created: outdoor string lights highlighting the round wrought-iron tables and chairs, feathery green ferns in large ceramic pots, and green starter vines swinging from wire containers hanging from the rafters. Large patio heaters lengthen the outdoor season. Double doors that can be slid back have been installed on the side of the coffeehouse, and everyone loves the seamless entry and exit Ren and Trey have created.

Renaldo had worked on his father's coffee farm in Brazil ever since he was a child—such wonderful memories of the pure, green-leafed bushes that produced beautiful red coffee beans. For years, the farm had supported their small family. He never really knew if his mother and father had wanted more children, but he was very happy being an only child. His father would take him to the fields, walking the red earth trails and teaching him all about coffee. The crisp morning air and frequent rainfall only made the days sweeter. Renaldo could still remember the heated discussions his parents started having about the "big" coffee growers moving into their region close to San Paulo. Their small farm just couldn't compete, but his father steadfastly refused to sell.

Renaldo would never forget when the local officials came to tell him his mother and father had been killed in an accident with a large farm truck. They had gone into town to get supplies. Happenings after that terrible day were a blur for Renaldo. He had just finished his secondary schooling when he learned he had inherited the farm free and clear. He seriously considered keeping it, but he wanted a fresh start. He sold the farm to the coffee growers for an unbelievable price and headed to the United States. He knocked around several big cities in America but missed the feeling of being connected to a smaller and more down-to-earth part of the globe. Finally, he chose to lose himself in the Midwest, near a small private college close to Chicago.

It had turned out to be an excellent decision. Renaldo was pretty rough in his mannerism and appearance, and by then he knew he was more drawn to men than women. The encounters he had had in Brazil had solidified his sexual orientation. During his wandering years, he had attracted all the partners he could desire. His brooding eyes and sadness-tinged demeanor drew others to him, and when he shared his background, it gave him a very mysterious aire.

Renaldo put his skills with coffee into play and worked at several coffeehouses close to the campus, where he improved his English as well as his native Portuguese and honed his knowledge of being a barista. It was in one of these shops where he had seen Trey playing his acoustic guitar. His rendition of Glen Campbell's "Faithless Love" shared his story of broken relationships. As soon as Trey had felt Renaldo's tentative attempts to establish a connection, he played Luke Bryan's "Crash My Party" with a few personalized words, signaling his acceptance, which resulted in Renaldo and Trey becoming a tight couple.

They rented a small apartment adjacent to the college and quickly developed friendships with others in the gay community.

They enjoyed the informal gatherings that seemed to spontaneously develop as their friends often dropped by. They, too, indulged in the parties held by those in their close circle, but their favorite was just spending time with each other. Renaldo displayed a tough exterior to others, but only Trey knew the soft heart of the man he loved. For once in his life, Trey found happiness within himself, and that contentment was evident in his songwriting.

As early graduation neared for Trey, the two often explored how they could stay together. Renaldo shared that he had sold the coffee farm his parents had long ago deeded to him. His proposal was to go to Meadowbrook and open a coffeehouse where Trey could write and play the music he so loved, and they could continue to be together.

Acting on their plan, Renaldo immediately rented a townhouse in a quiet, well-respected area of Meadowbrook, where he and Trey could come and go without issues. He quickly purchased a storefront in Brick Town, the hot spot for young and old to congregate.

They say, "Life imitates life," and Trey and Renaldo soon discovered a vibrant gay community right in Meadowbrook. They were able to establish new friendships, acquaintances, and allies in their lifestyle. Trey was at first thunderstruck and wished he had known this while he was in school. On second thought, he knew he was the one who wouldn't have openly acknowledged his orientation until he had left Meadowbrook.

Only one problem remained: both Renaldo and Trey wanted more freedom to be a couple. Although being gay had its issues, Trey and Renaldo knew that together they could surmount any obstacle. It was a relationship built on true love. They cared about and protected each other. Their goals were all American: establish a career, build a life together, acquire a home, and someday maybe even have children.

In no time, Renaldo had built a strong reputation for his expertise with coffee. He made sure there was a variety of fresh ground coffee each day at the Daily Grind, and patrons could buy the beans or ground coffees by the pound. Many of the elite or their event planners in Meadowbrook began to consult Renaldo on his perfect recommendations for their coffee or tea choices befitting an occasion. Eventually he began an expanded service where he would set up, man, or arrange management of a full-service bar for those events. He had done just that for Trey's father's Man of the Year Celebration.

Life changed quickly after Trey's dad was stabbed. Renaldo didn't have any idea how the future would turn out, but he hadn't liked seeing that detective quiz Trey, and he knew he would eventually have to wrestle with the detective himself. "That's all right," he thinks, "I know how to answer questions without revealing too much." As he had mentioned to the detective earlier, he had regularly served Ron his caramel macchiato with a double shot of espresso as he was on his way to the hospital. Doc would sometimes stop by, too, and sit at the bar to bend Renaldo's ear. Renaldo thought of himself as a "bartender," so he remained confidential about the tales he heard. However, it was so hard to stay calm when Ron started talking about his boys. Renaldo always found himself praising Trey's many talents. Doc would shake his head yes, but he always reverted to singling out Phipps and his achievements.

Renaldo had begun to feel very protective of Trey after several times of listening to Trey's dad. Why couldn't Doc Ron appreciate his namesake? Even if he wasn't geared like Ron, he was a stellar human being with many talents. Trey loved his family, but when father and son were together, there was obviously a strained tenseness in their interactions. The two were like oil and water.

Renaldo tries often to draw Trey out on the topic, but it never seems to work, and he realizes he doesn't have as much to lose as Trey. "Why don't you just sit down with your father and explain how your life has unfolded?" urges Renaldo.

"I don't believe my dad could handle a gay son. You've seen how he dotes on Phipps. He is all man this, man that, sports this, sports that! You notice he seldom asks about my music. He doesn't even come in to listen to my sets at the Grind. He's always at one of Phipps's practices or games."

"How about your mom?" inquires Renaldo.

"She knows. She was the one who said to be careful of what I say to Detective Finley. I think she may be as afraid as I am of Dad finding out for sure. Mom loves me so much, but sometimes I think she also worries about her standing in the community and country club. It is one thing to think someone has a gay son and another for her to openly embrace me."

"She's always been very kind to me," quips Renaldo. "Maybe we should start with her and see if she could act as our buffer with your dad. Oh, and I have another thought. Tom and Joey, I believe, would also help us. They really care about you. Does Phipps know?"

Trey shakes his head. "He must by now! We are so close that I should have confided in him, but I didn't want him to have to bear the burden of hiding the secret. He has to constantly live up to Dad's expectations, and anyway it's my responsibility to set the record straight—a strange twist on words—about all of this."

"There is one other person who knows—Cassy. She adores you, Renaldo, and she knows that we are a couple. We can be confident that she will protect our secret until we are ready to come out."

Renaldo arrives at the Grind the next day with a jumble of thoughts. Most of the morning, he finds himself distracted and searching for a simple solution to a complex human situation.

Finally, he realizes he must turn his attention back to the morning coffee crowd. Renaldo silently repeats to himself, "Trey means too much to me. I don't think I have a choice."

Chapter 16

THE SCARE AND THE FOREVER

Phipps and Claire –
Ten Months before the Stabbing

God, it was a perfect Friday night. I had cheered my heart out and was so proud of my quarterback. We had won the game by 14 points against last year's conference champs, and Phipps had one of his best games with 3 touchdowns. No less than four scouts from Division I schools were in the crowd, charting every move he made.

The dance to celebrate making the playoffs was filled with fun and friends and dancing to songs like Lady Antebellum's

"Champagne Night" and Morgan Wallen's "Chasin' You." When the DJ played our song, Luke Bryant's "To the Moon and Back," Phipps winked an "I love you" message and whispered, "Baby, let's get out of here. I just need to hold you and kiss you." He bent down and nuzzled my neck with promises of more.

The pickup's radio was blasting Brad Paisley's "Little Moments" as we held each other. "Grab the blanket in the back, Baby. Let's go down by the river and stare at the stars and our moon." Phipps pulled two White Claws from the small cooler and guided me to our favorite spot, where we could lie back and gaze up at the starlit sky. The river kept up its quiet gurgling as our hands began exploring each other's bodies and our kisses grew more insistent.

I'm not sure when it became a clear thought, but all of a sudden I looked into Phipp's aquamarine eyes, caressed his face, and revealed, "I want more of you—of us, Phipps."

"Oh, Baby, you know I want that more than anything—but you have to be sure; I don't want to lose what we have. You mean too much to me. I know they say we are just kids, but we have always been destined to be together." And I knew he meant it.

The darkening sapphire in my eyes signaled the answer, "Please, Phipps, make me yours."

He lovingly and gently undressed me as he stared into my eyes the entire time. He was as desperate as I was, but he kept reassuring me. "You are perfect for me; I'll never find another you." He slowly—very slowly—entered me and sought my eyes for a reaction.

I held him tight and begged, "More, Phipps. Please, Phipps, I want to remember this night forever. You and me—together—us."

I knew I was driving him wild—no wilder than he was driving me. We came to a crescendo together, completing what we had so longed for. Then we just held each other while sharing kisses that celebrated our union. Paisley's "She's Everything" was playing in the background.

The Morning After

Phipps knows his girl, his Claire, will be having second thoughts this morning. With their pent-up emotions spilling over, they hadn't used protection last night in the heat of the moment. "What if she is pregnant? God, I can't lose her. She's mine! She's my forever! OK, next steps? Think, Think."

"I'll call Tom. He's never judgmental, and I can use his advice, both medical and personal."

Over the phone, Phipps gives a quick synopsis of the crisis or possible crisis, and Tom assures him, "Come to the hospital now; I'll take a break, and we can talk."

"Tom, I have to assure Claire I will be there forever to protect her, to love her, to be like you and Joey," blurts Phipps.

"I understand, but you need a game plan?"

On his way to the hospital, Phipps goes right past Tom and Joey's house, and in the driveway sits Claire's lime-green bug. He slams on his brakes and finds a pen and a scrap of paper in the glove compartment. He writes a quick note, sharing what is in hisheart: "I love you, Baby!" He signs it with a single heart.

Tom and Phipps move to his office, and Tom quietly shuts the door. They earnestly talk for about an hour and a half, with Phipps sharing everything. "I know we are still in high school and have a long way to go, but I can't see a future without Claire in it. Plus, she wants to get her college degree—maybe even her law degree—and I dream of being picked up by a pro team after I graduate from college. A baby with Claire is something I see in our future, but this is just NOT the right time. We were careless, but I'll never regret sharing our love together. Help me, Tom," Phipps pleads.

"I never thought I would be saying this to a 17 year old—my favorite 17 year old to boot—but I think you have found 'the love of your life.' You look at each other the way I feel about Joey. There will be good times, sad times, the need-to-step-up times, but you two can do it. You want Joey to talk with Claire?" Tom asks.

Grinning, Phipps answers, "I think that is already happening. Claire's car was in your driveway earlier this morning."

"Well, then, let's get your future in order," he segues as he dials Joey.

Sharing with two adults who care so much about them is just what Claire and Phipps need to validate the important life commitments they are making. Their most heartfelt pledge is their vow to "be there," really "be there" for each other.

"We best address birth control!" Joey postures with a must in her voice. Claire blushes but knows it is the right thing to do. Joey calls her OB-GYN in Chicago and makes arrangements for Claire and her to meet with Dr. Jackson a week from Wednesday. Then she turns to Phipps, shaking her finger at him. "No more sex, Phipps, until we get Claire on the pill. Understand?"

"Yes, ma'am," he blushes.

Claire, seeing the question and concern still in Phipps's eyes, takes his hand and shares, "Phipps, I was so worried that I sought out Joey to help me secure the morning-after pill.'"

Phipps hugs Claire and whispers, "Part of me is happy, and the other part is sad. I can't think of anything I want more for the future than for us to build a family together. I'll never regret our first lovemaking, Baby. I love you so much; right now and forever, you are my baby," vows Phipps.

"And you are the man I want to share my future life and family with. I love you so much, too."

Tom and Joey both have tears in their eyes as they watch and hear these two being strong for each other.

After combing through such deep topics, Joey senses the need to lighten the mood. She claps her hands together and announces, "Let's go have some fun! We can get away, try new things, and just enjoy life. OK, all of you—that includes you, Tom—clear your schedule. I'm in charge. Chicago, here we come!"

An hour later, they are flying down the highway in Joey's Volvo, heading to the Windy City. Russ's "All to You" plays on the radio, echoing Phipps's thoughts, "I just want us, girl, you know I got us—Anything you need, my baby." His wink and kiss on Claire's forehead promise a great day and an even greater forever.

The two couples take their time ambling through the street carnival in downtown Chicago, eating cotton candy and hot dogs and playing carnival games. Claire playfully teases Phipps when he fails three times in a row to get the basketball through the hoop. So he grabs a football at the next carnival game and shows real skill in winning the top prize, a giant penguin, which he gives to Claire.

They continue to stroll through the arcade until Joey and Claire express a desire to go into a nearby music store. "Take all the time you need," Tom magnanimously says, as he and Phipps spy a car dealership and Harley shop down a block and across the street. "We'll just entertain ourselves. Call us when you are ready."

When they all reunite, the consensus is, "Food! We need food!" Walking along a side street, they spot Veniti's, a little Italian restaurant. Its glowing lights spill onto a small patio. Tom offers, "Let's try this; pizza sounds so good, and I could use a beer. There's even a table for four with an umbrella."

To complete the scene, an obviously Italian-looking waiter with a checkered towel on his arm beckons them, "Sit, sit. I can serve you right away. It's a beautiful night, no? Oh, gentlemen, how lucky you are to be with two 'bellissimo' ladies," he expounds as he throws a kiss with his fingers.

"I'm having such a wonderful time," expresses Claire. "It's fun to see just how much Tom adores you, Joey. You don't know what today has meant to me," and then looking at Phipps, she adds, "to us."

"Well, the adoration is certainly mutual," returns Joey. "You and Phipps bring us great joy. Some problems once in a while, but mostly just good times!"

"OK, you two, enough sappy stuff. Let's play this trivia game that's on the table. Girls against boys," suggests Tom. "It's all about Chicago!" He reads the first question, "Does Chicago turn its river green for St. Patrick's Day? You've got a 50/50 chance—yes or no?"

The evening progresses with much laughing, joking, and the waiter even joins in answering some of the questions before any of them can. Tom sighs and says, "I hate to break this up, but I do have to check in at the hospital tonight, so we need to start back." A collective groan, payment to the waiter, and a last toast to a perfect day and a great future sends them on their way.

Tom and Joey's love has always been strong and evident, and when they look at "their kids," who have become adults overnight, they recognize the same commitment they made two decades ago. Tom, holding Joey's hand, professes, "An always and forever, my dear."

Phipps kisses Claire lightly and then passionately, wanting the entire world to see Claire is his girl—his woman—now and forever.

Chapter 17

READY FOR COMMITMENT?

Several Months before the Stabbing

They have certainly become the talk among the students and staff; everyone at Meadowbrook High knows Cassy and Brock are dating. Anytime someone even sees them talking or walking together, they get a thumbs-up gesture accompanied by a huge smile. The boys especially enjoy teasing their coach, and Brock gives it right back.

"Got a date tonight, Coach? Ms. Carstens sure is foxy."

"Let's keep our minds on PE, shall we?" coaxes Brock.

"You're a lucky man. We really like her," chimes in several more students.

"She is fun, but during the day we have jobs and responsibilities, and I am trying to manage mine," counters Brock.

"Oh, come on, surely you can give us one little hint about her."

"I'll give you a piece of advice. Don't share details of your relationships. If the girl ever finds out, she won't ever trust you again. Now get that ball in play!" he gestures and runs down the court, showing he has closed the subject.

Cassy takes more ribbing from her female colleagues. "Saw you two out again last night; becoming pretty steady if you ask me," teases Ms. Black, the sophomore English teacher.

"The dart tournament at Murphy's Pub is a great hangout on Wednesday nights. It probably sounds silly; joking, laughing, and watching how different people throw their darts is very entertaining. It's one of our favorite stomping grounds," offers Cassy, wanting to steer the conversation in another direction.

One of the snarkier teachers turns up her nose and spouts, "It's still a bar and seems so inappropriate for two teachers. Surely you and Brock can find a better place to spend your time!"

Others comment on her rosy cheeks and ready smile. "You must have had a great night last night. Out with anyone we might know?"

"All I can say is he is good-looking and very attentive. I like those qualities in the men I choose," states Cassy.

On their dates, Brock and Cassy often share with each other what is being said about them and what questions are being asked. Earlier in their relationship, they had agreed to be very discreet and mindful of each other if they were going to be together.

In the community, their presence continues to grow. They walk the square on Christmas Eve, commenting on the sparkling red and green decorations, kicking up the snow with their winter boots, and huddling together while they sip hot chocolate at a small table in the community center.

On Christmas Day, Brock is invited to have dinner with Cassy's Mom, Megan, and several of her work friends. The serving platter holds the traditional turkey, and other bowls overflow with cornbread stuffing, garlic mashed potatoes, green beans, and cranberry sauce. Brock eats heartily, and Megan praises him for holding his own. They play cards and dice games, enjoy Christmas music and eventually dive into apple, pecan, and pumpkin pies. As it gets later and later, Brock knows he should leave, but he doesn't want this day to end.

Finally tearing himself away and heading home, he smiles as he remembers that next week is New Year's Eve and he will have Cassy to himself. He has it all planned. They will go out to dinner first at their favorite steak house, slip off to their number one dance spot, and make it back to his place where they can drink champagne and anoint the coming year in style.

"It feels so right having you here, Cassy, and it was perfect spending Christmas with your mom and her friends. Then tonight I am holding close the most beautiful girl I have ever known. Do you have any idea how much you mean to me?" They are entwined, toasting glasses, and looking into each other's eyes.

"Brock, you always make me feel like a million dollars. I do wonder, though, if your family is really disappointed you didn't go home for the holidays. Your sister has a little girl, doesn't she?

"Well, now that you bring it up, I had to promise I would bring this new lady in my life that I talk so much about out to meet them," puts forth Brock.

Cassy stiffens oh so slightly. Is this getting too serious too fast? She puts a smile on her face and offers, "That sounds great, but our school schedule won't loosen up until this summer. Maybe then."

Brock tries hard to look at the positive side of her reply, but once again he feels that what-don't-I-know warning course through his mind. "That's OK, maybe we can work out something sooner. I'm dying for them to know you, the perfect girl for me. My mom is gonna love you!"

As the clock begins chiming in the New Year, Brock and Cassy are locked in a sensuous embrace that ends with hot kisses demanding further satisfaction. Cassy pushes Brock flat on the couch and takes command. Her clothes are gone in a second, and she is tugging at his jeans before he can take a full breath; Brock is now naked, too. Cassy starts massaging his sac, rolling each ball with a deft touch. Brock hears himself growling, and his whole body stiffens as he begs for more. He cannot let her stop, not now. He grabs her hips to reposition her, but she scoots down and closes her mouth around his engorged cock. With precise movements of her tongue, she repeatedly strokes his shaft and circles the base of the tip. "Cassy, I am going crazy; I need to be inside you." Just then, she switches positions and lifts her legs around his head. She crashes down on him, closing the aching distance between them. Brock's hips begin gyrating as he tries to capture and hold her to his ever-intensifying sexual arousal. Every move she makes causes him to ache for more. His hands begin to explore her body, and he pulls her close so he can suck those hardened nipples. It is too much; he flips her over, beginning a heart-stopping rhythmic thrust that consumes both of them in flames of ecstasy.

Back in full swing at school, January and February are a blur. Both Cassy and Brock are busy teaching full time, seeing each other whenever possible, and just living life. On top of that, Brock is rehashing last fall's football season, trying to make changes for the coming year, and Cassy is grooming her cheerleaders for state competition.

As March comes in like a lion, Brock has his thoughts on California. He had grown up in Palo Alto, and like all the write-ups said, it was one of the best places in the state. It touts an urban-suburban mix, lots of restaurants, coffeehouses, and parks. His father for years has dealt in real estate, and they now lived in a beautiful four-bedroom, stylish home in a prime location of Palo Alto. Brock loves his father, mother, and sister, and he knows they love him. He thinks he has found the girl that will give him the kind of marriage his folks have. They are supportive of each other, still making each other happy and as far as he knows have been faithful partners. Brock and his sister, Jill, have enjoyed an excellent education. She has flourished on the wave of IT, becoming a sought-after web designer.

Brock had capitalized on his sports prowess, resulting in his playing college football. During his football heyday, his best friends were his teammates and coaches. Now he is where he has always dreamed of: a head football coach, a beautiful girl he is in love with, and now anxious to share all of this with his family.

Spring break is only a few weeks away when Brock rushes into Cassy's classroom during her lunch break. He is like a kid when he holds up his phone revealing plane tickets and gushes, "Cassy,

I've been watching the airfares, and a special popped up yesterday. Look! I was able to get these for practically nothing—we can fly to California, and you can meet my parents and my sister. Remember I mentioned she lives close to home, especially with her husband deployed in the Navy. You can also meet my niece, Lexie—-that's what we call her. It's perfect."

Cassy only hesitates a moment before giving Brock a big hug. "Oh, what a great surprise! How many days will we be there? I am looking forward to meeting your family, but I don't want to impose on them." Cassy knows from listening to Brock that they are well to do, and she is concerned about sharing her background. Maybe they harbor a vision of Brock with a socialite's daughter.

"Don't be silly. Like I said earlier, they are going to love you." He picks her up and swings her around, then looks toward the door to see if anyone is watching.

The three days they spend in Palo Alto are, in Cassy's mind, perfect. Brock's mother, Vanessa, who insisted Cassy call her Van, is welcoming and open. His father, Gabe, is a real gentleman and down-to-earth. His sister is like Brock, warm and so friendly. On the first night, they all just sit around the firepit drinking the family's favorite cocktail, vodka presses. Lexie, who just turned five, dotes on Uncle Brock, and he is great with her. He carries her on his shoulders, chases her around the fire, making her squeal, and even helps her create smores before she and Jill must leave. Cassy can't help but notice how comfortable and natural he is with her. She thinks to herself, "Brock will make a great dad!"

Brock finds himself bragging on Cassy, "She is the favorite teacher in the whole high school, and she really helps me when I encounter a tough student."

"Cassy, I can't believe you got him to think about anything but football," broaches his mother with a twinkle in her eye. "Even as a toddler, he was carrying around a Nerf football, forcing his father to play catch with him."

"Brock is a super teacher and an excellent coach. He develops his players' bodies *and* minds and makes sure they keep up their grades. He is well respected in Meadowbrook. I know you are proud of him, and you should be," offers Cassy.

"I am assuming you two met at the school? Brock told me he spotted you the very first day. Knowing my son, he made sure to follow up."

"Now, Dad, don't be telling all my secrets about how I schemed to get into her good graces," admonishes Brock in a cajoling way.

Cassy leans over and gives him a playful sock in the arm. "You stinker," she says, "here I thought you were after my teaching expertise?" Both his father and mother notice the fun connection they have.

"Yes, yes, I wanted that, too, but look at you. You took my breath away, and you were smart enough not to fall at my feet. I had had enough of that in high school," Brock shoots back.

"I can vouch for that," Van shares as she raises her hand. "That phone never quit ringing with girls calling to see, 'Is Brock available?' They never figured out he liked girls but just liked football more."

His parents let Brock and Cassy know they had invited people over for a backyard barbecue the next night. "Oh, Mom," sighs Brock, "we're here to see you two and Jill and Lexie."

"I know! It will just be some of your old high school teammates and coaches with their spouses. We can't help but show you off, especially with Cassy here. She deserves a real Palo Alto welcome. And I'll bet your coaches would love to hear how you feel now that you are a coach," puts forth his mother.

The barbecue turns out to be a lot of fun, and Cassy is a dazzler. She fits right in talking with the wives about their men and sports, shopping, careers, and families. These ladies do not pry, nor do they lean toward the intrusive; they just share and laugh.

Brock keeps looking over at his Cassy with pride; she could carry herself anywhere in any group. More than one of his former buddies slaps him on the back with, "Wow, Illinois obviously has more beautiful and talented women than I ever gave it credit for."

Brock and his former coaches talk for hours. They are so interested in where Brock has landed and the new ideas he is trying out with his high school team. They are very encouraging, making Brock feel like he has arrived as a coach. His mentor, who has driven down from Oregon to be here, especially compliments Brock. At one point, he asks about Tom Redford. "Do you ever see Dr. Redford and that other doctor he always talked about?"

"Oh, yes," Brock remarks, shaking his head. "They are both attached to Meadowbrook Hospital. Tom has a thriving practice and a wonderful wife named Joey. We see them quite often. They actually remind me of my mom and dad. Doc Ron, the OB-GYN, is very successful, too. He and his wife have two sons, and Cassy, before becoming a teacher, was their long-time nanny. Their second son, Phipps, is captain of our football team. He is definitely bound for Division I. He's a superstar, and I hope I can help him like you helped me. I can never thank you enough."

"No need, you are passing it on; that is my greatest reward," he says as he pulls Brock into a bro hug and slaps him several times on the back.

At one point, his father joins them, and they begin to reminisce about the many times several in this group had caravanned to see their hometown boy play. His father chides, "Brock, you were set on the University of Oregon the minute you read their football stats: 12 conference championships, 34 bowls, and 17 times ranked on the AP Poll. You and I both laughed at their name—DUCKS—but it turned out to be just the right program for you."

On their third night, Brock borrows his father's little sports convertible Audi and takes Cassy for a long ride up the coast. The sunset is a haze of vivid pinks, reds, and yellows. They don't talk much, just enjoy the warm temperatures and the breeze teasing their hair. At one point, Brock pulls the car to a stop at a lookout point. They get out of the car and sit on the hood to relegate the last rays of the sun into the ocean.

"What are you thinking, Cassy? Have you had a good time? We fly home tomorrow evening," reminds Brock.

"I have truly enjoyed it, Brock. Your mom, dad, and sister are wonderful people, and I can see how much they idolize you. And that Lexie is a doll; she adores you—and you adore her. They couldn't have made me feel more at home!"

"They like you, too. More than like you. My dad whispered to me, 'She's a keeper,' and Mom called you a treasure. Even my sister sent a text that said, '*She's perfect for you.*' Oh, Cassy, I know it's fast, but I sure hope we can build a future together someday soon," he says as he leans over and kisses her on the cheek.

His declaration hangs in the air as they drive to his home, and it lingers with Cassy all the way on the flight back to Meadowbrook. She keeps asking herself, "Am I ready to make a serious commitment?"

Once home, Cassy is driving herself crazy with what-ifs. "How can I be so confident in my professional life and yet so indecisive in my personal life?" Lamenting to herself, "Sex has always renewed me. Ron has been my aphrodisiac all these years, and now Brock may be my real future." Conflicted and frustrated, she grabs her phone and texts Jack, her BDF.

Cassy: *BDF – are you there? I need you.*

BDF: *What do you need, Babe?*

Cassy: *I need to come.*

BDF: *And you thought of me? Wow, I am impressed.*

BDF: *I'm driving. Give me five – and change into your tightest cropped T-shirt and your pink lace panties.*

Seven minutes had passed, and still no BDF.

Cassy: *BDF – are you there? I said I need to come. Where are you?*

BDF: *I am here – traffic was worse than usual. What's up?*

Cassy: *One of those days – and I need to come NOW!*

BDF: *OK, OK! Pinch your left nipple, Babe.*

Cassy: *Shall I take my T-shirt off first?*

BDF: *No, leave it on. Just play with your nipples through the shirt. Pinch your left nipple. Now circle it and imagine I am there teasing you with your shirt on. Do the right one, too. Pinch it, circle it. Imagine me there, kissing your lips and playing with your tits.*

Cassy: *Ahhh, yes. More.*

BDF: *Good, Babe. Now take off the T-shirt and cup your left breast as you slip your right index and middle finger under your panties and into your pussy. Are you wet for me?*

Cassy: *You know I am.*

BDF: *Good answer, Babe. Now caress each nipple with your wet juices. Tweak them. Enjoy the sensation. Imagine me smothering your breasts with kisses and nibbles. Touch your neck. I am there, making my mark with small bites and quick kisses.*

BDF: *Continue to trace the fingers of your left hand around your breasts while your fingers of your right hand trail slowly over your stomach. Enjoy the anticipation. Are you hot all over?*

BDF: *Dip your fingers again under your lace panties and find your clit. Circle it several times and enjoy the tingles. Push your legs apart. Slide your fingers through your folds and then enter your pussy again—imagining my fingers pulsing inside of you—stretching you for my cock.*

BDF: *Bring your wet fingers back to your clit—massage, circle it. Are the waves starting? Keep teasing your clit. Bring your left hand to your pussy, letting your fingers feel your heat as they pump faster and harder. It's me, Babe, my cock getting you close to the edge.*

He couldn't hear her scream, "I'm coming, Brock," as her body clenched her fingers, his cock. The spasms finally slowed. Several minutes later, she wrote,

Cassy: *Thank you, Brock. I needed that.*

BDF: *Cassy, I believe you did—now who in the hell is Brock?*

Cassy realizes she has some major decisions to make. And she knows the answers will change everything.

Chapter 18

MONICA –
HOW DID I GET HERE?

April, before the Stabbing

Although she is aware she often turns heads, Monica wishes it would have worked the same as when school boards were reviewing her credentials. Being a beautiful woman in a man's world certainly had its drawbacks, so much so she had had to move to Meadowbrook, Illinois, to become their superintendent of schools. Oh, yes, she is married, and many times someone in the community comments on how hard it must be for her to maintain a long-distance relationship. If they only knew, she is thrilled to be on her own. That marriage has died little by little as she garnered educational success. Plus, she longed to be around people who could excite her; being bisexual is both a joy and a curse. In the conservative education world, her sexual orientation certainly wouldn't help her if it was known.

She and her husband had never had children, so she has devoted herself to her passion, seeing students succeed. After all, it was her education that had catapulted her to Harvard, where she received her PhD and was very active in Delta Sigma Theta. Even at the university, she was considered a stunner, with her silky chestnut highlighted hair reaching below her shoulders, which she wore parted in the middle. Her heritage—a handsome black professional athlete father and her beautiful and intelligent Caucasian mother—gave her caramel skin, sable brown eyes with flint gray streaks, and an hourglass figure.

In this new job, as in her climb up the ladder, jeans and T-shirts have been replaced by tailored suits, high-heeled shoes, and button-up blouses. Her homage to her own, as well as others' femininity, is the various unique pins, ribbon ties, and jewelry she wears on her lapel, neckline, or wrist. Her favorite is a vintage oval pin, dark navy blue with rhinestones encircling it. The matching earrings are more dark-green than navy blue, ringed in rhinestones, a gift from her grandmother. They are a staple with her navy-blue power suit, double-breasted with gold buttons. A white long-sleeved shirt completes the look, and, of course, she has matching pumps. Black-rimmed glasses lend an air of authority while she is on the job. She is highly respected by everyone, as she has brought miraculous reform to the Meadowbrook school system. They have even recently received a Blue Ribbon Award from the federal government and hold the state's highest recognition on its report card. She values her administrators, teachers, and support staff and makes sure she lets them know it. Naturally, she belongs to or supports all the important organizations in the community: Rotary, Lions, Community Development, even the City Council, and various booster clubs. Very seldom does she have a night at home. That's why she relishes going to the state and national conventions for educators. It is a benefit she made sure was specified in her contract. Besides her own attendance, she had negotiated with the board for building administrators, on an alternate basis, to attend national conferences, knowing that it is a great learning environment but also grants them a small reward for their hard work.

When representing her school district at any conference, she makes sure she looks very professional. However, come evening and on her own, she can relax in shorter, provocative dresses teamed with sling-back high heels. Average in height at five feet six, she is short-waisted, and her long legs accent her slim ankles and sculpted calves.

Not long after arriving in Meadowbrook to assume her position as superintendent, she met with and assessed each of her principals. After all, they are her front line, and she must be able to trust them to carry out the school's mission. She has been pleasantly surprised with their dedication, leadership, and management skills. One in particular, the high school principal, stirs in her the feelings she hasn't acknowledged to herself in a long time.

This year is the high school principal's turn to go to the National Association School Boards' conference with Monica. She is the opposite of Monica in mannerisms and looks, but she is attractive in a sportswoman-type way. After a full day of going to sessions and connecting with colleagues, Monica is sitting at the bar in the hotel attached to the convention center nursing a Cosmopolitan when Jerri (short for Jerrilyn) approaches her.

"All alone?" Jerri inquires.

"Yes, I just needed a few moments to review all we heard today. We had some really good speakers with lots of information I'm hoping we can take back to the administrative team. I'm sure the board members who are here can also give us a good accounting of the sessions they attended."

"That is one reason I came over here—to thank you for this opportunity, Dr. Woodland. I really enjoyed the day. Just not sure what I'll do tonight with time on my hands." She gave Monica a questioning look that seems to convey more than just time on her hands.

"Why don't you start filling your evening by having a drink with me? We can share our thoughts about ideas to implement in our district."

There is an immediate attraction that neither can disguise as they volley back and forth in conversation. Jerri knows she can't make the first move. After all, this is her supervisor! As the evening progresses and the drinks keep coming, Jerri finally feels Monica's hand on her thigh. She carefully places her own hand over Monica's, giving it a warm caress, and moves her face within a few inches of Monica's. Their eyes are locked until Monica suddenly pulls back and turns to see the district's School Board President, Dr. Ron Phillips, coming into the bar. By the recognition on his face, he saw their intense positioning. Instead of coming across the room to greet them, as one would expect, he leaves without saying a word, but gives Monica a sinister eye.

Jerri obviously has seen him, too, and looks petrified.

"Relax, Jerri, we can take this up to my room in a little while. No one needs to know," reassures Monica. "We'll just sit here a little longer. Here is my room card," she motions as she pushes it across the bar. "Corner room, 8th floor, facing the front of the hotel. Come in about 45 minutes."

Jerri slides off the stool, clutching the card and shaking her head. "What am I doing?" she admonishes herself. "This is my boss, the one who evaluates me. I must be crazy to be contemplating this." But just like her boss, Jerri has few opportunities to be with the same sex in Meadowbrook. Plus, Monica is gorgeous and desirable!

In her own room, Jerri makes the decision: "I'm going for it!" She slips on a beautiful royal blue camisole with matching lace panties, then covers them with a sweat suit—no use to advertise this feminine side of her demeanor. Running a brush quickly through her hair and applying a thin sheen of blush on both her cheeks, she tries to curb the lust building in her body.

Monica, wearing a multicolored kaftan, answers the door at the first rap, wafting a scent like a beautiful garden of flowers. While Jerri stands just inside the room, Monica offers, "I can handle Phillips, so the night is ours. Although he is a well-respected doctor and serves as school board president, he has lots of skeletons in his closet that he wouldn't want exposed. He and I are kindred spirits when it comes to our private lives." Then she quietly locks the door.

Monica, however, acknowledges to herself, "He knows too much!"

While packing to leave the conference, Monica notices she has missed a call from her husband. Her mind skips back to how happy they had been in the beginning. She and Shawn had been married right after graduating from college and had moved to New York. He went the stockbroker route on Wall Street, and she taught at a private high school not too far from where they lived in their one-bedroom apartment. Life at first had been fun and exciting, but soon different interests and careers took a toll, and they steadily grew apart. She always wanted to share with him her challenges with students and some staff. He feigned interest; he didn't really want to hear it. He wanted to extol all kinds of financial facts and challenges, and she listened with half attention.

Monica chose to go back for graduate work. Money wasn't an issue then, and she qualified for several scholarships—as a black woman wanting to be a principal and then superintendent of schools. It had been an excellent decision as she proved her skills in leadership, but eventually she hit the "glass ceiling." Being a principal had come easily, but the superintendency was the good-old-boys' turf. She interviewed as the token female too many times to count and most often came in second.

Finally, in a conversation with Shawn, they had made the decision that she should take an out-of-state position in Meadowbrook. As their superintendent, she could establish experience to bolster her vita. Then she could come back to New York. Shawn made it clear there was no other place for a successful stockbroker with an eye to starting his own firm than on Wall Street. They could do the long-distance marriage dance that so many couples had to do to further their careers.

Monica dials the number and hears his voice. "I know you're getting ready to fly home; I know you love the conferences, but catch me up on how it's going in Meadowbrook. From your earlier emails, you seem to like it," posits Shawn.

"It has been a tough road, but we are really making progress. Most of my staff are willing learners and want as much as I do to show improvement. And this district is certainly not in the Big Apple, but it has its charms."

"That's great, Monica," Shawn genuinely offers. "Say, I know this will be a tough topic, and I will always care deeply for you, but I find myself wanting my freedom. Have you thought about our future together?"

There is a long pause on the phone before Monica asks, "Is there someone else, Shawn?"

"No, no, nothing like that. I often go out with the guys from work, and I find myself enjoying it more and more. You and I haven't really been together for quite a while! I mean, we seem to want different things, and maybe it's time we go our separate ways . . . ." Shawn says as his voice trails off.

"It hurts. It hurts my sense of pride and makes me feel like a failure in this arena, but I know it's true. College life was one way, and real life has turned out to be much different than we could have foreseen. In all honesty, you are just the one who called the question," sighs Monica.

"Well, my suggestion is to give it a couple of weeks, and we'll talk again. A marriage is not something we should easily end," offers Shawn.

"I agree with that," whispers Monica. "We'll talk. Goodbye, Shawn," she adds as a tear of failure slides down her cheek.

Who is the first person Monica sees when she gets home from the convention? President Ron Phillips—no surprise. They had scheduled this meeting to review some budget items before they had left town for NASB. Monica vows she will be her usual professional self unless Ron brings it up. Then she will be ready with a put-you-in-your-place retort. Sure enough, Ron saunters in with an I-caught-you grin. Monica stands up, offers her hand, and motions him toward the chair he usually sits in. She waits a moment to test him, then pushes the line-item budget over to him and starts to explain the items in question. It only takes a few minutes to validate the charges he had earlier questioned, so Monica begins to put her copy into her briefcase and stands up.

"Well, you are certainly cozy with some of your staff. It's a good thing none of the school board members saw you like I did!"

Monica very emphatically spits out her words, "I am friendly with all of my staff. I'm not sure what you want from me, but I caution you to tread lightly. You can speculate on what you think you know, but I am friendly with Winnie and several others in the community. And I don't need to insinuate; I can state! And which of us has the most to lose? You have your practice, a wife, two sons, and are a shoo-in for 'Man of the Year.' Yes, certain things could hurt my career, but I can always move miles and miles away. Can you afford to?"

As they stare down each other, Ron finally offers, "Let's just agree to keep everything professional. And private."

"Of course," Monica drawls and walks him to the door. Mission accomplished.

Her homecoming has presented one other looming problem for Monica. She isn't sure exactly how to handle this one, but she has thought before and is thinking now, it might be time to move on to another superintendency. Jerri has not approached her, but Monica can feel the subtle overtures every time she is around her, and with Jerri on the administrative team, there are far too many times they are together.

"Why, oh, why, didn't I follow my own rules?" Monica chastises herself. "I know better than to become involved with someone on my staff. I can't blame Jerri; I am her superior, and the onus is on me to draw that line. Maybe I should have a talk with her to explain myself, or will that just exacerbate the situation?" Monica, feeling tightness in her neck muscles and a headache ready to burst forth, tells herself to seek out Axel, the Ace to her and all the women in town. "I need a massage, and he is so good at working me in." Every person needs someone who will listen without judgment, and, most importantly, be confidential.

"Thank God, we now go beyond client and masseur!"

Chapter 19

BDF – LAS VEGAS

May, before the Stabbing

The Texts

Cassy: I will be in Las Vegas for a long weekend at the end of the month for a bachelorette party. (Definitely NOT mine!) Any chance of hooking up for a BDF on Thursday night before the others arrive on Friday?

BDF: Wouldn't miss it. How about the Alto Bar at Caesar's Palace (my hotel). I'll meet you at the bar and reserve us a private booth.

Cassy: See you Thursday night at 8:00!

BDF: PS - No "edibles" needed. Come commando. Plan on the "bestest" damn fucks!

Cassy and BDF

"I am going to enjoy this four-day bachelorette party in Las Vegas, especially since Jack Thatcher, my mile-high pilot and BDF, is meeting me tonight at 8:00 in the Alto Bar at Caesar's Palace, and the other girls won't arrive until lunchtime tomorrow," she says aloud to herself.

His teakwood-colored eyes and deep dimples promise an evening of fun and BDFs—best damn fucks. Plus, she just needs someone to talk with about her life and where she is going. "Jack is always a great listener and makes me think. He is more than a BDF. He's my therapist," she giggles, again to herself.

Cassy enters the lounge at exactly 8:00, knowing that Jack will be sitting at the bar nursing a Crown unless he has to fly out in the morning—then it will be a Coke.

"I can already feel my cock taking notice of Cassy. Every other guy in this bar is wanting to be in her, but goddamn, she is gonna come for *me* tonight," Jack mutters to himself as Cassy saunters toward the bar in her shimmery black dress that hugs her body in all the right places. "And that sexy plunging neckline will provide me easy access to her pert tits," he admits to only himself. Just as eye-catching are her open-toed, strappy, thin-heeled stilettos, showing off her long legs and slim ankles. Her blond hair hangs in ringlets past her shoulders. Is it a coincidence that Bublé's "Such a Night" is playing as she sports that same flirtatious smile she had on their Mile-High weekend?

The bartender sets a Cosmo on the bar with Jack's second Crown of the Gods. "Well, you obviously don't have to fly out early tomorrow," Cassy comments as she toasts her Cosmo to his Crown. "Good times all night!" she adds with a wink, knowing that Jack loves sex—great sex—as much as she does.

After a passionate welcoming kiss that includes sucking on her lower lip, the two banter back and forth for several minutes and then are escorted to a slat-shuttered private booth, where two more drinks and a charcuterie board await them. The Cosmo is especially refreshing—and inebriating—with its mango passion vodka and cointreau accented with fresh-squeezed lime and cranberries. And a Crown is a Crown, right? Cassy, however, tastes a hint of blood orange liqueur and lime on his lips. "I guess not all Crowns are the same!"

The bantering continues and quickly increases to teasing and flirting. Cassy's sultry gaze meets Jack's as his hands cup her face, drawing her into a deep kiss, forcing her mouth to open while his tongue battles hers for dominance. He then nuzzles her neck with butterfly kisses and small nips that make her shiver with excitement. His fingers slide through the V-neckline of her dress, fondling her right breast as he circles and then pinches her nipple. He replicates the touches with her left breast. Jack then leans down, pulling her right nipple to his mouth, swirling it with his tongue, licking and sucking until it is rock hard. Her left nipple deserves—and earns—his same attention. She moans, enjoying every stroke he makes on her body.

"Are you wet for me, Cassy?" Wanting to know firsthand—pun intended—he parts her legs, sliding his fingers through her folds. "So fucking wet, Cass!" She grinds against his fingers fucking her as he teases her clit with his thumb.

"Jack, don't stop. Please, don't stop! I need this; I am almost there." With a few more thrusts, he can feel her tighten around his fingers. Cassy cries out as a crescendo permeates her entire body, "Jack, I am coming!" Finally, catching her breath, she smiles at him, "You are definitely the BDF in my life. And we haven't even really started."

As Jack pulls Cassy into his arms, his visible bulge urges her to offer, "Let me pleasure you now, Jack!" She sees his cock grow even more as she unbuttons and then unzips his jeans. His erection jumps as she wraps her fisted fingers around his shaft. Her index finger circles the tip; she tastes the salty precum on her fingertip and then draws his cock into her mouth, sucking and releasing. Their eyes are glued to each other; nothing else—or no one else—interferes with this moment.

A gasp escapes as he fists her blond curls and rocks into her, guiding her mouth as his cock slides in and out, touching the back of her throat. "Goddamn, Cass, I am going to come fast and hard if you don't slow down!"

"Give it to me, Jack. I want to taste you. I want to see you lose control." He grabs her hair again, moving her head faster and harder, assuring a rhythm that expertly pushes him to the edge.

"That's it, Cass! I am gonna come." And he does, hard and fast, just as promised. She swallows every drop as his cum bursts into her mouth. He can taste himself as he kisses her.

She smiles that flirtatious smile, "Shall we take this to your room?" He kisses her again, pulling her into him as he drops several bills on the table and leads her to the elevators.

More of Cassie and BDF

Jack escorts Cassy to the elevators, his hand lingering on her back as he teases her earlobe with a promise of more to come. Cassy's face reveals her awe at the plush suite, and she walks directly to the huge floor-to-ceiling windows, letting in all the lights and glitter of the strip. Jack is eyeing the king-size bed and moves to order room service: a Japanese highball for himself and a Lychee martini for Cass and then sushi—shrimp tempura, soft-shell crab, and the house special (whatever that is, he doesn't care; he has the "house special" in his room where he is undressing her right now).

"Stay right there in front of the windows, Cassy. I want anyone watching to see what the sexiest woman in Las Vegas looks like— while I fuck her. Press your tits against the window." Jack continues to tease her earlobes with his nips and kisses as he circles her clit with his thumb. "How do you want it tonight—hard and fast or slow and easy?" he whispers as he slips two fingers in her core.

"Often," she quips. "I want to come often in all the ways you have to offer. Just make me come. I need it badly!"

"You got it, Cass. Spread your legs." As his thumb continues to drive her nub to new heights, his tongue replaces his fingers, driving in and out of her sex. "Cass, come for me!" Her hips battle his rhythm, pounding against his face.

"Don't stop, Jack. I'm close," she moans as her fingers claw at the window. She doesn't care who can see them; this is her night. She is getting what she wants—and needs. "Oh, Jack, God, Jack, this feels so good!"

There's a knock at the door. "Perfect timing, Cass. Time for a break." He tosses her a robe as he pulls on his jeans and responds to

CASSY PLAYS HER CARDS!

the second round of rapping. The server places the drinks and the sushi on the round table that has four royal blue velvet chairs. "Two for one on the drinks tonight, sir. Hope that is OK. No extra charge."

Jack and Cassy toast to the night so far—and the night to come. "Jack, this martini is fantastic! May I have a sip of your whiskey highball?"

"Absolutely, and I want to taste your martini on my lips." He removes her robe and pushes her back on the bed. "I like to see you naked." He takes the second martini and dribbles it from her breasts to the apex of her hips. He then begins kissing down her body, nibbling her tits, and down her belly. "Mm-m-m-m, you taste so good. Best drink I have had in a long time," he muses. Teasing her clit and her core with his tongue until she screams, he pushes his cock deep inside her.

"Harder, Brock, harder!"

And What's This About?

No planes to catch. No commitments in the morning. They both sleep in after a night filled with sex and escape.

Breakfast arrives in the room at 10:30: blueberry and Yuzu Soba Pancakes with whipped cream, pecan miso butter, and maple syrup for Cassy, and a champagne mimosa. Jack has the traditional steak and eggs with a Japanese bloody Mary.

He senses Cassy needs to talk, her pensive look giving it away.

Jack takes a sip of his bloody Mary and a bite of toast with strawberry jam. Cassie licks from her fingertips the jam that has drizzled down his chin. Jack presses a kiss on those fingertips and then asks, "So who the hell is Brock? I think he is pretty important to you—or at least could be. You said his name when we sexted and then screamed his name twice last night when you were coming. Time to spill the goods, Cass."

She stares into his eyes but says nothing. He waits, finally saying as he wipes a single tear from her cheek, "Come on, Cass. You know you and I are just a fling—all fun and sex—so talking to me about Brock is OK. Get it out. What's bothering you?"

"Oh, Jack, I don't know where to start. I have really messed up, and I don't know what to do."

"Go on, Cass, I am here for you."

"I just don't know what to think or where to take my future. I have been involved with a married man for eight years. Sex has always been fun with him—so have the trips and the gifts. I thought he was the one, but I am not convinced any more. Maybe I just liked the challenge—and the sex, of course. I am wondering if there is any future in it. Maybe I am still in love—or lust—with him, but now Brock has come into my life."

"So how is it different with this Brock?"

"For one, he isn't married." They both chuckle.

"And . . .?"

"And we are closer in age, and we have fun together. We work together. I like his family, and they like me. There just seems to be more of a future—a real commitment to us—maybe even a family."

After a short pause, she adds, "And the sex is fantastic!" Again, they both laugh.

"How would the married man take it if you broke it off?" Jack asked.

"I am not sure. He is so busy with his career and obligations in the community that sometimes I am barely even noticed. Other times, I feel like I am the center of his world. When he is with me, really with me, it's fun, it's great trips, it's fantastic sex. But . . . ," she pauses.

"But what, Cass?"

"But other times I think, 'What the hell am I doing?' I cannot see a future except for the fun trips, the stolen hours, the incredible sex—but I can't see a *just us*—there's the community obligations, there's the hospital, the country club, his wife . . . and two of the greatest kids in the world."

"A doctor, huh?" She nods affirmatively.

"And Brock? What do you see?"

"Possibility!"

"Talk more about that, Cass. What possibilities are you envisioning?"

"You are making me think too hard, Jack, but I know I need to go there, to think about *my* future—what *I* need and what *I* want."

Chapter 10

THE HAUNTING MEMORY

Ron is still in the hospital with no reason available for his unconsciousness. Seeking relief for her stress, Winnie lies under a creamy white sheet and soft coverlet on the massage table at the country club. Ace soothes her body with hot stones while a beautiful Mancini instrumental version of "Moon River" weaves sadness and happiness into her haunting memory of one day eighteen years ago.

Trey was just a toddler playing in the back yard when Winnie got the call from the other (really another) woman, letting her know that Doc was in love with her. Winnie knew Ron would never leave her, but she was so tired—tired of the dignified face she put on for others, tired of the makeup gifts he brought to her begging for her forgiveness and promising his undying love, tired of . . . just tired.

That day, she had dialed the only man she trusted. AG immediately recognized her tone of utter sorrow and stifled sobs. He quickly promised to meet her at their favorite art gallery in Chicago from their college days as soon as she could get there. After she hung up the phone, she contemplated backing out; she was just too tired, but she also knew he would hold her and make all the hurt go away. And Aunt Joey was an ever-ready babysitter. She would treasure having Trey to herself for a day or so.

Winnie could pick out AG anywhere, and she immediately saw him strolling through Gruen in River North. When their eyes met, Winnie ran into his open arms. He pressed his lips on her forehead as his arms stayed wrapped around her, whispering, "Winnie, it will be OK; I'm here now. Cry all you need."

They strolled through several of their favorite galleries and then stopped for dinner in a nearby boutique hotel with a French restaurant. Two glasses of Talbot Logan Chardonnay and a dinner of seared scallops infused with herbs, sweet potatoes with goat cheese, and a vinaigrette salad ended in dancing to the musical quartet. They laughed, she cried, he held her.

Their evening on the dance floor ended with Bobby Darin's "More." As they entered the small suite in the hotel, they softly hummed, "More than the greatest love the world has known, this is the love I give to you alone; more than the simple words I try to say, I only live to love you more each day."

Their eyes undressed each other's hearts as their fingers removed each other's clothes.

"Oh, AG, I think I made the wrong decision when I let you go and married Ron. He is certainly not the man I thought he was, nor even near the man you are."

"Oh, my sweet, sweet Winnie. You will always be my true love, and I will be here for you no matter where our paths wander. Now, come here. Let me show my love for you." He pulled her into his arms, removing the pins that held her chignon in place, caressing her hair falling now to below her shoulders, kissing first her forehead and then cupping her face with his hands. AG kissed her lips, first tenderly and then with a deep need to show how much he cared—truly cared for her—and wanting to take on all the hurt and stress she experienced with Ron. He expertly explored her body, gently and with love. His eyes were constantly on her eyes. He saw the hurt dissipate. He then entered her, slowly at first, then fast and hard, ending with satisfying gasps as their climaxes erupted simultaneously.

There was no embarrassment—just passion that unites two lovers of yesteryear with the promise of tomorrow.

That was eighteen years ago. Winnie has always known Phipps is AG's son, but how could she tell him now? Should she? And what about Ron? Or did she even care?

AG has always suspected Phipps was his son; he looks just like his grandfather—the same pronounced eyebrows that shaded the aquamarine eyes with lush lashes, same dark brown hair with just a hint of auburn, and the same birthmark that AG, his dad, and Phipps share—a small rectangular brown patch on the calf of each of their left legs.

AG has never missed a junior high or high school event of Phipps's. And he has never stopped loving Winnie, always there to hold her when she needed it, always there to wipe away the tears when Ron had had another affair that ended with expensive jewelry and empty apologies to Winnie.

Should he tell her he knows? Does she even know? What would be her reaction?

This morning he had attended the Ladies' Single and Double Tennis Tournament. As mayor of Meadowbrook, AG is expected to emcee the luncheon for this charity event and extend trophies to the winners of the singles and the doubles.

When Joey and Winnie come forward to accept their trophies for winning the doubles, he notes the sadness in Winnie's eyes. Both she and Joey thank him and the club for sponsoring this great event for the children in need in their community.

It is when Winnie stands and advances to accept the trophy for the singles that AG whispers in her ear, "Winnie, meet me at our boutique hotel this afternoon in Chicago. I think you're carrying a secret that's killing you. It's evident in your eyes. Please, let me be there for you."

Winnie nods a simple thank you to AG and then turns to the luncheon guests. "Thanks to each of you for coming out today for this annual event. You all know how special the children of Meadowbrook are to Ron. This is his favorite charity, and while Ron couldn't be here today, I will share the trophies and the success of this tournament with him tomorrow." AG knows then that he will be seeing Winnie in Chicago.

Winnie walks into the small French restaurant at 3:30 in the afternoon. AG is already sitting at the same table they had shared eighteen years earlier.

"I took the liberty of ordering the same menu items we had so long ago: two glasses of Talbot Logan Chardonnay and your favorite, seared scallops." She smiles; he remembers. "Of course, we are a little early for the dancing, not even sure the musical quartet is still around." She giggles, amazed that he has recaptured that day. "More than the greatest love the world has known, this is the love I give to you alone" runs through Winnie's mind as AG hums Bublé's "I'll Never Not Love You."

AG has already reserved the suite for them. They turn to each other as soon as they enter the room, and both blurt at the same time, "Phipps is our son."

"How long have you known, AG?"

"I have always suspected it; his birthday was nine months to the day after we had been here. And then as he grew, he looked more and more like my grandfather. I knew for sure at a little league basketball game when I saw the brown patch on the back of his left calf—exactly like the men in my family for the past four generations."

"Oh, AG, I have always wanted to tell you, but you had your family, and then Audrey got cancer. You just had too much on your plate. I didn't want to complicate your life."

He pulls Winnie into his arms, holding her, kissing her, undressing her. Matching his long-ago actions, he takes the pins out, holding her long hair in place. The cascades of raven locks are splayed on the pillow. "You are beautiful, Winnie. I love you. I love us. I love Phipps. I know it's complicated, Winnie, but we will figure it out. It's Phipps I am most worried about."

"Speaking of complicated, we have more to address."

"What else could there be, Winnie? Tell me."

"Well, I guess what I learned last night and what you now know for sure, it could be a solution to a real dilemma—even Phipps and Claire might be thankful to know in the long run."

"Come on, Winnie, spit it out. What happened last night?"

"I was home alone. Trey was playing at the Daily Grind, and Phipps was at football practice and then with Claire. Maya had the night off. The doorbell rang, and the Ring revealed Ava Davis at my door."

"Claire's mom?"

"Right. I invited her in. I asked if she would like a glass of wine. 'Unless you have something stronger,' she said and added, "'I think we both may need it.'"

"I fixed each of us a dirty martini—a very dry Broken Goose Martini—and she seemed to calm down. What she said, however, certainly didn't calm me down—at first."

"So what did she say, Winnie? Tell me."

"She said that Ron is the father of Claire, Phipps's girlfriend."

"And you believe her?"

"Absolutely, she even had DNA proof. Oh, my God, can you believe it? She wants us to meet with the kids and let them know that they are half-brother and half-sister and could in no way be together. I couldn't tell her that Phipps isn't Ron's—not until I could talk to you and be sure you knew that Phipps is your son."

"I am glad that conversation, which would obviously crush Phipps and Claire's relationship, does not have to take place, but boy, do we need to clean up this mess!"

AG reaches for Winnie. "It will all work out. Somehow! Some way! Some day! I am just glad you and I know the truth."

They laugh, she cries, they make love, he holds her. The sadness has left her eyes, just like eighteen years ago.

Chapter 11

NEW YORK – THE BEGINNING OF THE END

June, before the Stabbing

Winnie and the boys are in the second week of their annual three-week vacation in Europe, and both Claire and Renaldo are with them. That vacation has always meant a special time for Cassy and me—uninterrupted days together, sharing our own mini trips, and indulging in as many sexcapades as our imagination can dream up. This year has been bittersweet. I just learned that Trey is gay and that Cassy has known for several years.

I was scheduled for a conference in New York, so a mini trip it was to be. Cassy is due to arrive this afternoon. I am having a hard time this morning concentrating on the conference speaker. Just thinking about her has me trying to suppress a hard-on. It's a good thing that there are only two days left of this conference.

I booked Cassy and me at the Hotel Sienne on the Upper West Side because of its European charm and elegant suites. The Paris Aujourd'hui on the first floor is famous for its French and Mediterranean cuisine.

Cassy is sitting in the taxi on the way to the hotel when she sends a text to me.

> Cassy: *Deuce, I'm on my way. Can't wait to see you sporting your black silk boxer briefs.*

> Deuce: *Oh, Sass, it's hard waiting (in more ways than one)! ;)*

> Deuce: *Suite 414, left out of the elevator, end of the hall.*

> Cassy: *Wait until you see my new black lace teddy.*

> Deuce: *Surely it is as wet as I hope it is, and if my urgent need ruins your teddy, I promise to buy you new ones—in any and every color you want because I can't promise it won't happen again.*

> Cassy: *Promises, promises!*

Cassy and I cling to each other as soon as she enters our suite. She quickly sheds her clothes, revealing that promising, very sexy black teddy. I can't get my clothes off fast enough. We fall to the floor, smothering each other with kisses and words of passion, before I enter her and quickly draw her to an orgasmic crescendo that makes her cry out. At the same time, I arch my back and shutter with a crushing orgasm of my own.

As I help her up, I guide her to the spacious bathroom. "Look, there is a sauna next to the glass shower. How about I heat you up in style?"

Sass squeals and opens the door. As the heat rises from the steaming rocks, so does our enjoyment of each other's bodies.

We are both *au naturel*. "Touch me all over, Sass. I crave the feel of your hands. Yes, yes, that's it. Slide them back and forth on every inch of me."

"I love touching you, feeling your muscles, massaging your broad shoulders, working on your hips, but I don't know how long I can go without taking your wet member in my mouth."

"No, no, I get to touch you all over first. Your breasts are glistening, and I want your 'joy' mound to ache for me." I can't believe I get to caress and stroke this alluring creature before me. "Here, sit on my lap so I can kiss your eyes, nose, cheeks, and your breasts. I have to bury my face in them."

"If I sit, I want it to be on something big and hard," she teases.

"You got it."

Cassy eases down on my erection and circles her arms around me. I moan and wedge my face deeper into her cleavage. She sighs as she revels in the full length of my dick and pulls my head ever closer. She moves her hands up to rifle through my hair and direct my mouth to each of her peaked and wanting nipples.

We begin to move in a sensuous up-and-down motion as our bodies, wet with perspiration, slide in perfect rhythm and sensation to an inevitable climax. As we collapse against each other, we are quiet. It has almost been surreal. Such depth of sexual feeling and satisfaction.

Satiated but needing nourishment, we sneak across the street to Cappiano's for a "taste of Italy." Cassy looks fabulous in a body-hugging leopard-print pencil skirt and fawn-colored V-neck sweater. Her feathery hair is captured in a large crystal clip, although with that seductive cleavage, I can't believe anyone will notice her hair. I look pretty good myself. I have on black jeans that hug my ass, a white long-sleeved dress shirt with sleeves rolled up to my elbows, and sporting my Italian loafers. We make quite a couple; I can tell by the way people stare at us when we walk toward our table. I secretly think to myself, "If they only knew what we had been doing all afternoon—mmm, or maybe they do."

Cappiano's is a neighborhood favorite with its subtle lighting, dark wood tables and chairs, crisp white tablecloths, and a sizable selection of wines. An original brick wall covers one side of the room, and an old-fashioned wooden bar, deep brown bar stools, and huge smoked mirrors beckon diners to order their one-of-a-kind cocktails.

Pastas of every kind are their specialty, all with unique, flavorful ingredients. Cassy orders the caprese salad and cappellini cappiano, an angel hair pasta with shrimp, arugula, and light tomato. I have the house salad, but go all out with the Tagliatelle Pescatore, a shrimp, scallop, mussels, and calamari dish. It is served with a spicy garlic olive oil and cherry tomato sauce—one of my favorites.

Cassy, leaning over the table, captures my face in her hands and coos, "Let's go real Italian, Deuce, Chianti with dinner."

"Anything you want, Sass," I counter with suggestive eyes.

We drink, we laugh, we tease each other. As far as we are concerned, we are the only ones in this restaurant, and the waiter makes himself both attentive and scarce at the right times. Most of the evening, we have our heads practically touching, gazing into each other's eyes. We toast everything; as soon as one of us says, "Being together," the other says, "Great sex!" When one shouted, "Multiple orgasms!" the other countered with "Wonderful dinner!" By the time we stop, we are well on our way to being inebriated.

When the waiter comes with the dessert tray, we want them all. Probably should have gone with the tiramisu, as good one-night Italians, but Cassy wants the caramelized bananas with whipped cream. We decide to take it back to the hotel with a new bottle of chianti to go. Worth every penny!

Neither of us wakes up early; in fact, it's the sun peeking through the curtains that pushes us to open our eyes. Cassy's back is nestled against my chest; we are curled up like spoons, not really talking, just enjoying the moment. I nuzzle Cassy's neck and kiss her on the cheek, whispering, "I know you won't believe this, but I am hungry again."

"For what?" she asks with a smirk and a wink.

I laugh, "For you later, but now I need food. Let's go to that restaurant on the first floor. It looks promising."

Cassy jumps out of bed and begins to get dressed. "I'm starving, too. I need coffee—not that in-room stuff—real coffee. I'll race you getting ready."

We both hold hands as we go down in the elevator and enter the cafe. The Paris Aujourd'hui has a gorgeous dining room designed to evoke the elegance and ambience of a classic French bistro, with large windows overlooking one of the most beautiful old neighbor-hoods in New York.

As we enter, we can smell the coffees and morning breads. We select a bistro table by the windows and peruse the menu. The waiter arrives almost immediately, pouring sparkling water and pointing out the specialties.

"I'll have the orange-buttermilk French toast with bananas and cream and a tiger-stripe reserve espresso," orders Cassy.

"Didn't you have enough bananas last night, Sass?" I wink at her as she shakes her head. "I'll have the gruyere omelet with herbs and onions and your strongest black coffee," I order as I hand back the menu.

"OK, we can't spend all day in our suite like we did yesterday." Cassy puts on her fake pouty face as she places her napkin in her lap and arranges her silverware.

I cover her hand with mine and offer, "I will make sure we have a replay of that sex-filled afternoon, but we have to go shopping today for a new suit for my Man of the Year Party. I think I'll get the whole works, suit, shirt, tie, socks. I already have gold cufflinks to wear. You're the perfect person to help me. And don't forget," giving her my most suggestive smile, "we have to get you lots and lots of thongs for this week—edible if we can find them!"

"Oh, you are such a tease," moans Cassy. "Can't I get a pretty bauble, too? Something that will always remind me of New York."

"I'll buy you the prettiest bauble in the jewelry store, but now let's eat, Sass."

Back at the hotel we quickly change into appropriate wear to visit my personal tailor, Allan DaVinci. I want to arrive looking like I continue to be extremely successful because I am!

Allan remembers me, of course, and goes right to work, taking extensive measurements to assure the perfect fit. I explain to Cassy that this is known as a bespoke suit because it is tailored from a pattern made just for me. It doesn't take all that long, and Cassy is mesmerized by his expertise. I will have to go through multiple fittings, but it is well worth it. The hardest part is selecting the fabric; with Cassy's help, I choose Vitale Barberis in a deep charcoal. Then I pick out a ridiculously expensive white long-sleeved shirt. It clings to my torso, and I can tell by the look in Cassy's eyes that it is perfect. Some silk socks and a tie are next on the list.

Cassy comes toward me carrying a cobalt blue tie that she holds up to the fabric. "This is the one," she says with conviction, "and I'm buying it for you, Deuce. Every time I look at you during the party, I'll know a special part of you belongs to me." I pull her close and kiss her on the forehead. Everyone in the tailor shop stands by and waits for us to break the spell.

"Whoa, Sass, you have a lot more than a little of me. I just cannot get enough of you. You are mine!"

As we are taking a taxi to Tiffany's, I sense that Cassy's mind is somewhere else. I question the faraway look in her eyes. What, or who, is she thinking about? I do not say anything but wonder if she is questioning our relationship.

Coming back to the moment in front of Tiffany's, Cassy protests, "I was just teasing about the bauble, Deuce. My gift is being with you in this magical city."

"Look, I love spoiling you."

I know Cassy is completely captivated by the opulence on display. Everything sparkles as she moves from case to case filled with magnificent jewels. Finally, she says, "I would love earrings to wear with the pendant I received from Trey and Phipps."

"Your choice, Sass!"

She has a hard time deciding until her eyes land on a stunning pair of simple but elegant studs. "This is it," Sass says as she peers into the mirror, holding the diamond and pearl studs to her ears and looks into the mirror. "They will be perfect—pearls to match my own hair comb and square diamonds to complement the necklace."

"You've selected Tiffany's signature pearls in white gold with diamonds," smiles the clerk. "Excellent taste. Shall I wrap them up for her, sir?" the clerk questions as she turns to Deuce.

"Please do," I gesture, handing over my card.

Cassy's feet seem to be floating above the pavement when she walks out of Tiffany's holding a small blue bag with a white ribboned blue box tucked inside.

Zipping back to the hotel, we are ready for a late in-room lunch, and if I have a choice, a sexcapade that hopefully includes the circular tub. My dream becomes an instant reality when Cassy announces, "I am going to take a bubble bath in that great big, jetted tub."

"You just go right ahead, my Sass," I say with a fake bow and grin.

Busying myself, I select my attire for the evening at the theater, enjoying the musical *Hamilton*. I decide to wear one of my other bespoke suits. It's midnight black, and I'll pair it with a lavender shirt and deep purple tie, Cassy's favorite color.

I know Cassy is planning to wear a silk slip evening gown. It is shimmery silver and drapes over one shoulder. Her new pearl and diamond studs will look perfect, and I set them out for her. It makes me smile, remembering her delight in selecting them.

I can't help but hear her splashing around, so I quickly call room service and ask for a bottle of Dom Perignon to be sent up right away. I immediately undress and put on the plush hotel bathrobe just in time to answer the door, secure the bottle and press a tip in the steward's hand. I head to the bathroom with the bottle and two flutes.

Cassy's eyes are closed, but she feels me enter the water. When she looks up, I have a twinkle in my eyes and a glass of the most exquisite champagne coming toward her.

"Thought I would join you. You look so relaxed and happy."

"I am," she almost whispers as she sits up and takes the glass. "I'll have one, too." Cassy proposes a toast. "Here's to a wonderful evening with a wonderful man. And *Hamilton* just adds more magic."

As our flutes meet in the toast, I muse, "I'm looking forward to it, too, but right now I have something else in mind."

"What could that be?" she purrs as she scoots closer to me. "Can you enlighten me, kind sir?" she teases.

"Oh, yes, I have just the perfect 'entry' ready and willing." With those words, I grab her, push the bubbles aside and straddle her body. Beautiful and fragrant, too. "I want you, and my cock needs to be in you now."

The foreplay pushes both of us to a frenzied coupling and a wet and splashy climax. We laugh as we see most of the water is out of the tub and on the floor. "Well, that's what happens when we are having too much fun, too much Dom Perignon, and maybe not quite enough mind-blowing sex."

But my mind goes back again to Cassy's distance earlier in the day. Was she thinking about our future? her future? Brock Taylor?

Chapter 11

AXEL –
AN ADVOCATE FOR HIS WOMEN

No one would ever believe his name is Alfred; he is the epit-ome of an Axe, even Acel. He had just shown up one day in Meadowbrook with his table and credentials and started working to build a clientele as a masseur. In one of the nicer build-ings on the Brick Town Square, he opened a classic but understated salon. Off-white walls are accented with tall green ferns, soothing music plays in the background, and fresh water stands in several coolers with cucumber, lemon, or lime slices. Many salons he'd worked in over the years supplied cotton gowns and slip-ons, but Axel wanted to draw a select clientele, so he provided thick, soft white wraparounds, with an ocean breeze scent, paired with fuzzy slippers for the women, and soft brown robes with a musk scent and chenille slippers for the males.

Axel is six feet five with thick espresso brown hair cut short on the sides with a huge wave on the top that flops left when he is working. No one has ever seen him without his raffish short beard and mustache. His eyes are catlike—deep brown with flecks of gold that always have a hooded quality. His inviting lips are always curved into a know-it-all smile. Massive hands allow him to gracefully cover his patrons' smooth bodies with warm, scented oils. He loves his work but knows the real money is in house calls where the tips are always larger and the fringe benefits greater.

He is often spotted in his custom Trans-Am with an aggressive distributor curve, gold racing stripes and gold eagle's wings spread across the hood. This car forebodes danger and coiled excitement as it speeds around the city or flies down the freeway! He can count on the females of all ages to wave as he cruises by, wearing his tight white sleeveless T-shirt and, if he does stop by somewhere and steps out to lean against the car, he garners immediate attention. His white, very tight pants show off his ample masculine jewels.

Axel has also been smart enough to make an arrangement with the country club, really his best advertising, and it isn't long before almost everyone knows him and utilizes his *personalized* services. A few know and some at least surmise that he is bisexual. What they don't know is that he once worked on a cruise ship doing double duty until his promiscuous ways cost him his job. One of the staff members on the ship told him about a little town close to Chicago that was growing, friendly, and without a massage business.

He decided that was for him, and Meadowbrook has proved to be lucrative and amusing.

Taking time first to get established and build his customer base, Axel decides it's safe to indulge in his alter ego and seek assignations with some of the rough guys he's heard about. He craves their leather-bound bodies and take-me attitudes about sex. Trolling the out-of-town gay bars in the nearby fringes of Chicago, he usually gets lucky; after all, he is good-looking and has a killer body, ripped abs, and a firm ass. Using his smoldering eyes, he can signal his availability and readiness to play. His never-fail move is to lean way over the pool table to line up his shot. He can always count on hearing at least one or two cat calls: "Nice ass!" or "Love to tap that!" Tonight he is at the Twisted Spoke bar, where he fits right in with his black leather vest and hug-me pants, gloves without fingers, and steel-tipped alligator boots. Pounding music, lots of macho bragging, the click of pool balls against cues, and the smell of testosterone are a strong juxtaposition to his regular work.

The bartender, for a carefully slipped $20 bill, turns a blind eye as patrons slip into the backroom. Axel makes sure he never links too often with the same guy. He knows he must keep up his image; however, a guy is wired the way he is, so why fight it. His weekends are his own, and he can fill them anyway he likes. Perhaps it is this underlying personality that also draws women to him. That hint of danger, the loving caress of his hands, the soothing murmur of appreciation as he works each body part, and finally an unspoken guarantee that *all* his, and her, needs will be met.

Few would guess that Axel is a "card-carrying" advocate of women in general, but specifically for Winnie, Monica, and Cassy. The man loves women—truly loves them—and he hates the way most of them are treated by the men in their lives. Not for sex alone does he favor them, although he loves to satisfy his clients' and his own desires. He believes women are just the most fascinating creatures. Almost all the ones he sees regularly through his business are smart, funny, talented, dedicated, and devastatingly beautiful. He marvels at the way they maintain their attractiveness, raise their children, and stay married to some less-than-stellar men—real dicks. "Winnie must surely have her own good reasons for staying with Doc Ron, but knowing what I know it is hard to believe. Then there is Monica. She is still married to that jerk of a husband back in New York while she is here. Don't those men understand what beautiful women they have in their lives?"

Winnie - A Friend

Doc Ron's wife was one of his first clients, and he owes her a great deal since she is the one who spread the word to the country club crowd, especially the women, about his unique massage techniques. That anchored his immediate success.

Knowing everyone's secrets often makes Axel smile; if they only knew he had secrets of his own. He loves to hear Winnie gasp as she finally submits to the restorative pull of the massage. "Oh, Ace, more. Don't stop!" Axel never fails to enjoy what a beautiful woman she is, with the most supple and inviting body he has ever seen for a woman her age. He detects a sadness and anxiety about her that he longs to erase, and as they have grown closer and confided in each other, he feels more and more protective of her.

Today she is almost purring as he takes her head in his hands and begins manipulating the tight muscles in her neck. "You are still knotted up. What's going on?" questions Axel. "Try to relax even more and talk to me. I'm here for you," he says emphatically.

Winnie begins to feel more and more of the tension subside in her body and with just a touch of hesitation begins talking, forgetting to gauge her words. "It's my Trey, Ace. I love him so much, and I worry about him. His dad always wanted him to be a jock. Thank goodness Phipps has turned out to love sports. Ron always talks to the boys about being a man's man. For years, I have seen Trey cringe when that happens, but he works hard to not disappoint his dad. Were you there at the party when he played on his guitar "Hotel California" by the Eagles in honor of his father's award and everyone loved it?"

"Sure, sure, I was running in and out of the kitchen, trying to help, but I do remember Trey brought the room to a hushed standstill. He is very talented, and he obviously loves music. Doc Ron has had so many opportunities to be proud of him," poses Ace.

"Trey is just different in temperament and the way he wants to structure his life. I get so afraid Ron will continue to put all his praise and support behind Phipps, and Trey will eventually resent being the 'less favorite' and distance himself from the family. I couldn't stand that."

Axel thinks aloud, "I know exactly what Trey is going through. He wants acceptance for who he is and what he does. Doc Ron, just like my dad, refused to understand—or maybe he did but wouldn't admit it."

"Ace, I have to go in a few minutes; can you hit my shoulders once again? I really did need you today." As she gets up and moves to the dressing room, Winnie admonishes herself, "I best watch my mouth. What got into me? After all, my husband is lying gravely ill in the hospital. I am usually so careful to keep family secrets."

Ron - A Foe

Axel remembers the invitation he had received from Winnie to the Man of the Year Party. At that time, he had thought it over and had decided to be the bigger man and attend, even though he didn't have much use for Doc Ron.

When he had arrived, the house was jammed with well-wishers, and after hugging Winnie hello, he set about making himself useful. Everything clicked along, and right after the Man of the Year presentation, Axel had made a point of stepping up and extending his hand to Ron in congratulations. Ron gave him a look that telegraphed, "Wait, who are you? Why are you here?"

Axel started to say something, but Ron recovered himself quickly as he was in a crowd. He shook Axel's hand and quickly moved to the more important people in the room, clapping the men on the back and kissing the women's cheeks.

Axel knew he had been dismissed and disrespected. He hadn't felt deep anger like that in a long time. "I'll show you, jackass," he had muttered to himself.

Those same feelings erupt as Axel recalls Ron's last massage. He could hardly stand to work on Doc Ron. It was always an ear-splitting hour of hearing him brag about *his* life, *his* conquests, *his* importance in the community. Axel would always try to change the subject, but Ron would immediately steer it right back to something he thought made himself look good.

"You know I have the best OB-GYN practice in the Midwest outside of Chicago," Ron crowed many times. "I can go to any of those medical conferences and hold my own with the physicians at the biggest hospitals. They all want to pick my brain about the neonatal unit I started, and it is brilliant, if I do say so myself."

Axel would murmur sarcastically things like, "Oh," or "Wow," and would capitalize on the opportunities to push a little harder on Ron's muscles. "What a jerk this guy is," he often muttered to himself, hoping he didn't say it too loudly. Even though Axel couldn't stand the guy, he wasn't about to pass up a generous tip. And it was generous—this guy loved to show off.

"I have a perfect physician's wife and two sons. What is it the royals say, 'an heir and a spare'? Winnie loves our big house, the country club and all the money I give her to spend on whatever she wants. I know I am gone a lot, and she carries the load with the boys, but she still finds time to make me shine in the community."

Axel knew he was giving little digs, but he just couldn't help it. "How you must love her."

"When we were first married, I couldn't leave her alone. We had sex on every surface in the house and outdoors. However, being a strong male yourself, you must know how it is to be surrounded by luscious, tantalizing, and willing women all the time. It's hard not sampling the goods. I'm just glad Winnie treasures being a doctor's wife. Oh, I figure she knows, but is smart enough to be the doting wife."

As Axel recalls Ron's last message, he thinks to himself, "I wouldn't be so cock-sure of that, Ron, if I were you."

CASSY PLAYS HER CARDS!

Monica - Another Friend and More

Dr. Woodland, in a very short time, had built a strong relationship with Axel. She often cooed, "Ace, your hands are magic." It didn't take long before that magic snared them both, and Axel remains uncertain which one of them has enjoyed the after-massage activities more—Monica or him. Since Monica is married but her husband is hundreds of miles away, this has been a fun and exciting dalliance for both of them. She is beyond beautiful with her perfect body that molds to his like soft taffy.

Axel had already pegged Doc Ron's true character, or lack thereof; however, he doesn't know anything about Monica's husband. He never hears her talk about going back to that marriage, and he feels living apart like they do has to be a brave or maybe even dangerous move on her part.

He always enjoys listening to her talk about her position as superintendent. She really likes her job, and Axel has heard she is very good at it. He cannot believe the stories she shares, but it brings them closer, and Monica and he are building a strong bond as friends besides their sometimes-extracurricular activity. Axel is able to open up to her as well, sharing his disgust for men who take advantage of women.

Monica had only once talked about a short relationship she had initiated with another woman. She had never told Axel who it was, but several times voiced her anxiety over Doc Ron and his power as president of the school board. "God, the Doc probably knows something that he can use to ruin her career here in Meadowbrook," he mutters to himself. Slowly, it dawns on him: "If 'Dick Ron' had seen the two women together somewhere, it would present great blackmail material." Monica had intimated to Axel that she could say lots about Ron and his flings as well, but mudslinging had never been her style.

Today he is looking forward to seeing her for her weekly five o'clock appointment. Of course, so is Monica.

"This week has been a hell of a week," she thinks to herself, especially with the stabbing, all the questions and finger-pointing. She's so-o-o-o looking forward to Ace's de-stressing techniques. First, though, she slips her BMW coupe into the last parking space in front of her favorite bar and grill, Daze 'n Nites. "Thank goodness they serve food, too. If anyone from the community comes, I always have my appetizer beside my Cosmo," she giggles to herself.

She sips her drink, thinking about what she calls "a crisis a minute." She loves her job. However, the demands are almost 24/7: an AD accused of roughing up a student while stopping a fight, a teacher who'd let her license lapse, a newspaper reporter wanting a statement on why the district is running a bond issue now, and a student who has been found with drugs in his locker. Another Cosmo is in order.

Humming to Louis Tomlinson's "The Two of Us" playing in the background, her mind wanders to her husband, Shawn, and their recent Facetime conversation. Would she ever see him again? Would they ever connect again, or would this—whatever it is—ultimately end in divorce? That decision is on the horizon, and she knows what she needs to do, but it will put a final crushing blow to her one-time dreams of married life. She slides off the bar stool, grabs her keys, takes the last sip of her second Cosmo, and heads out for her very needed massage and perhaps more with Axel.

Monica starts to relax the minute she enters the parlor with its muted colors, green plants, and soothing music. This time it is Uriel

Vega with his melodic saxophone. Ace greets her with a kiss on both cheeks and whisks her back to her favorite spa room. Conversation isn't needed as he begins a tranquilizing manipulation of hot rocks on her neck and shoulders. He can see the tension in her muscles starting to dissipate and marvels, as he always has, at her radiant caramel skin.

When Monica repositions her body so Ace can massage her front thighs, she feels the change in his approach today—more like caresses, slower and deliberate. Her subtle sighs signal she is embracing the mood. As he nears the apex of her hips, she arches and invitingly opens her legs. His fingers circle her clit and then enter her; she hears him utter, "Monica, you are a fucking goddess." His urging fingers find her sweet spot and are soon replaced by his probing tongue, an aphrodisiac that brings guttural moans from both Ace and Monica. She explodes against his tongue, begging for more. He begins caressing her breasts, her nipples hardening at his touch. She feels his cock, hard as steel, wrapped in a condom, rub against her. He lifts her knees toward her shoulders and plunges his erection deep inside her, every thrust taking her higher. She clamps down around him, and he admits, "We both need this one, Monica. It feels so damn good!" After a final gasp, they both cry out and collapse in pure satisfaction. This isn't the first, nor would it be the last time, they seek each other to fulfill their needs.

And Then There Is Cassy

Axel places his magic fingers on Cassy's oiled body, removing her stress, but his thoughts only added to his. He could kill "Dick Ron" for what he had done to Cassy, robbing her youth and her innocence. Axel had become her confidante—the one to whom she turns to process her past and its connections with her future.

"Ace, where did you learn to be so attentive and to sincerely listen to people? I sometimes feel like I am taking advantage of you as my new-found therapist."

"Cassy, it's always just been a part of me since I was a young boy. I think my mother taught me how to really listen and tune into others' needs. She had a rough life, and she and I were incredibly close."

Axel's thoughts centered for a few moments on his own mother. She had been his rock. She had loved him beyond words. When he was younger, she had made sure to be home when he was, had helped him with his schoolwork, and taken him out to parks or trails where he could ride his bike or use his skateboard. His father had owned a gun store and kept long hours to feed his habit. He was a gambler and a drinker. His mother worked as a cashier at a grocery chain. She and his father had married right after high school, and neither one had any advanced secondary education. Both were gone now; he mourned his mother but still cursed his father. He came back to Cassy when he heard her voice.

"You're a fascinating puzzle, Ace, every bit a macho man, yet soft and responsive in a great way. Don't ever change; it's a powerful combination," she murmurs to him as she dresses and prepares to leave.

Axel vows to keep his knowledge of so many secrets to himself. He knows he will be contacted by Detective Finley since he was at the party when Doc Ron was assaulted, but hopefully he can maintain his stance as a bit player in this whole convoluted saga—and an advocate of the women in Meadowbrook.

Chapter 13

TWO TWISTS NOT EXPECTED!

September – after the Stabbing

As she stood looking down at Ron fighting for his life, her mind went back to the stir he had caused when they first met at the hospital. Handsome, personable, talented—he turned every nurse's head. Ava Davis had vowed not to be one of them. She had heard he was married, had a gorgeous wife, drove a fast car, carried a "bad boy" glint in his eyes, and had a twitch in his pants. And she remembers falling into his web.

Being the daytime in-charge nurse of Meadowbrook Hospital's birthing and neonatal centers at that time, she was constantly interacting with Doc Ron and his pregnant clientele. Doc and Ava steadily grew closer and closer in those early years as they compared decisions on the mothers and babies in their care. Eventually Doc Ron had asked her if she would be interested in filling in on occasion at his office. She jumped at the chance; she had bought her first house and wanted to make a few improvements and pay it down as quickly as possible. Most times she could only work in the evenings, and that fit into Ron's schedule just fine. The life of an OB-GYN was 24/7.

It had all started pretty laid-back with his saying something like, "Here, Beautiful, be sure to record these vitals," but escalated with a wink to "Wow, those emerald green eyes and auburn red hair could promise a fiery tryst with any one of your admirers—including me."

Ava tried hard to remain very professional, but she had to admit his attention made her feel important, and his appreciative looks at her body caused a throb between her legs and drenched panties. Oh, she had had several long-term boyfriends, but never anyone as handsome and playful as Doc Ron. She more than surmised that their professional relationship was heading for a collision, and she felt powerless to pull back.

One late night at the office, Ron had stopped by her desk as she was finishing the last of several backlogged records. He tortured her with his "Boy, you are fabulous" smile. "I'm starved and need a drink; my wife will be deep into sleep by now, and I hate to bother her by making a racket in the kitchen. Anyway, I am a lousy cook! Have you eaten?"

She hesitated a moment, then expressed, "I came straight from the hospital, so I haven't eaten either." He had her leave her car at the office, and they raced over to a hole-in-the-wall bar in the next town. The pub was famous for its burgers and carried any kind of craft beer you wanted. Doc and Ava casually visited about politics, hospital tales, and ordinary life as they devoured their food and sampled several ales.

When they pulled up to the office again, Doc Ron leaned over, looked intensely into her gemstone green eyes, and invited, "That beer just didn't do it for me. Can I entice you into one more drink? I keep a bottle of Woodford Reserve in my bottom desk drawer."

Ava, in her mind said no, but she heard "Sure" come out of her mouth. They were primed. Doc was kissing her the moment they entered the building, and she could see they were headed to his back office. Another drink was the last thing they were thinking about as their tongues battled for dominance. Their clothes fell to the floor, and their bodies throbbed in unison. Doc made sure Ava was wet and ready, and she surprised him as she grabbed his long, steel-like erection and guided it to her welcoming channel. They rocked back and forth, crashing into each other, savoring every moment until neither could hold back a thundering climax.

Oh, what a night that had turned out to be—in every sense of the word. The sex was mind-blowing; the afterglow was apparent for days; but the aftermath would last a lifetime!

The next day, Ava was anxious to see Doc Ron and hear what he had to say. What a letdown it had been when he treated her exactly like before. He never even mentioned their encounter, and his only acknowledgement might have been the wink he gave her. Days passed and it was she who longed for a replay, but he never let the opportunity present itself again. She had become just another one-night stand for him. She should have known better.

A month later when her always-reliable-and-never-late cycle failed to appear, she couldn't believe it. She fought with herself about what to do, but for her the decision was never in doubt. She would have *this child, and only out of absolute necessity would she ever reveal the father. Her final thought was, "That bastard will pay some day when the time is right."*

And Another Mom Has
Some of the Same Feelings

Every time Megan steps in to check on Ron, her mind revisits the past.

Ron and Cassy have never said a word to me about their affair. Oh, I know my daughter has a real appetite for sex, and so do I, so Cassy's behavior has never alarmed me. Cassy will settle down when she is ready. Hopefully, she will pick a better man than her father has been. God, years ago, when I met him in a bar, he was a biker and even held a job at that bar for a while. When I told him I was pregnant, he disappeared. We've had postcards from him occasionally, but nothing to pinpoint where he is. I tried for a while to send him news of his daughter, but I had no way of knowing if he ever received any of the communications.

Nursing has been the perfect career for me. I can support my daughter and have kept a roof over our heads. On the weekends, I still have had plenty of time to dance and meet partners at The Rusty Spur near the edge of town. I love to two-step to songs like George Strait's 'I've Come to Expect It from You' and 'It's Five O'clock Somewhere' by Alan Jackson. Thank goodness I was smart enough to not take those dates home. I kept my vow to never let a man take advantage of me again, and I didn't want Cassy to ever be put in an awkward position.

I know I am not a touchy-feely mom, but I love Cassy. I should not have let her grow up on her own, especially once she started school, but I have always been proud of her and vowed Cassy would have every chance to build a good life!

All of that crashed down on me last night. Jan, my best friend and a nurse at the hospital, and I went to the Rusty Spur to dance and drink. Jan looked at me in a strange way and blurted, "I have kept a secret from you for a long time. If I tell you, it may ruin our friendship, but you have to know he's just no good for her; he is married."

"What and who are you talking about, Jan?"

She stammered, "Cassy and Doc Ron. I never told you, but I know I should have—a long time ago. I saw them together when I was in Hawaii with my kids. They were more than 'together'; they were all over each other."

I couldn't believe what she said. I tried to rebut what she told me, saying that Cassy had always been close to the Phillipses, especially the boys. I tried to convince myself that Jan had it all wrong, but she just kept shaking her head, "I know what I saw."

I stood up and walked out of the bar. I didn't look back or say a word. I blame myself. I should have known after all the time Cassy had spent in that household that Doc Ron would take advantage of my beautiful girl.

He might be a great doctor, but there were just too many rumors about his screwing around. I know I should confront Cassy, but I cannot shake the feeling that Doc Ron enticed her with his money and fancy ways. At times it has been hard for Cassy to play in the same league as the other girls. She never had fancy new clothes or the latest shoes and jewelry. Her nanny job had given her spending money. The way she talked, she had always loved Trey and Phipps. It was Mrs. Phillips, not Doc Ron, who worked directly with Cassy about her nannying responsibilities. There was absolutely no need for Doc Ron to be involved at all.

As she checks on him a little later, she says in a disgusted voice, "I'm glad someone stabbed you; you deserved it. Will that be enough to stop you?"

Chapter 14

GUMSHOE WORK – SECRETS, INTRIGUE, CONJECTURE

Following the Stabbing and Many Interviews

Detective Mike sits at his desk at the Meadowbrook police station. "This place is actually pretty nice," he thinks, remembering the old days of working right on top of each other, desks back to back, phones ringing constantly, people escorted in handcuffs by uniform officers, and only the chief having an office with a door. The work hasn't changed, but at least now the detectives have cubicles with desks so they can leave out confidential files when they take a break for day-old donuts and cheap coffee. Right now Mike has papers strewn all over the floor, file cabinets, and in piles on his desk.

It definitely is time to sit back and try to piece together who had wanted to assault Doctor Phillips, especially since it was during his Man of the Year recognition party. "Whoever it was, they must have been plenty angry or upset over something," murmurs Detective Mike. He and his fellow officers, with plain old grunt work, have amassed a ton of information to decipher.

He starts by scanning the Man of the Year video and studying the still shots from the media team that documented the event. The photographer obviously liked her job; she made people feel comfortable as she snapped away and garnered some great shots. The videographer's work provided even more detail. Mike decides the photos speak for themselves; however, he notes, "I really need to talk to the videographer in person and determine for myself if there are details or clues that would surface."

Andy, the videographer, replies to Mike's call, "I am happy to come over now or anytime and bring the footage.

"Now will work great. I'll make sure our tech guy is available to produce a copy. I've already cleared this with Mrs. Phillips. We're ready to go," volunteers Mike.

As Andy, Mike, and the technician begin to scan the images, Mike poses questions to Andy: "I didn't see Axel, the masseur, in hardly any of this; do you remember seeing him?"

"Briefly, but very briefly. I know I saw him head to the kitchen a couple of times."

"Hmm, I wonder what that was about?" muses Mike. "I see the barista is everywhere, talking to people, monitoring the coffee bar, and checking in with Trey."

"Yeah, he is a friendly guy. I noticed that, too. He even stopped several times to talk to me," remarks Andy.

Mike laughs and postures toward the screen. "Don't you think Winnifred comes across as the ultimate hostess, and it looks so easy for her!"

Oh, she's a natural. I've filmed a lot of these types of occasions, and she is always in command."

At that moment, there is a closeup of Cassy. Mike laughs out loud this time and points to Andy, "I see you found the belle of the ball. Isn't she stunning? You and every guy there were checking her out."

Andy laughs, too. "I confess my camera did have a way of dwelling on her. She would make any guy's manhood stand at attention, including mine." He looks a little sheepish and intently returns to surveying the party scene.

When Mike and Andy finish, they both agree everyone moved about freely, in and out of the house, and no set pattern of interactions gave a hint of evil in the works. Mike then walks Andy toward the door and extends his hand, "We appreciate your help, and please check in if you hear or see anything you think would be of value."

"Will do. Good luck. Hope this helps."

Besides every guest having been interviewed by someone in the department, the caterers, band, newsmen, and servers had all been questioned. Mike knows his second in command would have compiled his thoughts from the various interviews, so he goes over to Gus's desk to get his insights. As he thinks of Gus, a crusty old buzzard comes to mind, but he knows Gus has forgotten more about police work than some will ever learn.

Gus greets him with his usual, "Hi, Boss, what do you need?"

"Nobody will ever be your boss, Gus," chuckles Mike. "I'm trying to piece together the info from the stabbing. I know you headed the interviews with all the hired help, so I wanted to get your thoughts."

Gus pulls out his small pocket notebook and starts thumbing through it. "There really wasn't anything that stood out to me. The caterers were busy keeping hors d'oeuvre trays filled and circulating. They did mention that this one guy volunteered to help them, and he seemed to know what he was doing. None of them could recall his name, but from others, I learned he was the masseur in town. The band was intent on playing, making the hostess happy. She had given them explicit instructions on what songs were acceptable. Each of the band members mentioned Trey playing with them and what a hit that had been. That gaggle of news reporters certainly couldn't give me any observations. They were too busy trying to outdo each other. And, finally, all the servers were from the local college, and they kept saying how much they were being paid by the hour. Not much to go on, Boss."

"Thanks, Gus," Mike says as he starts to leave. "Every little bit helps. See you later."

As Mike walks back to his cubicle, he engages in some speculation of his own. "It seems like Doc Ron and Cassy sent coded facial messages to each other, but it happened so quickly it might just be a detective's conjecture." He goes on to say to himself, "Many of the still shots show happy couples: Tom and Joey, Phipps and Claire, Brock and Cassy, Renaldo and Trey—they sure looked like a happy couple. AG and Winnie were together; however, Ron was busy being 'the man' so maybe AG was just being an attentive friend."

Phone records are easily obtainable for Detective Mike, but after reviewing page after page after page of the family's and close friends' and acquaintances' calls, only a few minor thoughts and observations surfaced. Mike summarizes aloud, "Phipps calls his girlfriend three or four times a day. Winnie talks to AG often; however, they are on lots of civic activities together, so maybe I am just trying to make a big deal out of nothing. Tom and Joey check in with each other at least once a day. Renaldo calls Trey quite often, but that could be due to changes in his music appearances. Doc Ron's cell phone is so constantly utilized, it seems like he talks 10 hours out of every 24—lots and lots of different numbers. It will take days to separate the ones that are business and the ones that are private. Of course, it is easy to pinpoint calls from his family. One other number pops up frequently; I'll have to check that one out. Wonder if Doc is being Doc and all the rumors are true."

Documents are irrefutably hard to deny, and Mike has chased down a few that demand further explanation. "I have copies of plane tickets for Cassy to Hawaii while Doc Ron was there for a conference, a rental agreement for an apartment for Ron in Chicago, and the college register shows no campus address for Cassy. Plus my team has confirmed that Trey and Renaldo lived together during Trey's college stay. God, the secrets this family seems to keep!"

As Gus passes by the boss's station, he hears him lamenting, "We've got some legwork to do. I need more information about Monica, the school superintendent, and I still haven't figured out the relationship between Winnie and AG. Oh, then there are still questions about Axel, the masseur, and the two nurses connected to Ron—Ava and Megan." Gus sticks his head around the partition and, with a friendly growl, demands, "Time for a break."

After what must have been his fourth cup of coffee, Mike heads to the hospital to check in with the day officer who is assigned to Doc Ron's room. His charge is to compile the 24 hours of each day from whoever has been stationed there. Mike spots Officer John Statin, who is, from all indications, a good officer, and thinks to himself, "I have to remember to support his rise in the department."

"Hi, John, how's it going?"

"Well, Mike, you've done this before—long periods of nothing, and then everyone shows up at once. Mostly it's family members and whoever is with them. Then the doctors, lab people, and nurses are constantly checking on the patient. We just try to make a quick note of those and the time they go in and out."

"Good, good," encourages Mike. "I know you all do your best. With Doc Ron not regaining consciousness, everyone is baffled, including me! OK, give me a quick rundown of family—and anyone not family or medical who has been here."

"Here's the list; stop me if you have questions:

1. Most frequent visitor is his son, Trey. He comes every day at odd hours. Stands there, seems like he's talking, then leaves. When he is not alone, Renaldo, the barista, is with him. He never says anything that I can tell, but he wears a scowl the entire time.

2. Second most often is Winnifred, his wife. She comes midafternoon; if not, then she usually comes in the evening accompanied by the mayor. AG seems to be comforting her, but it's hard to tell since I am usually outside the door.

3. Son Phipps is always with Claire Davis, and they talk openly to Doc Ron. They keep trying to cheer him up, just in case he can hear them, is my supposition. That's it for immediate family. Haven't seen his mother or father from what the nurses say. Some peripheral people have been by.

4. Meadowbrook's superintendent, Dr. Woodland, walked by one day. She asked me if there was any improvement. I shook my head, and she went on. Don't know if she was here for someone else and just checked in or what.

5. The masseur who moved into Meadowbrook a few years ago and opened a massage salon stopped by. He asked me if I knew how Doc was doing. I told him, as far as I knew, he was about the same as when he came in, but if he needed to know more, he could ask Dr. Jensen. Only thing is with HIPPA, there probably isn't much the doctor can tell him. Maybe I should have told him to ask Doc's wife.

6. Several staff from his office have visited but not stayed when they found out he still wasn't responding. Listening to them talk, I could tell they are worried about what is going to happen to his practice if this goes on too long.

7. Same with school board members—they arrive in twos so as not to warrant someone saying they were having an illegal meeting. They were chatty, giving all kinds of scenarios of what they would have to do to temporarily fill his position.

8. Finally, all of us have seen Miss Carstens here at odd hours. She checks to see if he is alone, then steps in and

holds his hand. When she leaves, she often has tears in her eyes and never speaks to any of us, not that she needs to. Kind of puzzling.

"Anyway, Chief, that's the report. Hope it helps us solve this case. It's a weird one. Who stabs someone when they are being honored? I guess if you want to hurt someone, it's as good a time as any."

"Well, I am not the chief, but I really appreciate your good work here. Be sure to pass it on to the others. Looks like we all have to keep digging. I'll stop by again. Thanks, John."

Working on his list of individuals to check on, Mike's mind dwells on the two nurses. "Cassy's mom, Megan, seems to be well thought of, but is what some would say "rough around the edges," drinking and going to bars. Ava, the head nurse at the hospital, is a mystery, especially about the father of her child." He sighs, "There is always plenty of gumshoe work for me—even with a team to back me up!"

Mike hopes Doc Ron is coming out of his coma-like state. Last time he had checked, Ron's vitals were good, and he seemed to be wavering between awareness and unconsciousness. "Surely the doc can give me some definitive clues to point us in the right direction."

Mike tries to see Ron at the hospital, but a nurse assistant is changing his bed linens. Then later that evening when he comes by, the night nurse, Megan, is busy checking the readouts on Doc's machines. With no major changes in his vitals, Mike is surprised to see Megan continue to hover over his bed. Based on her expression, he questions, "What am I missing? There's obviously more to this story."

Since it is close to the end of the day, Mike decides he will go back to the station and plot out his next day of interviews. He reviews several files, shuts down his computer but not his mind, and heads to the stairs when he sees the town's anointed busybody coming at him. He silently groans as she puts a triumphant look on her face and gushes, "Just the person I wanted to see. Detective Finley, I felt I just had to come. You remember my grandfather was a decorated policeman, and I learned so much from him. Today's officers don't seem to have his persistence or insights; of course, that excludes you and me."

Mike gives another silent groan, and points to the chair beside his desk. "I do remember you were the one who found Doc Ron and alerted everyone."

"Well, I certainly wasn't upstairs prying; I just wanted to give him my congratulations. You can imagine what a fright it was for me to find him that way. I know you've been in Meadowbrook for a long time, but nobody, absolutely nobody, knows the people here like I do. I wrestled with myself about coming in because I was sure you would want to interview me, so I said to myself, 'Just get in there. Save him a trip to my place.'"

"Thank you. That is thoughtful. Please enlighten me."

"First of all, I did not see anyone in his office when I went in, and I was so shocked that I ran out immediately. However, on second thought, there were a couple of huge houseplants by the bookcase and a small door on the left side of the room—probably a place to store paper, ink, toner, etc. You'll check for evidence there, won't you?"

"Yes, I've already ordered a second forensic team to comb the office. In the heat of a fresh crime scene, items or clues can be overlooked."

"Good, good. It never hurts to be extra thorough. That's what my granddad always said, rest his soul."

"Now as to people, a couple of quick observations. Like I said, I hate to pry, but people are always confiding in me, and I'm very observant myself. Take that former nanny of theirs, the Phillipses, I mean. She knew that house backward and forward. Who knows what went on through all those years? Then there is his wife, Mrs. High and Mighty. If I were you, I would ask her why she is so often seen with the mayor of our fine city. Now, his two sons—I don't believe they would ever harm their father, but I'll just bet they could really give you tidbits that might open up this case."

Mike is trying his best to hold on to his smile as Miss Busybody is speaking right into his face. So he settles for, "You make some very good points. I have started my interviews and am as anxious as you to know who and why someone would want to assault the doctor."

"Mind you, I'm not trying to tell you how to do your job, but lots of new people have moved into Meadowbrook, and some of them look very sketchy. It wouldn't hurt to check out their backgrounds."

"Anyone specific you have in mind?" Mike asked and hoped she had no answer.

"I hate to point fingers, but that new football coach rides a Harley Davidson and hangs around with his students. Then that masseur, who moved in, roams around the city in his funny-looking car—bet he thinks it's cool—and goes into women's houses. He even does business at the country club. I'll have to admit the new barista has opened a great coffee bar, but he wears all that black, and where does he get all his money? Oh, I'm keeping you. I can see the office is thinning out. Forgive me. I had to do my civic duty. I am certain my observations will aid you in your work!"

"We are grateful for any information or tips we receive, so thank you for coming in. Drive careful now," Mike admonishes as he ushers her toward the police department's front door. "I'll certainly call you if I need more information."

"And don't you worry, Detective, if I think of something I've forgotten, I'll come right in."

Mike feels a silent groan coming on again.

Chapter 15

AND SO THE TRUTH UNRAVELS

t isn't just Ron's life that is in a "death watch." If someone had taken the temperatures of those surrounding the Doc, they would have been red hot. Secrets had reached a crescendo and were ready to spill out. Everyone's life would be changed to some degree—and some a lot of degrees.

Ava is now struggling with how to tell her daughter that the boy she is seeing is probably her half-brother. She had kept assuring herself all these years that something like this couldn't happen. She had chosen to keep Claire in the dark. Even when Claire and Phipps began dating, Ava was certain it would run its course, and Claire could go off to college and find her future husband. Now Ava realizes she has no choice. Last night, Claire confided in her mother that she had started using birth control for protection because she now has an intimate relationship with Phipps. Ava is crushed but tries to remember to be the supportive mother she had never had. "Why didn't I tell her sooner? I was foolish to think this would just work itself out," she chastises herself. To keep her mind from spinning out of control, she segues into something ordinary.

"Where did you get the prescription?" Her voice has more of an edge than she wants it to, but part of her hurt is that Claire hadn't come to her when she needed help.

"Mom, you have been so wonderful. I just didn't know how to tell you, so Phipps and I talked to Tom and Joey. I am on the pill now, and Phipps and I plan to be together forever. I promise we'll finish high school and then college before we get married."

Ava is trying hard to look at this objectively; she knows the Redfords have handled the situation with care and solid advice, but this is HER daughter.

"Oh, don't look like that, Mom. We'll keep our promises. You'll see."

"Claire, I'll always love you no matter what happens. However, I think—no, I know—it is time I told you about your father. Hesitantly, she begins by saying, "What I have always shared with you is true. This man and I were only together one time, and you were the joyous result. I have been thankful every day of my life that I have you as my daughter. The only regret I have is you could not enjoy a true father-daughter relationship because he was already married."

Claire was not unduly surprised; her mother had told her years ago about a tryst that had resulted in her birth.

"Has something changed, Mom? Can you tell me now? You know, I've always wondered."

"I'll tell you, but it will break your heart, and I'm not sure if you'll ever be able to forgive me."

"Oh, Mom, we've been through everything together. What could it possibly be? Just tell me."

"Doctor Ron Phillips is your father!" For much longer than it seemed, there was total quiet in the room. Ava had tears running down her cheeks as she watched the full truth of the situation dawn in her daughter's eyes.

"No! No! No!" screams Claire. "That's Phipps's dad. That can't be." She kneels before her mother, who is sitting in a dining room chair, and clasps both her mom's hands in hers. "Tell me, tell me it isn't so!"

Ava mumbles, "It is. Oh, honey, I am so sorry."

Claire stands up with a trance-like stare. She walks slowly toward her bedroom, slams the door, and bursts into tears. She flings herself across her bed as she feels her heart break into a million pieces.

And across Town

About the same time in another household, a shattering conversation is set to be very revealing. Winnie is home from visiting the hospital and feels she has to tell Phipps the truth about his father. She cringes at the thought because she knows how proud Ron and Phipps are to be father and son. And truthfully, she doesn't want to appear less in Phipp's eyes. Her sons have been her crowning achievement, and she's not sure she could handle the recriminations that might result from the well-kept secret.

At first, she thinks she will do it alone, but on reflection, she believes AG has a right to be there, too. He arrives first, takes Winnie in his arms, softly kisses her, and states, "Are we ready?"

"No," sighs Winnie, "but I'll feel better if Phipps knows the truth."

"Let's hope he can absorb it without lots of turmoil."

Just then the garage door opens, and in strolls Phipps. He throws his letter jacket on the nearest chair and yells, "Mom, where are you? I'm starving. Practice went extra long."

"In here, Phipps, in the kitchen. I'll warm up some of the lasagna Maya fixed yesterday."

As Phipps enters the kitchen, he sees AG, gives a wave, and with a short hello, takes a seat.

"Phipps, while this gets warm, AG and I need to talk to you."

"Geez, Mom, you sound so serious. Did something happen to Dad?"

"No, no, nothing like that; however, it is about your dad. Many years ago, before I met your father, AG and I were a couple, and ever since then we have connected off and on over the years."

"That sounds pretty kinky, Mom. Why do I need to know that?" He casts a smirky grin in AG's direction.

"Well, honey, I didn't think a lot about it myself, but throughout the years as you've grown into a fine young man, I have had lingering doubts about your paternity. Maybe I was too afraid to do anything because it would so disrupt our lives, but you have a right to know the truth. So recently I had a DNA test done. There is no doubt that AG is your father. That's why he's here."

Phipps stands up, drops his fork, gives them both a cold stare, and shouts, "I don't believe that! You two are just trying to pull me away from my dad, and what a 'convenient' time to tell me. Dad's still in the hospital. He can't even talk to me. I'm sure he'll have a few choice words to say about this ruse," he shouts as he stalks out of the room.

"Well, that went well," AG postures. "I didn't even get a chance to say anything."

"AG," Winnie grabs his arm, "we have to give him time. This is a huge shock. He'll need time to process things and work out his anger. Ron has always favored him, as you well know, and we just shattered his world. He'll come back with more questions and concerns. We've got to be ready to answer them and to deal with Ron. Phipps is right. This will severely wound Ron's pride, and he'll want to fight back."

"This is just one of the first steps in putting things right, Winnie, but why does it have to be so intense and break so many hearts? I also have two kids who need to know they have a half-brother. I keep asking myself how they will accept this."

Winnie and AG embrace as each is lost in their own thoughts.

Later at Ava and Claire's Home

Both Ava and Winnifred, separate from each other, had made the same vow to themselves to be honest and be available as their cherished children, really young adults, begin to face the unimaginable facts that are now affecting their lives.

Ava, for her part, had always hoped that Claire would be well on her own and that Ron could smooth the way when the truth came out.

Winnifred, for her part, kept secretly denying the tell-tale signs that Phipps was AG's. She had faced enough recriminations in her early life and shied away from upheaval. She had always just kept treading water and enjoying the good things in her life. Now she had both Phipps and Ron to face!

Ava is more than surprised that evening when Winnifred calls, saying she needs to talk to her about Claire and Phipps. Yes, their kids had been dating for some time, but the families interacted in different spheres, so contact was usually limited to circumstances where many people were involved, like the Man of the Year Party.

Ava invites Winnifred to come over, but she is not sure how Claire will react in her current state. Ava is further flummoxed when Winne announces she will bring AG and try to bring Phipps. What did she mean, "try to bring Phipps," and what had she meant, "important background about Phipps"? This could turn into a real fiasco.

As Winnifred hangs up the phone, Phipps is walking toward her, shaking his head. "Mom, how could you get us in such a mess? Were you ever going to tell me the truth? I feel—huh—betrayed. So betrayed."

"Of course, honey," breathes out Winnie. "I tried to force myself a hundred times to just verify my suspicions, but watching you grow and be such a loving son to whom you thought was your dad, I just couldn't pull that away from either one of you. Even when I knew for sure, the words would get stuck in my throat, and I couldn't stand to hurt you. I love you so! Please, please, I hope in time you can find it in your heart to forgive me."

"Does Trey know?" demands Phipps. "I assume Dad doesn't know?"

"No one knows except AG and me, and now you," assures Winnie. Phipps stalks off again, but Winnie follows him to his room.

"Phipps, there is even more that you don't know."

"I have to see Claire, Mom. She is the only one I trust right now. She won't care who my dad is or isn't. She loves ME!"

"You are right! Phipps, *we*—you and I—need to talk to Claire *and* her mom."

"Why, Mom? Why is it important that you and I talk with Claire?"

"Phipps, like I said, there is more to this story than even I realized until last night."

"Come on, Mom. What are you talking about? I'm not sure I can handle any more surprises or secrets. My brain is twisted in denial."

Phipps grabs his jacket and heads to the door. "I told you I need to see Claire. What the hell do you and her mom have to do with this?"

"Can you, please, trust me just a little bit longer, Son? I am only trying to put things right. I have already called Ava and asked if we could visit with her and Claire."

The Real Truth

Ava coaxes her daughter out of her room, "Phipps and his mother are on their way here."

Claire, wringing her hands, says with tears cascading down her cheeks, "Phipps is now my half-brother. How could this happen to me? Mom, I'm not sure I can face him. I must end our relationship forever. It's too much, just too much."

"My beautiful girl, you owe it to Phipps to see him. Can you imagine how he will feel? Just like you, because it is happening to him, too."

The ringing of the doorbell announces the Phillipses have arrived. Ava opens the door, and there stand Winnifred, Phipps, and AG. "Come in," motions Ava. Tension permeates every corner of the room as they all wrestle with their own thoughts and questions. In fact, they are all just standing there looking at the floor.

Finally, Ava motions for everyone to sit down as she takes a seat herself. "I need to explain that Claire's father is Doc Ron, the result of a one-night stand years ago. I am so, so sorry, Phipps. I should have been honest with you and Claire when you first started dating. Your dad doesn't even know, and your mom just learned last night. I told Claire this morning. What a mess I have made in your lives. You are a half brother to Claire." Claire looks up at Phipps with red, tear-stained eyes, and a sob rends the air.

Everyone is stunned. No one speaks until Winnie says with relief, "This is wonderful! The truth is unraveling."

Everyone but AG looks at her like she has lost her mind. Phipps finally dials into the facts, grabs Claire, and starts his own story. "Claire, Mom just told me that Ron is NOT my biological father; AG is. It's a long story, but that can wait. The most important thing is we are not related at all."

"Oh, Phipps, are you sure? This is too hard to follow. I think my heart had actually stopped beating, and when I saw you, I couldn't stop crying." Tears are still cascading down her wet cheeks. Tears of pain may now become tears of joy if everything they are saying is true.

"Yes, it is true; we are not related. I have always known we were meant for each other. This just proves it."

Phipps and Claire stay locked in each other's embrace as Ava, Winnie, and AG move to the other room. They try to fill in the blanks for each other; however, they are thankful that their past foibles haven't spoiled the future for two wonderful kids. Winnie assures Ava that she knew her husband was a philanderer, and Ava apologizes again for letting it happen. "I do have to be honest though. Claire means everything to me, so I have never regretted the outcome."

All that is left is for them to fill in Ron when he regains his health! Something they both dread.

At the same time, they hear the roar of Phipp's pickup speeding away from Claire's home. Winnie sighs, "I am sure they are on their way to Tom and Joey's to sort out all of this."

As Winnie and AG leave Ava's, Winnie ponders her son's future, while Ava says a silent prayer of thanks for this turn of events.

Chapter 16

AND IT JUST KEEPS UNRAVELING

Cassy and Brock have just left Eldorado's, their favorite Mexican restaurant. Sometimes they need a fun, casual atmosphere after their long days at school. The Mexican food is authentic and always excellent, especially the Nachos Cameron, homemade nacho chips topped with grilled shrimp, sauteed onions, tomatoes, bell peppers, and guacamole, accompanied by sour cream and pico de gallo. They wash the nachos down with tequila margaritas and savor the fresh lime and salt on the rim. The music of Selena, Shakira, Ricky Martin, and other Latin singers have them dancing. Their favorite is moving together to Enrique Iglesias's "Hero."

Both Cassy and Brock are dedicated to their students, Brock often stepping into the role of a surrogate parent to his players who have less than ideal home lives. Cassy has long held a real affinity for Brock's star player, Phipps, and his Claire, Cassy's cheerleading captain. They seem like a well-matched couple. Cassy wonders what she had missed during her high school years when she was so involved with Ron. Sex was her thing then, but had she failed to foster a love relationship? If she were honest with herself, the answer had to be yes. But Ron had taught her to be a woman. Doesn't that count for something?

Once they get back to his condo, Brock and Cassy have the windows wide open, and they are dancing and laughing as they sing to Blanco Brown's "The Git Up," playing on the radio. Cassy looks beautiful tonight as she does the cowboy boogie in her short-sleeved yellow and white striped sundress that hugs her waist and accentuates her bust. It comes just above her knees, and she wears it with her favorite red leather cowboy boots. Of course, Brock doesn't care about all of that; he just knows he likes what he sees and loves to laugh and make love with her.

They grab two craft beers and go out on the deck to watch the sun go down. The conversation takes a serious turn when Brock professes, "Cassy, lately we've talked around the subject of marriage. I realized today that is exactly what I want. You in my future, full time!" He moves within an inch of her pert nose and beautiful eyes, almost daring her to deny their ever-deepening connection. "We can laugh and dance through life. I love you. Let's make this—*us*—permanent."

Cassy knows he is right. Questioning and almost admonishing herself in her mind, "Why am I hedging? What am I waiting for?

Ron has never even hinted at a real commitment. And I can't be the reason for destroying the boys' happy home life. Brock is perfect, drop-dead handsome, a considerate, dynamic lover with a killer body, and he has a career, not just a job. We really like to do the same things: being with friends or just sitting and talking. It's not just about the sex, although that is mind-blowing. He has become my everything." And she knows now she is his, too.

"King, I love you, too. But I can't go forward without sharing a secret I have carried forever." She lowers her head and moves to sit down. "Come here," she beckons with a wave of her hand. "I can't agree to anything until I have been totally honest with you. I graduated from boys to men very early in my life. Sex made me feel happy and powerful, and probably, if I'm honest with myself, I was at times searching for a father figure. Several years ago, I started a long-term relationship with a married man. I can't blame him for all of it, but he was like an aphrodisiac."

Cassy can see Brock's muscles tense as he locks his jaw and rolls his fists into a ball. "I'm not sure I want to hear this, Baby." Brock pushes the words through his gritted teeth. "I'm not naïve; I assumed you had other men in your life, just like I've had other women. But swear to me this isn't still going on!" He reaches over to grab her forearms; she winces, and Brock drops his hold. "I would never physically hurt you, Cassy; you have to know that, but thinking of you now with someone else drives me crazy."

His voice is strained as he admits, "I have sensed your resistance sometimes as we grew closer, but I just kept hoping I was wrong." A cross between a worried and angry look forms across Brock's face. "Cassy, does this someone still hold a place in your life? I'm not sure I can stand the answer, but I must know."

Jumping up, Cassy turns Brock's face toward hers and says over and over, "NO! NO! NO! Believe me, I have broken it off with him. I know my future lies with you, and I am thrilled."

"I get it—it's someone right here in Meadowbrook. Am I right? Tell me who it is. It's not Doc Ron, the guy you worked for so long as the family nanny, is it?"

When Cassy doesn't answer, Brock knows he's nailed the truth. He stands up, grabs the rail of the deck, and mutters through gritted teeth. "Stabbing wasn't good enough for him. I could kill him!"

"Brock, please don't say that. You can't mean it. I promise, I'm yours now and forever."

"I love you, Baby! You are mine, and I am yours," Brock murmurs with conviction as he picks her up and takes her to his bedroom. They are locked in a fever of wanting and possessing.

"Get naked, NOW, Baby. I need to be in you. You need to know that it is our—yours and mine—future. Just you and me."

Cassy hurriedly removes her sundress, seeing her King's smoldering eyes turn even darker as he reaches for the front clasp of her lacy bra and jerks her matching lacy panties from her body. "Baby, I am going to make you come like never before, and I want your eyes open, knowing it's me, Brock—*your* King, *your* future, *our* future. I'm gonna make you forget he was ever in your life."

The intensity of his kiss is matched by her eagerness. "King, please, now! I need you as much as you need me." This jolts her for a moment as she processes that she really does want Brock—for much more than sex.

"Not yet, Baby! We have some connecting to do. Look at me, Cass!" His kisses go to the sensitive skin of her neck and then to her granite-hard nipples, where he licks, sucks, and even nips and then soothes with his tongue. His fingers dance over her body and go to her very core. "God, baby, you are so wet for me.

"Oh, yessssss!" Cassy pleads, "Brock, I actually hurt for you right now. Please, please." He circles her clit several times, his pressure heightening her demand.

"Open your legs for me, Baby. I need you to watch me as I feast on you." He flicks his tongue on her swollen nub as his fingers enter her, sending spasms of want through her entire body.

"Brock, I am coming!" she screams as he continues to push her desires. He enters her, their eyes meeting as their bodies lock in a connection they cannot deny.

"Stay with me, Baby. I want to come at the same time you do," Brock begs as every plunge takes them higher and closer to a crescendo of not just sex but love. She watches him shutter as his head flies back, and her own orgasm milks his pleasure. "Cass, you are mine. You always will be mine!" he declares.

They lie with their bodies intertwined and their eyes committing to a future that is theirs—only theirs.

On the other side of town, sitting on their deck, is another couple with ties to Ron. They had closed the Daily Grind and headed to Renaldo's about 7:00 P.M. They were going to open a bottle of wine, grill steaks and marvel at the miracle that they had found one another and hoped to be "fully" together. Trey knows it relies on telling his father, as soon as he is out of the hospital, that he wants Renaldo in his life full time. He dares to hope that his father, for once, can really see who he is.

Trey, thinking about all of this, is in a pensive mood, and Renaldo tries to lighten things with a bottle of Merlot and funny stories about patrons who had been at the coffeehouse today. "This group of five women was already what you would call, 'four sheets to the wind' when they came in demanding coffee. They wanted big mugs, with strong black brew. They kept saying they couldn't go home to their husbands and kids in their current condition. I teased them about where they had been and what they had been doing. That sent them into further peals of laughter, and everyone in the shop was laughing with them."

Renaldo is rendering all the fine details when Trey interrupts, "Thanks for trying to cheer me up, Ren, but every time I go through the scenario of trying to get my father's approval of our relationship, I get cold feet. Dad has always idolized Phipps because, in my father's words, 'Phipps is a real man's man.' I'm sure he doesn't mean to hurt me or belittle me; however, I'm known as 'the artsy one,' as Dad always calls me. I don't measure up as Ronald Edwin Phillips II's son. My mother, thank goodness, loves me just the way I am, and you've seen how she accepts and enjoys us as a couple. It's the same with Cassy, Joey, and Tom! Why can't all people just take us as we are?"

"I don't know about all people," observes Renaldo, "but society has made great strides, and I like to think it will just get better and better. Your father does love you; that's apparent when I'm around him. Maybe we need to give him the benefit of the doubt. His eyes light up when he sees you playing at the Grind. He may not understand music like he does sports, but I would like to think he sees your talents, too."

"I love him. Always will, but I'm old enough to know he's not perfect either. My father has a wandering eye—and dick—and sometimes it's hard to ignore, especially when I watch him and Mom together. Of course, there have been rumors all along, but I just choose to ignore them."

"Trey, you need to know, I will never let anyone make you feel 'less than.' Sports are not the measure of the man; sexual orientation, for that matter, is not the measure of the man or woman. It is your heart, your caring, your talent that make you just the right man for me."

"Ren, you make me feel loved and accepted. It's something I have dreamed about for so long. How lucky we were to find each other." He gives Ren a quick kiss and announces, "I'm going in to take a shower before we grill these steaks. Want to join me?" he says with a beckoning look on his face.

"In a minute," Renaldo replies as he playfully slaps Trey's passing ass. "I'm going to finish my wine." As he looks out over the neighborhood, Renaldo feels a sense of belonging that has eluded him for so long, just like Trey had shared. Ren has always wanted to build a good life, and he reaffirms to himself, "I won't allow anything to come between Trey and me!"

As Trey is heading for the shower, the doorbell rings. His immediate thought is, "Shoot, who can that be? I had X-rated plans for Ren and me."

Trey opens the front door. Phipps questions immediately, "Can Claire and I come in? We have a lot to tell you—things you cannot even imagine have happened."

"Of course. Ren is on the patio. Do you want him to hear this, too?"

"Yes, the whole 'famdamily' needs to know cuz everyone in Meadowbrook is going to know we are not the family they thought we were." Phipps pulls Claire close to him and kisses the top of her head. "Come on, Baby, we can do this."

Ren, walking in from the patio, turns with a questioning look to Trey but quickly welcomes Claire and Phipps. He offers them a glass of wine and then remembers they are still in high school, so he offers, "How about a Coke or sparkling water?"

"No, maybe later. You are not going to believe the day we have had."

"Spill it, Bro. Tell us what is going on."

Trey is astonished when he hears their story. He cannot believe that Phipps is AG's son and Claire is his sister. He smiles and hugs her. "Claire, welcome to this crazy family. I always wanted a sister, and you are perfect!"

Thinking back to his earlier comments about his dad, Trey asserts, "I don't care who our dads are, Phipps. We are still brothers, forever. We share a history no one can take away from us. Maybe that explains why we are so different from each other, you 'jock,' you." He gives Phipps a strong, affirmative hug.

"Well, with all this news, I might as well spill the beans about my life."

Phipps interrupts, "Pleasssse, Trey! I know Ren's role in your life, and Claire and I love that you two have each other. Boy, this town is going to be talking about us for years." They all laugh as they join in a group hug. "We'll take those Cokes now and toast to all our futures. Who knows what will unravel next?"

Chapter 17

HOSPITAL PUZZLE

etective Mike Finley has reviewed the party video over and over to see who was in the main room at the time of the incident—and who was not. He and his team of detectives have interviewed, more than once, those who were at the party. He has followed up on the solid evidence about affairs, one-night stands, grievances, secrets, and anything else he could think of.

He knows the woman who alerted everyone about the stabbing is just more of a busybody than an assailant. She had been snooping upstairs when she found Doc Ron with the letter opener—a knife, she thought—in his back. Of course, she claimed she had just gone up to congratulate the doctor, but she had shared way too many details about the upstairs of the Phillipses' home to have gone directly to Ron's office.

Having the weapon has certainly not been any help in identifying the guilty party because it had been wiped clean of fingerprints. In following up on its origins, it had turned out to be a gift given to Doc Ron by the former nanny, Cassy. She maintained the inscription was a homage to all the time she had spent with the boys. Debatable—why hadn't she given it to the family instead of just to Ron? Evidence has certainly established that Cassy and the Doc were involved in some type of illicit relationship. As to who knows what and who doesn't, he isn't sure yet. He will have to keep digging.

As to a motive, almost anyone he talks to seems to have a reason to be angry with or dislike the Doc. It is an oxymoron that so many "loved" him, and it seems just as many "hated" him—many of them the very same people. The real question is who would benefit from stabbing him, and were they out to kill him or just give him a warning of some type? Mike has done his due diligence in checking backgrounds, hunches, and innuendos thrown out by the interviewees, but he has that gnawing feeling he's missing something. Talking to himself, he muses, "Who would be capable of using violence to assuage their anger or solve an issue?" He lets out a subtle laugh, "Anyone! Haven't all these years taught me it could be anyone, and often the most unlikely?"

Establishing opportunity is a quagmire because the appearance, reappearance, and non-appearance of individuals in the video run the gamut. The house and grounds were wide open, and people were constantly milling about. No video could catch all the "goings on" at such an event. Sitting there rocking back and forth in his office chair, a thought strikes him. "Could it be?" he whispers. He grabs his jacket, leaves the building in a rush, and heads to the hospital. He has to talk to Ron; surely he is alert by now. If Ron can just give any slight detail of who stabbed him, it might be exactly what is needed to clear this case.

When he gets off the elevator on the fourth floor, the first thing Mike sees are four policemen, the doctor caring for Ron, and Dr. Tom Redford. They are huddled together, and their hushed conversation has an urgency to it. As he comes toward them, he hears Ron's longtime physician say, "But he was recovering. He was doing much better; I expected him to be OK. This can't be! We must find out what happened."

"What's up?" asks Mike.

His attending doctor looks pale and drawn. "He's dead. I can't believe it. He's dead!"

All of them stand there for a moment, dumbfounded and seemingly lost for words. "How could this happen?" poses Dr. Jensen, shaking his head. "He should have made it! Not one of us here at the hospital thought he was in grave danger of succumbing to his wound. Something happened—something totally unexpected must have happened."

Detective Mike hates this turn of events. He puts his hand on the doctor's shoulder and promises him they will get to the bottom of what transpired. "Please, all of you, this is now beyond a crime scene; it is a murder scene!" To the officers he says, "Guard that room. Absolutely no one except the doctor or who accompanies the doctor is to enter that room. We will follow up after the body is removed."

Mike next turns to Tom and explains, "Doctor Phillips's wife and sons need to be notified. Would you like me to go to them, or since you and your wife are so close to the family, would you prefer to break the news? They will have questions, of course, but let the doctor or me handle that if necessary."

Tom agrees he and Joey will go to their dearest friend's home to tell Winnie and the boys the unbelievable news. Tom calls Joey and can't help but cry as he's driving to pick her up. She is distraught and crying when he arrives, and they fall into each other's arms, clinging with unfathomable sadness. Eventually, they know they have to pull themselves together and be strong to handle this heartbreaking task.

When Tom and Joey pull into the driveway, they notice that both boys' vehicles are parked there, too. Hesitantly, they ring the bell, and Winnie opens the door to greet them. Her demeanor changes the minute she sees their faces. "What, what is it? Is something wrong?" gulps Winnie.

"Are the boys here?" asks Tom. "I think you better get them!"

Even though Tom and Joey shared the news in a very calm and caring way, it was like a lightning bolt hit the room. Winnie, Trey, and Phipps spring up, start grabbing coats and car keys, and ignoring the Redfords, charge out of the house to rush to the hospital.

Dr. Jensen, the doctor the family had used for years, sees them coming as he stands by what had been Ron's room. They can see the room is empty. Turning to the doctor, all three begin firing questions. Finally, with a weary look and defeated stance, he answers, "We honestly don't know what happened or what went wrong. You know I would tell you if I knew. I am so very, very sorry. We will do all we can to find the answer. Of course, we'll do an autopsy."

In unison the three beg to see Ron, and as the doctor is a long-time friend, he takes them to the hospital morgue. It is a surreal scene as the three take in Ron's lifeless body, the boys breaking into gut-wrenching sobs and Winnie openly crying.

News of Ron's death spreads like wildfire. Sentiment seems to be that the person who did the stabbing had not meant to kill him, but the question still remains: "Who did it? Who murdered Doc Ron?"

"Is there a chance that one of the persons I suspect of stabbing Doc Ron really wanted him dead and has now completed the job?" Detective Mike is thinking out loud. "How could they? An officer was always posted by the door to his room, and the nurses and doctors were constantly in and out checking Ron's status. Family members showed up at all hours, and close friends, whose names appear on an approved list, only stayed a few minutes." Mike mutters to himself, "Who would have had access, a reason, and an opportunity to inflict a fatal assault on the semi-conscious Ron? Besides the family, Cassy Carstens is the one who came to Doc Ron's room most often and, according to the officer on duty, appeared at times to be talking to him and holding his hand. However, the evidence from the Man of Year Party never put Cassy off the main floor, and she was still downstairs when the alarm was sounded from the top of the stairs."

Detective Mike hates the thought, but he will have to go back and talk to guests, servers, caterers, and bartenders to verify that he and his fellow officers hadn't missed an important clue. In his conjecture, he had narrowed it down to Renaldo, Trey's partner; Brock, Cassy's boyfriend; and Axel, the masseur, who is close to both Winnie and Monica. On second thought, it could be anyone; there were so many moving parts and very few solid leads. "Maybe it is time to rattle a few cages," ponders Mike.

Interviewing the caterers and bartenders a second time adds very little to what is already known. They all look incredulous and declare, "We simply set everything up and came back to tear it down." The caterers go on to say, "We've done myriads of parties for the Phillipses over the years, and nothing seemed out of the ordinary this time."

The servers vow, "We made sure the champagne was flowing, and the trays were always full of hors d'oeuvres. We also kept the bar stocked and were ready to mix every kind of drink imaginable. We were continuously swamped," chime in the bartenders. "Remember, it was an open bar."

One pattern has emerged: no one remembered seeing the masseur anywhere downstairs during the presentation of the award or right after. Of course, he could have just come to say congratulations and gone home. Talking to Renaldo, Detective Mike mentions that many attendees had seen Renaldo tending the coffee bar, but few could place Axel at the party after the opening ceremony. Mike wants to watch Renaldo's expression and read his response as he inquired, "Did you happen to notice Axel at the party? You were situated where you could see most of the room and most of the guests."

"Honestly," replies Renaldo, "I was really busy at the coffee bar making specialty drinks, and I spent the rest of the time with Trey, so I'm sorry I'm not any help. I just don't remember."

Mike believes his next step is to corner Brock. He is lucky; when he locates him, Brock is just finishing football practice and heading to the locker room.

"Hi, Brock, I'm Detective Mike Finley, and I'm now re-investigating both Doc Ron's stabbing and now his murder. How well did you know Doc Ron?"

"I know who you are, Detective, and I can tell you straight up I hardly knew Doc, and I didn't do anything to him. I can't say I liked the man for good reasons, but I never touched him. My girlfriend, Cassy, worked for them as a nanny in her high school years, but let's face it, we didn't run in their social circles. I saw him occasionally at special functions or something for the boys. His son, Phipps, is my star player, but you already know that. I'll bet you've already checked out my background. There was nothing before I came to Meadowbrook, and there has been nothing since I moved here. If you want the real perpetrator, you'll have to look elsewhere."

Axel wasn't hard to find either; he was at his massage business, and when he sees Detective Mike step in, he goes to him and inquires, "How is the investigation going? Do you have some promising leads?"

"That's why I'm here. I'll get right to the point. In reviewing the video of the Man of the Year Party, you are seen coming into the house, but nothing after that? How do you explain that?"

"I was in the kitchen for quite a while helping the servers and caterers. I could see they were struggling to keep up, and in my cruise ship days I had to fill in for all kinds of jobs."

"What's bothering me, Axel, is that none of those individuals you mentioned remember seeing you in the kitchen," pushes Mike.

"You think I'm lying? Wait a minute, that's bullshit! I've been through this before with people lying about what I have done—making accusations that weren't true."

"I know," counters Mike, "I checked your HR records with the cruise line, and you were let go for issuing physical threats to co-workers and being quick to lose your temper."

"That's a lot of BS! That's not how it went down, and unless you have some real evidence that I did something, get out of here."

Mike's cell phone begins pinging just before he turns around to leave. He had already decided to give Axel time to cool down and answer rationally and give Renaldo time to rethink his less-than-convincing disclaimer about the party, and Brock to realize Mike probably knows quite a bit about Ron and Cassy's longtime affair.

Answering his phone, he hears Ron's doctor say, "Can you please come over to the hospital immediately? We've had some very disturbing results show up in Doc Ron's labs."

"The autopsy isn't done, is it, Dr. Jensen?"

"No, no, not yet, but the labs can certainly answer one of our questions: what killed him?"

"I'm on my way. Be there in a few minutes."

Detective Mike, Dr. Jensen, several lab technicians, and key hospital administrators talk for more than an hour. There is no question Ron has been poisoned. The culprit used cyanide, which most likely caused a heart attack. His blood tests earlier had shown he was improving. When the technician went in to get more blood in the morning, he found Ron dead. His heart monitor was turned off. Obviously, it was someone who had access to the poison and access to Ron. It's such a mystery because Ron was guarded 24/7. Only hospital personnel came and went freely, and any action they took should have been noted on his chart.

Dr. Jensen keeps chastising himself. "Even though I have been diligent in ordering blood samples and searching for answers, I failed to keep my patient alive. How could this happen here?" he moans as he resumes pacing and shaking his head.

At this point, Detective Finley states, "I believe I have narrowed the list of those who most likely stabbed Doc Ron, but my gut tells me it's not the same person who poisoned him. It looks like we are dealing with two separate perpetrators. Can any or all of you help me gain access to records of who treated Ron and which nurses and orderlies were on duty? I know that could be quite a list."

"All of us will help," said Dr. Jensen. "This is so unbelievable. I really must connect with his wife, Winnie, and give her an update on what we have learned."

"I think we should wait until we know more," cautioned Mike. "It's difficult to say, but he is already gone; final arrangements are being made for the funeral, and I'd like to secure further evidence before we stir up a storm or scare off the culprit . . . or culprits."

Everyone, even the head hospital administrator and PR spokesperson, agrees a couple of days won't make any difference, and it will give them time to scour the medical records and personnel assigned to Ron's care.

They are now looking for a KILLER!

Chapter 18

THE FUNERAL

Walking in a fog, Winnie is making funeral arrangements. Her boys have been her constant companions and given her four strong arms to turn to. Of course, the funeral will take place at the Meadowbrook United Methodist Church, located downtown. The Phillipses have been members since coming to town, and Ron served as a lay leader. Financially, they more than supported the church's work, and they are highly thought of by Pastor David. He had already been to the house several times to comfort the Phillipses and to ascertain any special requests for the visitation and the funeral.

Ron had never discussed death with his family members, so Winnie and the boys are having to deduce what he would have requested for his funeral. Ron's parents were gone, and being an only child considerably narrowed those who would have had a say in the arrangements. Joey and Tom are the voices of reason, and they, like many others, loved Ron in spite of his shortcomings.

An obituary filled with Ron's accomplishments is easy to draft, and all involved believe that Ron would have wanted memorial gifts to go to the Meadowbrook neonatal unit; it is extremely costly, has to be routinely updated, and Ron had supported it for years. Ron had died on Tuesday, and his visitation is scheduled for Friday with a funeral on Saturday morning, so anyone who wishes could attend. Rumors are running rampant about what might have happened or about who might have done this to Ron. Detective Mike and Ron's doctor had agreed to put everything on hold until after the funeral. The family and the community needed time to assimilate this tragedy.

The morning of the funeral dawns cloudless, warm, and beautiful. Just like the "Man of the Year Party," everyone who's anyone is there, and then there are many, many others. With the church filling up right away, soon there is standing room only. Winnie and the boys with the Redfords enter the church and take the front pew as a hush comes over the crowd. Winne is in a tailored black suit. She wears a large black hat with a subtle dotted veil that gives her an appropriate and distinguished look designed to preserve her privacy. Many were curious to see if she showed some real emotion. Both Trey and Phipps are wearing deep navy-blue suits with cream-colored shirts and navy ties. Joey and Tom, holding hands, come down the aisle in dark charcoal attire. Joey's hat is a pillbox design with a short veil.

Yes, Claire was really Ron's daughter and could have sat with the family, but she chose instead to be with her mother a few rows back.

Even though there had been the suggestion of memorial gifts rather than flowers, the church is absolutely saturated with bouquets of every kind and color. The overwhelming fragrance assails the senses of the attendees the moment they step through the door. Really it is a beautiful sight with the pearlized white casket at the front of the church, large candles burning in a halo glow, the pastor and assistants in their formal robes, and the beauty of the church itself with its stained-glass windows. The service is befitting of Ron's status with several accomplished soloists singing timeless hymns and an assembled choir doing the same.

The eulogy Tom gives is heartfelt and personal, leaving most with tears in their eyes as they remember the man.

"I was blessed to know this man since our college and medical school days. We stood up for each other at our weddings. My wife, Joey, and I are godparents to his and Winnie's two sons, Trey and Phipps. He and I worked side by side at the same hospital all these years. He was complicated, but aren't we all?

My dearest friend, colleague, and skilled doctor was amazing when it came to saving fragile newborns. He helped many couples realize their dream of having a family. His altruistic side came out in the establishment of the updated NIC-U at Meadowbrook, which many of you favored with your memorials in his name. Thank you.

He loved his family, supported this community, and served as a volunteer in too many capacities to count. His most apparent was being the School Board President, and he was recently honored with Meadowbrook's Man of the Year trophy.

I, as many of you, will miss him every day. We must make sure we give his family all the love and care they deserve. Godspeed, Ron."

Somehow, Winnie, Trey, and Phipps make it through the reception in the visitation hall of the church. The ladies' guild, with the help of church members, has provided a stellar array of finger foods, and the flowers were moved from the sanctuary to the hall. The family stands for a good three hours, just meeting and thanking people for coming and letting them share their memories of Ron. Some want to talk about his hospital work, some want to extol his philanthropy, others want to share little vignettes that make the family laugh. Winnie is especially comforted with kind words, as she is now viewed as the grieving widow.

Very soon it is time to proceed to the burial, and the line following the hearse snakes for miles through Meadowbrook. Winnie has recently purchased two plots side by side. She had certainly not had any inkling she would need them this soon. She, the boys, Claire, Ren, and the Redfords ride in the lead limousine right behind the hearse. It's very, very quiet during the ride to the cemetery. Everyone appears to be in their own quiet reverie, or maybe it's still too much of a shock to be fully processed. After all, he was supposed to recover.

The graveside service is short but meaningful: a few Bible verses, a stirring rendition of "Amazing Grace," and a call for remembrances from those gathered around. Trey steps forward to say just a few words. His voice is strong but low. "I speak for me and my brother. We have had the best parents in the world. Every day we will miss our father and vow to be there for our mother." He looks down at Winnie, who sniffles and puts a handkerchief to her eyes. What Winnie had most feared hasn't happened. No one has touched on the family's many secrets, and for that she will be eternally grateful. This is no time to try to explain a gay son, an unknown daughter, and a son who is not Ron's.

She inwardly sighs, "What does the future hold—good or bad—happy or sad?"

As the minister draws the service to a close with a prayer, Winnie, Trey, Phipps, Joey, and Tom each step forward and place a white rose on the casket before leaving. In the limo taking them home, Winnie is thinking what a blur the day has been. Everyone always talks about their wedding, how fast it is over after all their planning and preparations. Well, most funerals certainly don't give you much time for planning, and the emotions either. The surroundings are surreal, thus making it even harder to assimilate. Right now, she is worried about her boys and how they will cope. She leans over to them to give each a huge hug and whispers, "I love you both so much, and I know your dad did, too. I couldn't have made it through today without you."

Both boys answer at the same time, "Oh, Mom, we love you, too. We're here for you!"

Winnie then turns to Tom and Joey. "I know thank you is not enough; however, it truly expresses how much I value your help and friendship. You knew Ron as well as I did. Tom, Ron would have loved that eulogy. You really captured the essence of the man."

Joey was sniffling as she placed her forehead on Winnie's. "We'll be here for you, too, just like the boys."

At the house, Trey and Phipps have changed their clothes, checked to see if Winnie is OK and disappeared to be with Renaldo and Claire. Tom and Joey have gone to the hospital to check on his patients, and then the two of them are going to stop for a drink. They have invited Winnie, but she just wants to be alone. She stands in the great room, thinking of all the events that have taken place here—the parties, the holiday celebrations, the Man of the Year recognition and . . . . She starts talking to herself as she sips on a Godmother— amaretto with vodka. Normally she would not have indulged in this drink; too many calories, but today is an exception. She has to have something to soothe her thoughts.

She knew she had truly loved Ron at first. He had shown her such passion and caring. His joy at the birth of their two sons still made her smile. Maybe, if this had to happen, at least he never knew Phipps was not his biological son nor that Claire was his child, and it will give Trey the peace to live his life as he chooses.

Then questions start to surface that make her uncomfortable just thinking about them:

Will my boys really be all right?

Ron and I made up a will after the boys were born, but is it still valid? Where is it? Do we have a lockbox at the bank?

I never had to work after Ron's practice was established and thriving. Will I need to go back to work? As a couple, we never talked finances. Ron handled all of that.

Phipps will be heading to college soon, and we paid for Trey's, so I will need to pay for Phipps's education. I wonder if Ron had money set aside for that. And what about Claire? Doesn't she deserve something?

Am I still a doctor's wife, or is that automatic prestige gone?

Will I have enough money and energy to keep this house and the grounds going, or should I consider selling it?

I'll have to arrange to have a stone placed for him. What would he want? Well, it is too late for him to protest, so thank goodness the boys can help with that.

What about his practice? Will it die a natural death? Maybe Tom knows someone who wants an established practice.

Had all those women crying at the service been crying for the doctor or the Casanova that graced them with his attention and, let's face it, his body?

As she continues sipping her drink, she makes a mental note to call their attorney. At the same time, she has to admit to herself that recently Ron's conquests had begun to really bother her. She says aloud, "Every woman wants to feel she is the number one love in her husband's life." She hadn't felt that in quite some time. As she lies back on the sofa, the enormity of what has happened finally hits her, and she feels hurt, abandoned, and scared. Tears stream down her cheeks.

What would her relationship with AG become? Would he want to be in Phipps's life? She remembers seeing him at the funeral, but he seemed to purposely step back, letting us be the family everyone expected.

Her Godmother drink finally begins to do its job, and she falls into a troubled sleep. That's where the boys find her when they return home. They cover her with a quilt, kiss her on the top of her head, and go to their rooms. They, too, feel sad, abandoned, and full of questions about the future.

Chapter 19

THE ARREST

All the re-checking and re-interviewing had finally paid off. The letter opener that had served as the weapon had not shown any fingerprints, and as Detective Mike knew from the earlier report, the house showed "a million" fingerprints. That was an exaggeration, he knew, but that was how it had felt when he read the printout.

He wasn't sure what had prompted him to send the fingerprint crew back to Doc Ron's home office to check all the surfaces, especially those behind his desk, except that logically the assailant had to be behind Ron. Otherwise, Ron would have noticed him or her in the room. Mike pulls out the photos taken of the office and registers that there were two large plants positioned against the wall on either side of the desk. A hunch hit him. He put a call in to the lead man of the crew and asked him to be sure to pull fingerprints from in and around the plants and walls.

Several hours later, Mike is delivered a beautiful thumb print of one Alfred Axel Nilsson found on the bookcase partially covered by the huge Dorado Dracaena plant that sat to the right side of the desk. It could have easily concealed a person.

Not wanting to waste any more time, Mike, accompanied by two uniform officers, again tracks down the masseur. Axel is just getting into his car when he sees Detective Finley walk up. Axel registers the two officers and the determined look in Mike's eyes as he pulls out his badge, asserting, "Alfred Axel Nilsson, you are under arrest for the stabbing of Dr. Ronald Edward Phillips II." Mike then proceeds to read him his rights. Axel has a defiant look on his face, but he doesn't put up any kind of struggle as the officers handcuff him and lead him to the patrol car. He doesn't even profess his innocence. He knows what he has done. And even gladder that he had done it.

Riding to the station, Axel opens up, "Well, I did this town a favor when I gave that SOB a warning, and that's all I did. You can't pin his murder on me. I just wanted him to realize he wasn't the 'adored Romeo' he thought he was. Him and his constant sexual conquests were hurting some of the most elegant, talented, and caring women I've had the pleasure to know. They deserve better!"

As he is booked, Axel lets Detective Mike know he will call his high-powered lawyer as soon as he can. "I can easily have him post my bail, and I will be out in no time. He's helped me out before. Anyway, I didn't kill anyone."

Axel's attitude makes Mike grind his teeth. He'd seen guys like this before, and it was a good bet this one would skip out on his bail and disappear. Time would tell.

Megan was trying to rest. She had worked the night shift at the hospital for years but had never gotten used to sleeping through the day. She knew she was a dedicated nurse and was so proud of her work record, but she also realized it was a matter of time before it all came crashing down.

She had always been extremely proud of Cassy. Talking to herself, she asserts, "Yes, my Cassy was sexually active for quite some time; however, she has turned out to be such a great person, earning her teaching degree and working at the high school. She has a steady, respected boyfriend, one who will marry her, and together they can build a happy life and family." Something Megan had never been able to accomplish. Her thoughts are of Cassy.

Cassy had come to her right after her trip to New York. She had had the hardest time telling her mother about Ron and the scope of their relationship. With Brock in the picture, Cassy knew she had to break free, but she wasn't sure she could or that Ron would let her.

"Mom, I hate that I have hurt you, Cassy's bowed head and cracking voice signaled how remorseful she was. "You don't deserve any of this, but I was so afraid I wouldn't be able to resist the intoxication of being with such an experienced and polished man. I must take some responsibility; after all, I loved the trips, the jewelry, the flattery—what was I thinking about being with a married man? You have always been there for me, and I know you will always be there. Please, please say you forgive me. I love you, Mom."

Megan embraces her daughter; both have tears in their eyes, and Megan smooths her daughter's hair as she vows, "It will be all right. You'll see. Everything will work out." Megan is more worried about what Cassy has or hasn't told Brock. Either way, it could turn out to be a disaster. "Have you told Brock about this?" opines her mother.

"He knows who and that there was an affair, but not any details. He made me promise it was over, and I really don't want to give up this chance for a real relationship," whispers Cassy.

Megan, having heard the scope of Doc Ron's involvement with Cassy, is livid. She hadn't let Cassy know how hurt and angry she is, but no matter how Cassy had become involved in this long-term illicit affair, it is Doc Ron's fault. How could he have taken advantage of her young, impressionable daughter? That was what she had been when it started—a girl! He was a devil! He was an adult; he knew better. He was the one who should have said no. Megan couldn't even think about it, particularly when, for years, she had watched his "moves" at the hospital. He was so smooth and what Cassy had said, "polished." Ava had never told her directly, but Megan was pretty sure Ron was Claire's father. No wonder Ava never wanted to talk about it; he had gone right on with his family and never even acknowledged his responsibility. Surely, he knew. How many others had he trapped or toyed with? The thought alone made her sick.

She knew it was wrong, but she was glad someone had stabbed Doc Ron. She was sure he would recover; after all, she took care of him every night on her shift. Megan knew what had to be done. She didn't see any other way to stop the temptations or prevent them from blowing up and ruining Cassy's chances for a "normal" life. Megan formulated a plan. She made mental notes of who could help her, researched how to do it, and took time to begin accepting what her actions would mean for her. She vowed, "I will do anything for Cassy—my daughter—the only good thing that came out of my long-ago screwed-up marriage."

Getting the cyanide had been relatively easy. A credit card and the internet, and she had daily access to a syringe—something no one would miss in the supply cabinet. She calculated as best she could the amount of the poison to put into Ron's IV to induce death. Her biggest dilemma was how to pull it off without anyone seeing her. She put her hand in her scrubs and felt for the key card that let her in the side door that most of the nurses used to enter their locker room.

She planned to enter there in her scrubs and walk authoritatively but quickly to Ron's room. Her plan was to use the syringe to place a lethal dose of poison in his IV, banking on enough time to exit the hospital before anyone would be alerted. After midnight in the wee early morning hours, few people were in the hallways, most patients were sleeping, and the nurses were at the station prepping for the day's required treatments and medications, so she felt confident she could pull it off. The issue was the police officer guarding Ron's door. She'd just have to take her chances.

It had worked exactly the way she had calculated. The officer had been engaged in an animated conversation with an orderly about some sports team and was so used to seeing hospital personnel he barely took notice of her both times she passed him. As she drove home, her heart did a flip, and she whispered to herself, "I am a MURDERER!"

How she managed the coming days, she couldn't fathom. She had stood by Cassy and Brock at the funeral and had said all the right things. She did feel a twinge of guilt when Winne personally thanked her and Ava for their care of Ron while he was in the hospital.

Now she lives in fear and resignation. Each day since he died, Megan has expected a knock at her door or the police coming to the hospital looking for her. Today is the day! She hears the doorbell ring. Her heart skips a beat as Megan opens the front door and sees Detective Mike Finley standing with his badge in his hand. There are two uniformed police officers with him—the same ones who had been with him when he arrested Axel. "Megan Carstens, you are under arrest for the murder of Dr. Ronald Phillips II." He proceeds to read her her rights. The officers cuff her, and she goes to the patrol car as if in a trance.

On the way to the police station, Megan confesses, "You know it was almost a relief to see you come today. I really hated to kill a doctor, but I absolutely went crazy when I heard about him and Cassy. I had to do it to save her! You understand, don't you?" she motions with her hand toward Mike. The detective just shakes his head. Standing at the station while Megan is booked, he reflects that the two of the oldest and most prevalent motives in the world for murder had found their way here—anger and love.

Would Meadowbrook ever be the same?

Epilogue

5 YEARS LATER

Cassy and Brock

Cassy's eyes are glued to the TV in the great room. There is Monica, larger than life, leaning against her BMW convertible, and Axel, her Ace, walking out of the doors of the Western Illinois Correctional Center in Mount Sterling, free after serving five years for the stabbing of Dr. Ronald Edwin Phillips II, her Deuce. Cassy hadn't realized until right now what an impact Ace had been in her life. Oh, he was always the best masseur she had ever had, but he was really the one, *the one* that started the transformation in so many women's lives in Meadowbrook, most of all hers.

Axel had confessed taking things into his own hands because of the constant negative impact the Doc was having on the important women in Ace's life: Monica, professionally blackmailed by Doc to keep her sexual life a secret; Winnie, emotionally blackmailed with all of Doc's affairs and more; and, yes, me, a naïve young woman who had been . . . . Exactly what had he done? Tricked me into believing I would be the next Mrs. Ronald Edwin Phillips II? Tricked me into a long-term affair—with the same trips, jewelry, and promises he had used to pacify Winnie, his wife and the mother of the two boys I adored?

God, how stupid I had been! Thank God Brock came into my life, showing me what a real relationship could and should be. Our wedding had been small and so meaningful—a destination wedding in Hawaii, with my favorite two boys in attendance—Phipps and his Claire, Trey and his Ren. Tom and Joey had been there, too; Joey, the perfect matron of honor for me. And Brock's mentor and former coach was elated to be the best man—well, second best to Brock. Brock's mom, May, and dad, Steve, and his sister and her daughter had flown in as well. It was the perfect wedding—those close to both of us observing our exchange of vows on Secret Beach at the Makena Cove on Maui at sunset and then sailing the ocean for our private wedding dinner—fresh seafood with champagne with elderflower liqueur, and key lime pie, instead of a wedding cake. The stars overhead promised a perfect beginning for our new life.

"Mommy, Mommy, pwese, Tommy and I're hungwy! Daddy said we coulds have a picnic outside. Mommy, pwese!" the miniature Cassy pleads.

"Yes, Ali, we get to have a picnic in the backyard—but only after I tickle you and slobber you with kisses," Cassy chortles as she picks up Ali and swirls her around the room.

Brock, with Tommy sitting high on his shoulders and clapping his small hands, enters the kitchen from the mud room, ducking to be sure his clone doesn't bang his head on the archway. "There are my two favorite girls!" he exclaims as he kisses each on the forehead.

"No mo' kisses, Daddy! I wants Awee to see the swaprise. Come on, Awee. Youse will wuv it! Mommy, did you makes the sami-ches? Peanut butta for me and jewee for Awee? Chips? Cookies, too?"

"Yes, little man, I did. Let's go see the surprise that you and Daddy have been working on," she promises as she looks into the eyes of her man, her Brock, her King. "Life is good," she thinks. As the four rush to the new playhouse Brock (and Tommy, of course) had just finished, she adds, "No, life is perfect."

Claire and Phipps

"Claire, Baby, hurry up! We have lots to share with Mom and AG, and they should be answering any second," Phipps motions to his wife of one year.

"Good morning, Phipps and Claire. So glad we can con-nect. We don't always have the best internet connection on this cruise down the Danube," answers Winnie with AG waving in the background.

"Hey, Mom! Hey, AG—mmm, Dad," replies Phipps, while Claire flashes the biggest smile in the world. Phipps kisses her temple and then adds, "We have lots of news for you! And you two are the first to hear it."

"Ahhh, that's sweet," Winnie shares as she throws them each a kiss. AG provides a two-finger salute that shares his thanks in being recognized as Dad and included in the conversation.

"So, let me introduce to you my husband, the newest player for the New York Giants!" Claire declares with a wide-sweeping introduction that shows how proud she is of Phipps. "He will be backup quarterback, but you will definitely want to come see him, even if he is standing on the sidelines this year," she continues. "But you just wait; he is going to be the star soon."

"We knew you could do it, Phipps—get picked up by a pro team. We just didn't know which one was going to get you. Congratulations, Son," AG relates, excited that Phipps is seeing his dream come true. "I know it will be a lot of work, but you are used to giving your best to get your best. We are really proud of you!"

"Yes, we are thrilled but not surprised—and, you know, Phipps, that I am going to worry every time you get on that field," Winnie adds.

"Ah, Mom, no worries; I will be fine. And now I want to introduce to you, Claire Phillips, my wife and the next Madeleine Albright of Columbia University. Georgetown wanted her, but Columbia got her! She starts classes next week," Phipps gushes as Claire blushes.

"Oh, my God, this is fantastic news! Things cannot get any better than this, can they?" Winnie responds rhetorically.

"Well, actually, they can, Mom. We have more news—unexpected but *the* best news ever!" Phipps draws Claire into a close hug and kisses her temple as he continues, "We are pregnant! In about seven and a half months, you two are going to be grandparents. Again, you are the first to know, so we are begging you to keep our secret until we can tell Trey and Claire's mom."

Tears of joy slide down Winnie's cheeks as AG hugs her tight and kisses the top of her head. "Phipps and Claire, whatever you need, we are here for you. Your mom and I want to be the best grandparents in the world and the best parents for you, two of the best kids in the world. Do we know if it is a boy or girl yet?"

"Not yet, and we have not decided if we want to know. We will probably cave—at least, I know Phipps will—but we are holding out at this point. We are going to start looking for a larger condo or townhouse—maybe three bedrooms—so when you come to help with the baby, you can stay with us."

"We will be there as often as you want and as long as you need us. We cannot wait! Maybe we can shop for the nursery when we are back in the States for Trey's wedding. We would love to buy whatever you need," AG offers, and Winnie affirms with additional tears and smiles.

"Speaking of Trey, how are their ceremony plans coming?" Phipps asks. "We definitely want to fly back for their nuptials and all the festivities that go with it."

Trey and Ren

Both Trey and Ren stand in the Daily Grind's archway leading onto the patio. Their guests, having been personally greeted by the wedding hosts, Tom and Joey, anticipate a night filled with love and laughter for this special couple. It is a perfect sunset as the lights laced through the open rafters twinkle and the candle lights dance on the tables decorated with crystal vases filled with white full bloom hydrangeas. In the background, the guests hear "More," sung by Bobby Darin—something old.

They are in identical light gray tuxedos with silver gray lapels and matching vests. Each sports a pastel yellow tie against his crisp white shirt and a single blue rose pinned to the lapel—something blue. Silver cuff links with their initials, their wedding gift—something new—to each other, just adds to their model-like appearances.

Not wanting to miss a moment of the ceremony, together Trey and Ren walk hand in hand toward the far end of the patio, where an almost full circle double wrought-iron arch stands with large floral arrangements of white hydrangeas and lilies accented with yellow and blue roses attached to each—the perfect frame for the couple's vows.

Standing under the archway, Trey and Ren cannot help but laugh as Cassy and Brock's three-year-old twins toddle down the aisle—something borrowed. "Tommy, waits for me. I hafta drop the peddals for good luck. You has to swo down, pweese!" Ali begs as giggles follow her down the aisle.

Tommy, dressed in a tuxedo like his "Uncle" Trey, tugs on the platinum wedding bands tied to the ring bearer's satin pillow. "Awee, you has to huwee up. We's gonna be late for da wedding! Evwyone is here!" And the crowd's giggles continue as they see Ali and Tommy grab the hands of their "uncles," Trey and Ren, who hug the twins and point to "Uncle" Phipps, Trey's best man, dressed in a matching tuxedo. He escorts Cassy, their mom and Ren's "best woman," down the aisle, radiant in a smoke white gray sheath with silver sequins on the neckline and sleeves. When they reach Trey and Ren, they hug them both. Cassy asks, "Are you ready for this?" taking Ali in her arms as Phipps hoists Tommy on his hip.

Trey and Ren respond with wide smiles that promise a future filled with love and laughter. "Definitely! Let's do this."

"Welcome, friends, families, and loved ones." AG pauses and smiles at Winnie before he shares, "We are here this beautiful evening to celebrate the marriage of Renaldo Antonio Mendez—Ren, our soon-to-be son-in-law and favorite barista to all of us—and Ronald Edwin Phillips III—Trey, our son and all of Meadowbrook's favorite musician.

"I have asked Ren and Trey to each share a poem that symbolizes their relationship and promises of forever." He turns to Ren. Everyone chuckles when Ren begins with "I promise you always—each and every morning—fresh coffee made from the finest Brazilian beans with a dollop of cream and one teaspoon of sugar, just the way you like it."

Once the laughter dies down with the setting sun, Ren takes Trey's hands into his and looks into his green eyes and shares, "Trey, this is my paraphrase of St. Therese's words of wisdom and love.

"She said, 'May today there be peace within. May you trust that you are exactly where you are meant to be—with me. May you not forget the infinite possibilities that are born of faith in yourself—and in me. May you use the gifts that you have received and pass on the love that has been given to you—and to me—to us. May you be content with yourself—and me—just the way we are. Let the knowledge settle into your bones and allow your soul the freedom to sing, dance, praise, and love—with me. It is there for each and every one of us. I will love you always, Trey."

There is a hush—and not a dry eye—as Trey begins to strum his guitar. "Ren, and these are my promises to you:

I will love you forever and a day.
It was your smile from across the room.
It was your first hello and your hand on my shoulder.

It was your words that inspired me to be me, just me.
Was it happenstance or fate, we will never know but
I knew then I would love you
Forever and a day!

It is your coffee in the early morning hours,
Your nods of encouragement and acceptance throughout
the day,
Our reflections each evening center on us—you and me.
Is it happenstance or fate, we will never know but
I know now that I will love you
Forever and a day!

We know there will be rain and even storms,
But there will be rainbows and sunshine
As we go through this journey together.
Will it be happenstance or fate, we do not need to
know because
I will love you
Forever and a day! Always!"

There is a hush, and again, not a dry eye.

Tom and Joey

Tom and Joey cannot believe how their lives changed overnight. Their Victorian home is now filled with the laughter of children, after a night of terror and struggling with the unknown.

A year ago today, a car accident ended the lives of two doctors, both at Meadowbrook Hospital: he, an oncologist, and his wife, a pediatrician. Two lives snuffed out needlessly by a drunken driver led to major changes in Tom and Joey's life. They had known they were the official guardians in case something happened to their two friends, Trev and Tiff; they just never expected it would ever happen.

Laney, now three, and the twins, Easton and Weston, now five, call Tom and Joey Mommy and Daddy. They are surrounded with all the love two parents can promise them. They have "aunts" and "uncles" with Phipps, Claire, Trey, Ren, Cassy, and Brock—all who adore them, and "cousins" with the Taylor twins, Ali and Tommy, and baby Lucy, Phipps and Claire's new baby. And they are awaiting the arrival of Ren and Trey's adopted son, Turner. Gram Winnie and Gramps AG have their hands full as "the family" just keeps growing.

"Hiwa, Daddy, push me hiwa," Laney pleads as Tom pushes her on the tire swing, hanging from the giant oak in their backyard.

"Daddy! Daddy! Watch us!" The twins echo Laney's pleas. "Mommy taught us how to do flips!" Tom smiles at Joey as she completes her own backflip on the trampoline. She places her right palm over her heart as Tom does as well, a silent "I love you" they now use often as the chaos of three preschoolers takes command in their home.

"This is how it should be," Tom reflects. "Joey and me, and a house full of kids.

Jack (BDF)

Jack (BDF), you ask. His wings have been clipped. More about that later.

THE END
(OR MAYBE A NEW BEGINNING)

Wanna' Taste of Their Drinking Habits?

(If you drink, don't drive. Not even in a golf cart or on a bike. Enjoy with Absolut responsibility.)

Winnifred Phillips

- Very particular about the drink and the glass

- Most glasses had been purchased when she and the boys were in Europe

- When at the country club, Winnie has an added splash of pear liqueur

  <u>White Diamond Martini</u>
  Served in a chilled Orrefor Martini Glass

2 ½ oz of chilled Absolut vodka

Dash of chilled dry vermouth

Garnished with lemon twist/lemon swirled on edge of glass

Broken Goose Martini

Served in a chilled Lenox Martini Glass

1 oz Grey Goose Vodka

1 oz Broken Kettle Gin

3 Blue Cheese Stuffed Olives

Shaken not stirred/strain

Glass pick for olives

Gin & Tonic

Served at the pool in the heat of the summer

Served in a Williams & Sonoma Cocktail Glass

2 oz Bombay Gin

4 oz Tonic

Splash of lime juice, ice

Wine

Served in Baccarat Wine Glasses

Beaux Frères Pinot Noir

Ribbon Ridge Pinot Noir

La Jota Howell Mountain Merlot

Mayacamas Cabernet Sauvignon

Champagne

Served in a Lalique Champagne Flute

Dom Perignon with Elderflower liqueur

Dr. Ronald Edwin Phillips II - The Deuce

- Partial to only one drink—scotch!

Scotch
    Served in Waterford Whiskey Glass
    2 fingers - neat
    4 fingers double
    Glenlivet 18
    Macallan 18
    Macallan 25 on special occasions

Irish Whiskey - OK in a pinch
    Served in Waterford Whiskey Glass
    2 fingers - neat
    4 fingers double
    Jameson Reserve
    Bushmills Original

Champagne
    Only on special occasions
    Any glass would do for him
    Chilled
    Dom Perignon, Vintage Champagne

Cassy Carstens -
Our one and only "Sassy Cassy"

- With the gang on the sand, in college, and with Brock

  <u>Beer</u>
  Cold and out of the can or bottle
  Coors Light
  Busch Light
  Budweiser Light
  Corona - with lime (special parties or dates)
  Michelob Ultra (when she is watching her figure)

- With Ron (Cassy's Deuce)

  <u>Cosmo / Cosmopolitan</u>
  Mikasa stemmed crystal martini glass (her preference)
  2 oz Tito's Handmade Vodka
  ½ oz triple sec
  ¾ oz cranberry juice
  ½ oz fresh-squeezed lime juice
  2-inch orange peel/twist/ice
  Shaken

- With girlfriends & other teachers

  <u>Mimosa</u>
  Served in champagne flute
  2 oz fresh-squeezed orange juice
  2 oz champagne or Brut

<u>House Wines</u>

- With Brock (Cassy's King) and his family

<u>Vodka Press</u>
   Served in a small tumbler with ice
   Swirl a lime wedge and a lemon wedge around the inside
   of the glass
   2 oz Grey Goose vodka
   2 oz Sprite
   2 oz Club Soda
   Stir gently and garnish with lime wedge

- With Jack (Cassy's BDF)

<u>Mango Cosmo</u>
   Served in a stemmed martini glass
   3 oz Malibu Mango Rum
   ½ oz fresh-squeezed lemon juice
   1 ½ oz cranberry juice
   Shake with ice, strain, and garnish with lemon peel

<u>Lychee Martini</u>
   Served in a stemmed martini glass
   2 oz lychee juice
   3 oz vodka (Your choice. Our favorites are Absolut and
   Grey Goose!)
   1/2 oz vermouth
   1 lychee for garnish
   Shake with ice, strain

Trey & Renaldo

- Unique blends of coffee beans found by Renaldo (mostly from Brazil)

Coffee

    Dulce Signature

    Subduction

    Parceiros do Cafe

    Sitio Baixadao

Specialty Drink at the Daily Grind!

    Daily Grind Blue Refresher - Beat the Heat!

    Served in rainbow splash glasses

    ¼ cup Blue Curacao syrup

    2 tbsp lemon juice

    1 tbsp lime juice

    1 tsp ginger juice

    ¾ cup sparkling water

    Shake and pour over ice

Cocktails

    Black Russian

    Served over rocks in pre-chilled Old Fashion Glass

    1 oz Absolut vodka

    1 oz Kahlua coffee liqueur

    ½ tsp lemon juice

    Cognac - Ren introduced Trey to it

    Served in glass snifter

    Palm it to warm it and release its natural flavors

    Remy Martin is Ren's—and now Trey's—favorite

Claire & Phipps

- Phipps - whatever beer was on sale or in the fridge at home

- Claire - would take a can of beer, but never drank all of it; on special occasions would drink a Skinny Girl Margarita

  Skinny Girl Margarita
  > Served in a Solo cup on the beach

Axel (Cassy's Ace)

- Learned during his cruise days - authentic tequila comes from Mexico

  Tequila
  > Served straight up
  > Don Julio, Patron, or Jose Cuervo - whatever is available

  Mezcal - on *very* special occasions
  > Served straight up at room temperature
  > Del Maquey Chichicapa or Montellobos

Monica (The Superintendent)

- District business, if appropriate, drinks Sauvignon Blanc wines from New Zealand

  White Haven or Oyster Bay

- On her own time

  Godmother
  > Served on the rocks in Waterford Whiskey Glass

½ glass Amaretto

½ glass Grey Goose Vodka

Wow!!!

Tom & Joey

- Drinks preferred are low cost and thoroughly enjoyed

Wines

    La Crema Sonoma Coast Pinot Noir

    Infiniti Malbec

    Josh Cellars Chardonnay

    Sterling Napa Cabernet Sauvignon

- Tom - drinks what his dad has always drunk

Manhattan

    Served in a Manhattan tumbler

    2 oz Glenfiddich Whiskey

    ½ oz sweet vermouth

    2 dashes bitters

    Shaken with ice and garnished with brandied cherry

- Joey - loves drinks with little umbrellas

Pineapple Coconut Martini

    Served in a chilled stemless martini glass

    1 ½ oz coconut rum

    1 oz pineapple schnapps

    1 oz pineapple juice

    ⅓ oz grenadine syrup

    Garnish with pineapple ring infused with rum

    Shake and strain

Mike Finley, the Detective

- Any brand of coffee donated to the precinct by corporations like Walmart, Amazon, Chevron, etc.—hot, strong, brewed all day so it is thick and stands on its own!

- On his own time

  Beers
  > Budweiser (for many years) and Bud Light (recent switch—watching his weight. Oh, yeah, what about the donuts!)

  Cocktail
  > Served in any glass in the cupboard
  > Jack Daniels - Old No. 7
  > On the rocks

AG (Andrew George)

- Acquired taste in college for local craft beers

  Craft Beers of Chicago
  > Half Acre
  > Two Brothers
  > Goose Island
  > Moody Tongue

  Cocktail
  > 7 & 7 Highball
  > Served in classic highball glass
  > 2-3 oz Seagrams 7 Whiskey
  > 2-3 oz 7UP
  > Over ice

Jack (Cassy's BDF)

- Loves to explore drinks

<u>Crown Royal Special</u>
Served in two lowball glasses filled with ice
Double shot of Crown Royal, divided
1 cup freshly squeezed blood orange juice, divided
Stir and serve

<u>Japanese High Ball</u>
Served in chilled tall glass; add ice cubes and stir for 30
seconds; pour out any water
1 part Japanese Suntory Toki Whisky
3 parts club soda
Stir the whisky and ice 13.5 times clockwise; gently add
club soda down the sides of the glass; stir gently and
drink up!

**Remember, like it said on a cocktail napkin we saw – "Drink
Responsibly! And to us that means 'Don't spill it!'"**

About the Authors, M R Westover

Both M and R are "rewired" schoolteachers and administrators. They enjoy the Florida sun, the fall in Iowa, walking on a sandy beach anywhere in the world, an occasional trip down the river, and spoiling their grandkids.

They want to thank their families and friends for their patience and support during the writing of this book, and they hope they will have as much love for us as we continue our journey with Jack, the BDF! Oh, and watch for *You're the One!*